SEAL Team 6
bin Laden and Beyond

- J. L. NARMI -

International Standard Book Number (ISBN): 146361098X
Library of Congress Control Number (LCCN): 2011916021

11-1

INTERPRETATION OF THE PRINTING CODE: the rightmost number of the first series of numbers is the year of the book's printing; the rightmost number of the second series of numbers is the number of the book's printing. For example, a printing code of 11-1 shows that the first printing occurred in 2011.

— *Printed in the United States of America* —

TABLE OF

CONTENTS

PartI

Part II

SEAL Team 6: bin Laden and Beyond is a novel that will send chills down your spine with its real-time setting of events currently unfolding in the Middle East. *SEAL Team 6: bin Laden and Beyond,* dares to go where many other novels deem too politically uncomfortable to venture or even discuss. Events that seemed implausible just a few short months ago are now unfolding at lightning speed before the eyes of the world. One does not need to make a great mental leap to consider the book's events as distinct possibilities of things to come in the days after bin Laden.

The focus of the novel follows a thread through historical events to modern times and is interwoven with the realities of sovereign politics and the emotional drain on the characters described. Historically relevant background of the Middle East region invites the reader to invest their attention in previous events and apply them to an ever-changing situation. The lines between fact and fiction are blurred as the characters and plot assume a reality complete with political personalities and diplomatic strategies.

U.S. Military Special Forces have a long history of working behind the scenes, hidden from public view, to prevent serious world events from becoming a reality. *SEAL Team 6: bin Laden and Beyond*, is simply the next possible set of events that could occur in a world with groups intent on avenging bin Laden's death.

A narrative of progressively increasing tension is punctuated with enthralling military action and intrigue. *SEAL Team 6: bin Laden and Beyond* picks up where many news stories end, and allow people to have a vivid image of the possible operations of our U.S. Special Forces. The overarching tension between characters, countries, religions, and agendas contribute to the drama within *SEAL Team 6: bin Laden and Beyond*.

We live amidst a delicate balance of tolerance and intolerance, conventional and unconventional, and those who want to change the world through democracy and peace and those through war and terror. *SEAL Team 6: bin Laden and Beyond* will prompt the reader to think about the consequences of failing to prevent cataclysmic events from occurring and will take the reader behind the scenes into the dark world of international diplomacy and special operations.

> – *Ronald E. Narmi*
> *Rear Admiral, U.S. Navy Ret.*

--------------- ACKNOWLEDGMENTS ---------------

I would like to thank my editorial team, especially Alec, who remained focused and on task during the editing process. Alec also provided expertise to properly describe Naval procedures and terminology that made this work more credible and realistic.

I send a tremendous amount of thanks to my brother, a retired Naval Admiral, who provided intellectual and emotional support while writing the book. His experience and expertise were invaluable to the completion of this work.

– *Jon L. Narmi*
*Author, **Seal Team 6:** bin Laden and Beyond*

*This novel is dedicated to members
serving all branches of the U.S. Military,
especially the nameless and faceless members of
all U.S. Special Forces committed to the protection
of the sovereignty and freedoms of the
United States of America.*

Part I

SEAL Team 6: bin Laden and Beyond

CHAPTER 1

GREETINGS

GENO GENELLI BLASTED OPEN THE DOOR OF OSAMA BIN Laden's bedroom with his fellow SEAL, Fats Walker, and other SEAL Team members early in the morning hours of May 1, 2011. Bin Laden had heard shooting in the compound below and was awake. He shoved one of his young wives in the direction of Geno and Fats as he was reaching for his trusted and constant companion, an AK-47. Fats shot the young wife in the leg. Geno shot bin Laden in the chest and finished him with a head shot as bin Laden fell to the floor.

"Pleased to finally meet you," Geno said to the corpse. "You murdered my cousin in the 9/11 attack on the World Trade Center, you bastard. Bag and tag him," Geno said to two other members of SEAL Team 6. The entire world would soon know about the exploits of a very secretive U.S. Navy SEAL Team.

Bin Laden's compound had been under prolonged surveillance by the CIA for several years. This situation played into the CIA's bumbling reputation, as the press had a field day speculating why it took the CIA

SEAL Team 6: bin Laden and Beyond*

so long to verify that bin Laden was in the compound.
The real situation was that, over this extended time,
the CIA had been able to mine many al Qaeda secrets
by observing the comings and goings of couriers,
placing tails on them, and searching their network.

Accordingly, bin Laden had become expendable
through the law of diminishing returns. The CIA had
mined all that they thought they could from the
compound and now called in the military to take bin
Laden out. These secrets would become very valuable
to America in the reprisals that would surely come from
al Qaeda now that the military had killed their leader.
Sometimes it is better to ask questions and gather facts
before shooting than it is to shoot first and ask
questions later. The CIA had gotten as many questions
answered as they thought they could, so they turned it
over to Special Operations for their shot.

SEAL Team 6 loaded bin Laden's body on the
helicopter, along with treasure troves of laptop
computers, CD ROMs, flash drives, books, manuals,
and anything they could gather from the operation,
including three of bin Laden's wives who were living
with him at the compound.

SEAL Team 6 quickly lifted off to return to their
launch base in Bagram, Iraq. Bin Laden's body was
taken back to Bethesda, Maryland, for autopsy and "safe-
keeping" along with JFK's brain and other unknown

- 2 -

treasures of the American government. A mock burial at sea was conducted aboard the USS *Carl Vinson*. The CIA kept bin Laden's body because they were not willing to risk any conspiracy theories about whether or not bin Laden had been killed. They were never going to display or show the body to the public, although it was in storage for viewing by key senators, members of Congress, and agency directors if the CIA ever needed to pull an ace out of the hole for funding or clearances. Espionage and counterintelligence is a dark and dirty world. It is always best not to take any chances.

The CIA's trove of intelligence gathered from the bin Laden compound was key in ramping up the Kill-Capture program conducted by U.S. Special Forces. In these kinds of operations, overhead drones circle suspected al Qaeda hideouts or gathering points, while observers key in on targets for groups like SEAL Team 6 to take out. Except for the notoriety of the target, the bin Laden raid was simply another successful mission by teams like SEAL Team 6. The Kill-Capture program count had reached nearly twelve thousand over the past two years, compared to six thousand during the previous two years. Taking out bin Laden was not anything out of the ordinary for teams like Geno's; only the target was special.

Geno was glad to have bin Laden out of the way, so that the military could move on with more pressing issues. Al Qaeda had made their threats after the death of bin Laden and everyone expected that, but events were rolling so rapidly and violently in the Middle East that it was difficult to stay in "real time".

For example, the peaceful demonstrations that brought down the government of Tunisia escalated with moderate violence in bringing down Mubarak in Egypt. Libya became engulfed in a deadly civil war with thousands of casualties, leading to NATO providing a no-fly zone coupled with targeted offensive bombing raids. The United States was getting in deeper.

Then came Syria and all of its bloodshed. The CIA, other intelligence agencies, and the Joint Military Command felt that these falling dominoes of repressive dictators could be contained if they fell in an orderly fashion without presenting a clear and present danger to the United States of America.

However, CIA and Special Forces were stretched to the limit with these uprisings and the current Kill-Capture programs. The present administration was calling for a buildup of Special Forces from its present level of sixty thousand troops to one hundred thousand by the year 2015, but that did not address the stretched needs of today's Clear and Present Danger principle.

The Clear and Present Danger principle became the official U.S. national security doctrine in 1919 when the Supreme Court limited the right to free speech if it posed a clear and present danger to the security of the United States of America during times of war. This wartime footing scenario is why the George W. Bush Administration lobbied so hard to have the War on Terror declared after 9/11. Such a declaration allowed the Bush Administration to establish many activities, such as communication monitoring, military tribunals, and offshore interrogation and detention centers.

What was the clear and present danger that everyone was concerned might happen? Under the present circumstances the entire Middle East region might blow apart. Israel, Iran, Saudi Arabia, and Yemen were the concerns linked to the Clear and Present Danger principle. Israel was constantly in the crosshairs of Hamas, Hezbollah, Iran, and Syria, along with an alphabet-soup of many other Arab terror groups. An attack on Israel was an "official" attack on the United States of America. The United States was not required to respond to "routine" skirmishes and conflicts against Israel, but if a significant war or nuclear attack came, the United States was obligated to become involved. Israel was an obligatory action point in the rectangle of these four parties.

Saudi Arabian oil is the lifeblood of the Western world; hence, one may look on Saudi Arabia as the pump of the rectangle. Any credible threats to Saudi Arabia must be taken as a threat to U.S. national and economic security. This "policy" would bring the United

States to war with other factions if Saudi Arabia or its Royal Family were attacked or threatened.

Iran could be called the wild card or the joker of the rectangle, depending on your point of view and the Iranian President's remarks of the day. Iran is an ancient and proud nation tracing its roots back to Persia and Darius the Great. However, the Iran of today seems to be fixated on two things: destruction of Israel, and the sponsorship of terror, mayhem, and nuclear arms proliferation.

Yemen was becoming a very dangerous area of the world. The country was nearly lawless because of its heritage of being used as a whipping boy for the British, Iranians, and warlords of its own invention. Al Qaeda had deliberately set up shop in Yemen after being driven out of Iraq and was recently coming under heavy pressure in Afghanistan. The "American al Qaeda", Anwar al-Awlaki, the mastermind behind the Fort Hood shootings and the Detroit "Underwear Bomber", had moved his operations to Yemen. Yemen has also become a fertile breeding ground for Hamas, Hezbollah, and various other extremist groups. The American Administration had beefed up its drone program in recent months in hopes of taking out al-Awlaki. Yemen was the least stable corner of the rectangle, because Iran had provided ample funding to keep al Qaeda and warlords well supplied within Yemen.

A disruption of balance within this rectangle could

wreak havoc for the United States at any point in the future, and that is exactly what happened after bin Laden was killed. The rectangle was reeling out of control and the United States felt gravely threatened. Though they did not know it, Geno Genelli and SEAL Team 6 had two extremely dangerous missions staring them in the face. The balance of power in the world and the safety and security of the world were uncertain. No one knew how extensive and far reaching the damages would be, other than "extreme" at a minimum.

Containment of geopolitical events happening in these areas of the Middle East was the issue of the "Big Dogs" up top, and Geno was ready for anything except for the three-ring media circus that was occurring in Washington, D.C.

What Geno cared about was the way the administration had completely blown the cover of SEAL Team 6 to the entire world! Geno was ticked, big time! SEAL Team 6 had been buried extremely undercover in very deep Black Operations since the late 1980's. SEAL Team 6 did not exist in any official acknowledgment of the United States Navy or American government. A cover story of misappropriation of funds, personal misconduct, and other issues had been created to disband Team 6; that is, take it into very deep "black" operations.

It became "SEAL Team 6 this and SEAL Team 6 that," in the media after the takeout of bin Laden.

Then, to top it off, the President wanted to meet personally with the team to thank them for what they did. What they did was do their job!

"I respect the President," Geno said when all this happened, "but I'm not a pawn in some reelection campaign. Does the guy have a clue of the danger we and our families could be in if our faces showed up on the cover of *Time* magazine? I mean, for God's sake, leave it alone. Go thank the helicopter pilots! Go thank the deckhands on the *Vinson*! Leave us alone! We have people that would love to track us down and kill us for a payback. Some dumb ass inside the administration is going to leak a photo or a name, and then we're screwed."

Reporters were flocking to the headquarters and training facilities of SEAL Team 6 like bees to honey, sniffing for any tidbits of information about the team that they could break to the public as "news".

My God, sir, please, Mr. President, Geno thought to himself, *please, Secretaries and Suits, leave us alone! We're going to have some real heavy-duty assignments coming up because everybody knows these guys aren't going to take bin Laden's death lying down. We'll probably be off on another deadly mission before you can say DEVGRU Navy SEAL Team 6.* Geno shook his head at the thought. *Jesus, how are we going to focus on a mission when we are worried about our families back home?*

Little did SEAL Team 6 leader Geno Genelli realize what lay ahead for him and his team. Bin Laden was a routine takeout mission. They rehearsed these missions hundreds of times with various nuances that allowed the team to succeed even through unplanned adversity, such as 6 faced when they lost a helicopter in the hard landing on the bin Laden mission. These missions became routine, auto reflexive, but still dangerous. What lay ahead for Geno and his team was not in the training manuals, and the stakes could not have been greater.

America and the world would soon learn what was waiting in the days beyond bin Laden. However, when challenged, as Geno liked to say, "Let's get it on!"

CHAPTER 2

WALKING A TIGHTROPE

THE "CONTAINMENT" ISSUE INVOLVING THE SAFETY AND security of the West revolved around America-friendly kingdoms in the Middle East, notably Jordan and Bahrain. Bahrain is Saudi Arabia's neighbor to the east via a twenty-five-mile land bridge, and Jordan is a neighbor to both Syria and Israel. Bahrain is oil-rich and Jordan is oil-poor. The U.S. Navy Fifth Fleet is headquartered out of Bahrain. Jordan is host to friendly surveillance efforts for the West and provides a buffer between Syria and Israel. Jordan and Bahrain are two kingdoms that differ in economic wealth, but share a common role as buffers in the region. Meanwhile Lebanon, another country in the region, is dirt poor.

Jordan's King Abdullah II, who is recognized as a serious leader and was chosen as the fourth-most influential Muslim of the Arab world in 2010, rules over a constitutional monarchy that maintains ultimate control through an upper house of government that he appoints. Moreover, King Abdullah II retains absolute veto power over any legislation passed by both houses.

This arrangement is about as close as one can come to democracy in the Middle East except for Lebanon. Jordan remains a staunch ally of the United States, unlike Lebanon. Like many other leaders in the Middle East, King Abdullah II was educated in the United States and was very familiar with American freedoms and values. He put his power and nation's safety on the line when he committed troops to the coalition organized by Margaret Thatcher and George H.W. Bush during Gulf War I. Jordan and King Abdullah II are valuable assets of containment for the United States.

Israel's neighbor, Lebanon, has a democratically elected government dominated by the deadly Hamas organization that Iran backs. Hamas spent a great deal of human currency and money from Iran winning the hearts and minds of the Lebanese people. The West was stunned when they won free elections in Lebanon, which forced the West to rethink their tactics throughout the region. Perhaps brute force was not the only option to use as a strategy for containment in the region. General David Petraeus took note of the Hamas victory and implemented a "Hearts and Minds" policy in Iraq after the troop surge in 2007 that won the war in Iraq and in Afghanistan today.

Bahrain is a mini-Saudi Arabia of sorts. It has relatively few people and immense oil wealth. In cooperation with the United States, Bahrain has built up a significant military force, most notably its Air Force.

Bahrain serves as a geographical buffer to Saudi Arabia on its eastern border. Iran has long made threats to Saudi Arabia and Bahrain because of the conflict between Sunni and Shi'ite Muslims throughout the region. Sunnis govern Saudi Arabia and Bahrain even though their countries contain significant percentages of Shi'ite Muslims. Bahrain is 70 percent Shi'ite while Saudi Arabia is 15 percent. Iran has long made territorial claims on Bahrain, even attempting to annex Bahrain as a province of Iran in earlier days. Therefore, the geographically small Bahrain is of immense importance to Saudi Arabia and the West.

Saudi Arabia's immense oil fields lie in the eastern part of the country, and that region is predominately Shi'ite. Bahrain, fearful of becoming a pincushion in the battle between Iran and Saudi Arabia, consulted with Saudi Arabia before allowing the U.S. Fifth Fleet to place its headquarters at Manama, as part an Iranian buffer strategy.

Saudi Arabia is a country with a split personality. It has been a friend of America and the West for decades because of one primary thing: oil! The Saudis had it and needed someone to build its infrastructure and the West wanted the oil and was willing to build the infrastructure. So the West built and controlled the oil fields entirely until 1973 when Saudi Arabia got its first 25 percent stake in the national oil company, Aramco, as a reward for Saudi support of Israel in the

1973 Yom Kippur War. Islamic extremists have never forgiven Saudi Arabia for the unholy act of supporting Israel against the Arabs. The Saudis assumed full control of Aramco after further negotiations in 1980.

That 25 percent reward became very costly for Saudi Arabia over the years, as they also battled fundamental terrorists within their own borders that sought to overthrow the ruling monarchy. This also explains to some degree why Saudi Arabia looks the other way on some Muslim extremism that emanates from its borders. Fifteen of the 9/11 hijackers were from Saudi Arabia, a fact not lost on the West or American Special Forces members like Geno Genelli.

Saudi Arabia is also home to something more sacred than oil in the eyes of all devout Muslims: Mecca and Medina. The Islamic prophet Muhammad received the message of Islam at Mecca and began preaching Islam there. Hence, Mecca is considered the holiest site of all Islam. Medina is the burial place of Muhammad and Muslims consider it the second-holiest site of Islam. Saudi Arabia proclaims itself to be pro-Islam, as one would expect, and makes these two holy sites available to Muslim pilgrims from around the world. This universal Muslim accessibility through Saudi Arabia to the Holy Shrines increases the risk that militants can take root and set up operating posts or safe houses within the country.

Saudi Arabia has built an immense military force for a country its size. The justification given is that they must protect the holy sites from infidels of the West and keep them accessible to all of Islam. A significant amount of their weaponry has come from United States defense contractors. Therefore, its military leaders have had vast exposure to the West and they know about Western ways; most of their key officers were trained in the United States or by American contractors in Saudi Arabia. The Saudi Air Force and military might as well have *Made in the USA* stamped on every jet and piece of meaningful equipment.

The ace card of this situation for the United States is that the USA also knows nearly everything there is to know about Saudi Arabia's military structure and its equipment and what can disable it. This is a significant insurance policy for the United States if Saudi Arabia or Bahrain were to launch attacks against Israel or other America-friendly states in the region.

The majority of the Saudi Royal Family and most of the high-level government bureaucrats have also been educated in the West, primarily England and America. Saudi King Abdullah traveled regularly to London and Cleveland for his cardiovascular treatments and surgeries. The Royal Family and bureaucrats also frequently vacation in the West. As a result, Islamic radicals consider the royals and their bureaucrats agents of the "Great Satan".

WALKING THIS TIGHTROPE BETWEEN THE VARIOUS FACTIONS of the Middle East requires skill, patience, and money. The United States frequently makes "royalty payments" for base leases and other services provided under the radar screen in the Middle Eastern sector of the world. For this reason, the State Department must be skilled and rely on the CIA for accurate information. The participants such as Jordan, Bahrain, and Saudi Arabia have to be able to "win by losing" occasionally along the way, as does the United States while Syria and Iran often seemed to "lose by winning". The "good guys" have to stay focused on the big goal: balance and security for all, rather friend or foe.

The U.S. State Department and the American military high command must remember the Arabic proverb, "An enemy of my enemy is my friend" before they take any knee-jerk action.

The ingredients of radical Islam, true Islam, oil, the West, Israel, hedonism, capitalism, and political agendas can create a lethal combination if not mixed in the correct proportions. Geno, SEAL Team 6, and other Special Forces are often called upon to clean up the mess when the portions are not properly mixed. And a big mess was brewing prior to bin Laden's final days, and his death provided accelerant. Geno Genelli was about to become a busy man.

CHAPTER 3

MEETING OUR MAN

GENO GREW UP IN HOUSTON, TEXAS. HE WAS A SECOND-generation Italian American. His father was a full-blooded Italian and his mother was half Italian, half German. The heritage of both his mother and father was of Sicilian descent—Palermo, to be specific. Sicily and Palermo had a "Mafia" reputation. In fact, that was why his great-uncle Giuseppe and his grandfather Vito had fled the island in the late 1800's. There had been a local Mafioso dispute involving the young men, and they knew they had to flee or be killed.

Giuseppe and Vito landed in New Orleans, as many Southern Europeans did. Northern Europeans entered the United States almost exclusively at Ellis Island in New York City. The Genelli boys quickly learned that "southern hospitality" was not granted to dark-skinned Italians. They quickly made plans to get out of the port city of New Orleans. Giuseppe had heard there were some Mafia connections in the Kansas City area and headed north, working his way as a track layer on the Illinois Gulf Railroad.

Vito had had enough of the Mafia. He was much more conservative than Giuseppe, less of a risk taker, and was looking for some normalcy, if that were possible as an Italian immigrant in a foreign country. Vito had heard of opportunities in Houston, Texas, and headed for Houston to find work. He found a job on the Texas Southern Railroad scooping coal from coal bins to coal tender cars used to fuel the giant steam engines of the day. It was backbreaking work. It paid a dollar a day, but was an honest job and he had no association with the Mafia.

Vito was happy and saved as much money as he possibly could to bring his sweetheart, Katarina, to America. He had been forced to leave her in Sicily because of his quick getaway. Vito, instilled with a strong work ethic, earned an honest living, would not tolerate lying or cheating, and raised a fine family in America, including Geno's father, Mike. Mike married a strong-willed German girl by the name of Gertrude, sweetly called Dolly by her family.

Dolly was a very religious Roman Catholic and always turned to God and Saint Jude, the patron saint of lost causes, whenever she faced the difficulties of life. Mike was not a particularly religious man. After all, he was an Italian male at heart and real Italian men didn't "do" church, except for festivals. In Italian tradition, Mike was the father and leader of the family. Dolly, the German, was more subtle in her ways, but she could be quite stubborn when she wanted to be. Dolly insisted that the children go to Catholic schools, attend mass, and say the rosary daily.

Geno was the fourth of five children, sort of a middle child. Yes, he had heard all about the middle child syndrome, but it was no bother to him because he had quite a "motor" inside of him that just kept him going full bore most of the time.

As a child, Geno had the mandatory paper route of the day. The family of seven needed the money, and he worked for a time as a carry-out boy at the local grocery. However, as he gained more independence, he spent a lot of time around the nearby Gulf of Mexico. He loved the water and became an accomplished ocean swimmer in his teenage years. He was able to sneak away from home because it was difficult enough for his mother to keep five kids under control during the 1970's and '80's, especially Geno with that motor running inside of him.

Geno played sports off and on in high school, but he liked real-life action, and that's what eventually led him to the Navy. It seems that at the ripe old age of nineteen, he had used his fake ID and was working part time as a bouncer at a local bar. He got a little carried away one night bouncing a guy out of the bar, and the guy pressed charges. The judge gave Geno the proverbial choice of going into the military or going to jail.

The judge's offer was a no-brainer for Geno. In fact, it was a passport to adventure for him. He went down to the local recruiting station and joined the Navy because he thought the poster of a U.S. Navy SEAL he saw was cool and that it was something he would be good at. After all, it probably involved water and adventure. What more could a nineteen-year-old kid full of testosterone want?

Maybe Saint Jude or his mother's rosary had arranged this deal, but he was willing to grab it since he had been given the chance. I mean, c'mon, how else would this have happened out of thin air? God must have wanted him to do this. At least, that's what he told his mother to pacify her.

Dolly was just happy to see her little Geno get some discipline and structure in his life before he did something that would really get him in trouble. After all, in the Navy, aboard a ship out to sea months at a time, how much danger was there? Little did devout Dolly know!

The U.S. Navy SEAL program is a fifty-two week "survival" program—survival of the fittest and the mentally toughest. A lot of guys can get into shape to do a hundred push-ups, a hundred crunches, run five miles, or the like, but can they do it in ice-cold surf? Can they do it without sleep for twenty-four to thirty-six hours? Can they do it with little or nothing to eat or, more importantly, to drink for twenty-four hours?

Can they do an entire hell week of it? The majority could not, but Geno could, and he thrived on it!

SEAL is an acronym for sea, air, and land. SEALs like to be called SEALs. The mouthful of their full title, United States Navy Sea, Air, and Land Teams might be admiral-talk or Pentagon-talk, but a SEAL is a SEAL and they are damn tough. Geno was a pure SEAL, and if you call him otherwise with the right mix of alcohol and testosterone, you might get jacked in the jaw! SEALs know no limits and that's just the SEAL himself! Put a team of SEALs together and nothing is impossible in their eyes.

The U.S. Navy uses terms and descriptions that are far more professional sounding when speaking about SEALs: "Our SEALs will go anywhere to accept any mission that is necessary to defend the United States of America. Our SEALs are a deterrent to terror and warfare around the world. They protect and defend America's interests, whether it's a ship in port where innocents may be endangered, or it's on the high seas, or rather, it is in the bowels of a building in some far off enemy secured location. With proper training and preparations, no mission is impossible for our SEALs." The last sentence was especially true in Geno's mind because he had "been there, done that" many a time in his career.

Geno was a tried-and-tested U.S. Navy SEAL. He missed Gulf War I in the early '90's, but he hadn't missed much since. Like all BUD/S recruits—that is, Basic Underwater Demolition/SEAL School—Geno had to earn his way up the SEAL food chain to be entrusted with the "Black Ops" of SEAL Team 6. You don't turn a rookie loose when the security and secrecy of the United States government is at stake. Team 6 is the best of the best and filled with the highest level SEALs from all other SEAL teams.

Most BUD/S recruits don't graduate from SEAL training. The dropout rate is normally 80 percent. Only men are permitted to become SEALs due to the extreme physical demands of SEAL training and assignments. Geno liked the macho appeal of that. These men were truly some of the finest and toughest men that America had to offer for its defense and deterrence. Navy SEALs are some of the most feared and respected warriors on the face of the earth.

The Navy suspected they might have something special on their hands with Geno during his BUD/S training. As mentioned, BUD/S is as much or more about mental toughness than it is physical strength. Quitting or giving up on ANY element of BUD/S training will get you bounced out of the program immediately. There is no leeway or bend because, in a real exercise, a fellow SEAL must have absolute faith that his teammate will not quit or fail the squad. Again, these are not ordinary missions and these are not ordinary men. They are like Superman, "faster

than a speeding bullet, more powerful than a loco-
motive, and able to leap tall buildings in a single bound,"
and SEALs are trained to confidently think they can
accomplish nearly the same.

The internal strength generated by extreme physical
training and their quiet confidence makes a SEAL a
SEAL. Geno's BUD/S class was progressing normally
like any other, and the dropout rate was a standard
75–80 percent.

Geno was doing as well as anyone in the class.
In fact, he led all recruits in the water exercises and
training. He was an accomplished ocean swimmer.
The farm boys from the Midwest and the city slickers
from New York had never seen a real body of water,
let alone swam in it. Ocean swimming was a lot
different than doing laps at the local YMCA. There were
currents, crosscurrents, and undertows to deal with.
It required tremendous stamina and skill, something
Geno had. On a given training exercise, the recruits
were loaded with full gear, taken two miles out to sea,
and told to swim ashore. The gear weighed seventy-
five pounds and the recruits were dressed in full
camouflage: boots, blouse, and all.

The BUD/S normally do this in pairs or a group to
simulate a real drill. Geno and Fats Walker dutifully
went overboard when the instructor told them to do so.
As a safety precaution, other instructors were on duty

in Zodiac boats along the way to rescue anyone who got in trouble. Giving up and getting help meant you were booted out of BUD/S. But hey, it beats drowning, and maybe the chief is in a good mood today and he'll cut me some slack, but they never do. Instructors continually tempt, threaten, or cajole recruits into quitting just to see if they are mentally tough enough to survive in real-time missions or if will they break and endanger the mission or their teammates. Recruits that take the bait admit their own defeat, follow the tradition of Drop on Request, and ring the infamous ship bell three times announcing their departure.

Fats was struggling right off the bat. He was a land-lubber from Iowa and his body build carried a certain amount of excess even for a guy in "SEAL shape". Some guys are just built that way. Geno had swum ahead but was keeping an eye on his teammate. Geno saw Fats was struggling, and then saw him go under the waves. His natural buoyancy due to his body build helped him pop up, but he was starting to flail and panic. He went down a second time and popped up again.

Geno knew there was a problem, but there were instructors there and the class was nearly 90 percent done with BUD/S. Going back to help Fats was the natural thing to do, but given the ocean swells that day, Geno wasn't sure that he could go back to get him and then get to shore himself. Also, there was that 90 percent of training that he had already completed, and he didn't want to get bounced from the program because of Fats. He thought to himself, *Let the instructor pick him up.* But the instructor in Fats' zone didn't seem to be moving toward him. Geno didn't know the Zodiac's motor had died for some unknown reason, and the instructor could not get to Fats. Fortunately, Geno's "leave no man behind" instinct kicked into gear, he went back to get Fats with the risk of being kicked out of the program himself.

The BUD/S legend says that Geno swam back to Fats and got him stabilized. He was coughing and flailing up a storm due to the water he'd taken into his lungs. Once Fats stabilized, Geno somehow got him back to shore. The instructors had decided to sit back and see how this all played out. They were impressed, to say the least, and Geno had just accomplished the golden rule of combat, particularly SEALs, to leave no man behind. The instructors thought the kid had real potential.

Not only did Geno complete that leg of training, but Fats did too because Geno got him to shore. Fats and Geno formed a lifelong bond on the Silver Strand shores of Naval Amphibious Base Coronado that very day. Geno and Fats would team up many a time again in their careers, and Fats might someday be able to return the lifesaving gesture to Geno.

CHAPTER 4

A BUDDING SEAL

THE U.S. NAVY SEALS CAME INTO BEING IN 1962. GENO had joined the Navy after his bar-bouncing experience at the behest of the local judiciary shortly after his nineteenth birthday in 1995. Corny as it may sound, he was a bi-centennial baby, September 23, 1976, to be exact. He did his basic training through Great Lakes Naval Training Center in Chicago. Given the time of year of his "encouraged" enlistment, he arrived in time for the blasts of winter off Lake Michigan. Training was frigid, to say the least, and little did he know that this would not be his first winter chill as a future SEAL.

He completed basic like most recruits. "Break 'em down and build 'em up" is the mantra of all the services. The U.S. Navy was no different in that respect. The difference was that the Navy seemed to attract recruits that were more self-disciplined, industrious, and had higher levels of education. Maybe it was the allure of simply knowing that they were more likely to have a warm cot and hot food every day aboard ship. Geno excelled in basic—if anyone really has that as a goal when joining. In fact, he ate it up. Spit-shined his shoes, kept his locker in impeccable order, gave crisp salutes and crisper "Yes, sirs" and "No, sirs".

Geno outperformed during basic training, which enabled him to be considered for the fifty-two-week training program for SEALs. Each SEAL receives extensive specialized training in all aspects of air, sea, and land operations. Geno was given advanced specialized training in underwater demolition, because of the days he spent swimming in the Gulf of Mexico as a youth. Geno loved underwater demolition because it was fun to play with plastique and other explosives. It gave him a thrill to be in danger, he didn't have to worry because he had Dolly saying the rosary for him back home ever since he'd entered SEAL training. Geno feared nothing but he had made one concession to Dolly, and that was when at all possible he would wear the gold Saint Christopher medal and chain, the patron saint of mariners and travelers, that she gave to him after he completed basic training. Geno's concession to Dolly made them both feel better.

After advanced demolition, he received additional advanced training in hand-to-hand combat and close-in fighting. SEALs are trained to be as quiet as can be. The favored method of a SEAL kill is a wrench of the neck or a slit of the jugular with a hand over the enemy's mouth. "No gun, no noise, no unwanted attention" is one of the SEAL mottos. "One strike, one kill!"

is another. SEALs and SEAL teams often develop their own mantras based upon the personalities of the team. Geno's personal motto was "Let's get it on" and, being from Texas, he liked to order his men to "saddle up".

At the age of twenty-two, Geno got his first assignment, SEAL Team 7, based in Coronado, California. It was an assignment that gave him mixed feelings. San Diego was one of the greatest places in the world to live with boringly pleasant temperatures and blue skies. San Diego on the West Coast, what was going on in Asia for the SEALs? *Not much,* Geno thought. The action in the 1990's seemed to be on the East Coast out of Little Creek, Virginia, and he wanted to be where the action was.

There had been a war in Bosnia for the East Coast SEALs to take part in. Also, there had been Gulf War I and the ongoing clean-ups and takeouts from that. Then there was the usual checking and laying of undersea listening cables throughout the Baltic ports just to make sure the Russians were not feeling their oats. There were cables throughout the English Channel and Mediterranean Sea as well, since allies spied on each other to keep everything honest. There were interesting assignments to the Arabian Gulf waters from time to time, but San Diego and Asia? Other than the routine missions to Russian North Pacific ports, North Korea, and our friends in Japan, there didn't seem to be much going on from the West Coast, but Geno was excited to get going with his SEAL career. His motor was running! *We're here, San Diego!* he thought. *Batten down the hatches and grab up the women and children, Geno's in town!*

The movies often portray Navy SEALs and other Special Forces as macho bar-busting-up types, but nothing could be further from the truth. These men are trained to conduct operations in anonymity, unless the Defense Department needs some hype from the press. Operations are never discussed or disclosed to anyone except within the Special Forces community. As the chief says during training, "You work the way you drill and you drill the way you work! No screwin' around or you'll slip and blow your cover sometime when your life or your team's lives may depend on it. I find out any of you slimes are screwin' around down in Tijuana or in sailor's row in Diego, I'll cut your nuts off and you won't have to worry about BUD/S or a frickin' piece of tail; you'll be a frickin' eunuch! We've got our ways of blowin' off steam and you better stick to 'em or I'll have your ass now and forever!"

Geno had gotten the message, as did everyone else in BUD/S. SEALs gathered in SEAL-designated watering holes and might catch an occasional piece of strange, but that was it. There had been many a spy or Black Ops personnel brought down by a whiff of perfume and a comely look. Chief always said, "If you're going to fool around, do it at home, or don't do it all.

Fooling around may kill you or your buddy or both."
Geno always did what the chief said.

It is a fact that spy agencies regularly use beautiful
women in a game of cat and mouse when trying to
gather information or to get a guy to become a double
agent. Geno had had a fling or two, but nothing serious.
He was a middle child and had grown up un-showered
by heaps of attention, which allowed him to become
the independent person he was. He wasn't a loner per
se, but he knew that SEAL life wasn't conducive to
family life. He didn't want to be worried about a wife
and kid back home. His mother, Dolly, was family
enough for him. He didn't worry about her, she worried
about him. He was now with his SEAL brothers and he
liked it that way.

SEAL Team 7 wasn't as boring as Geno thought
it might be. They had their share of ops off mainland
Russia, China, and North Korea, as well as insertions
into Colombia to assist in the ongoing drug wars of
South America. Occasionally they did some black ops in
the Philippines and were at the cutting edge of "advising"
the Philippine National Army fighting the rebels of
the Moro Islamic liberation front in the Southern
Philippine Islands. They made a key discovery for the
DOD and CIA, which the CIA monitored: a small but
growing group of Islamic fundamentalists operating in
the remote islands of the Philippines. This find became
vastly important after 9/11. SEALs and Special Forces

were key in neutering those elements post-9/11. They knew who they were and where to find them. Let's just say they turned a few heads, slashed a few throats, had some night kills, and eliminated a lot of Islamic fundamentalists in the process.

The press heard some highlights from DOD press releases and the like, but that was more about providing good news for the American public and working up war fever post-9/11. Geno had done well, logging thirteen confirmed KIAs and was key in helping to wipe out the local command and control of the Moro Philippine branch of al Qaeda. His actions in the 9/11 campaign in the Philippines resulted in getting him transferred to the elite SEAL Team 6 in Virginia. These were the elite of the elite and most likely to take on the most difficult assignments.

SEAL Team 6 was known as the Navy's premier counterterrorist unit. Geno took Arabic language classes while training for Team 6. He wasn't fluent, but like most guys, he could get his points across with the locals, and more importantly, he could listen and have a good idea of what was going on. He had grown up with his mother and father speaking Italian when they wanted to talk about something they didn't want the kids to tune in on. He didn't like that, so he sure as hell didn't want to be in a long hot war not knowing what was being talked about around him. Once again, this proved another plum for Geno when it came to mission assignment and his growing leadership skills.

At the time, SEAL Team 6 wasn't really SEAL Team 6, or so the U.S. government and military said. The U.S. Navy, DOD, and the CIA had "dissolved" 6 in the late 1980's over misconduct issues. They used this as the perfect cover to form a deep operational team known as DEVGRU—United States Navy Special Warfare Development Group. Perfect! The anti-military wing of Congress got their pound of flesh and the government got what they wanted—dark and deep! So DEVGRU, or 6, was the hottest unit, and Geno was there. He was happy as a crawfish in a Gulf of Mexico pie.

Something happened on 9/11 though, that Geno took personally. His cousin Tom from Iowa was trying to make a name for himself, working on the upper floors of one of the Twin Towers for a firm known as Cantor Fitzgerald. A total of 658 of their 960 employees got wiped out that day, and it hit home. Geno was pissed, and his motor was in danger of blowing! He knew he had to calm himself down and focus for the next mission that he knew would come, but he was pissed and it was now personal. Hell hath no fury like a lethal killing machine with personal skin in the game!

Geno went sort of Rambo on the next campaign back in the Philippines. It added to his legend and stature within the SEALs and got him selected for SEAL Team 6, setting him up for the most important mission of his life and one of the most important missions of the

Western world. Because of this mission, he would earn many medals and citations, including the highest award the U.S. Navy gives to its troops—the Navy Cross. There was talk of the Congressional Medal of Honor, but that's not Black Ops style, so Geno had to make do with his service's highest honor. But Geno didn't care about medals, crosses, or stars. He just worried about the mission whenever he was out and about, and getting home safely with his men.

CHAPTER 5

THE CALL

JUST WHEN HE THOUGHT HE HAD SEEN IT ALL IN HIS **SEAL** career, Geno would get a call that would rock the world. Islamic fundamentalists were planning to kidnap the King of Saudi Arabia and several members of the Royal Family! The unthinkable and impossible could be pulled off during this Arab Spring movement even though the Saudi Royal Family had their finest and most loyal soldiers surrounding them. Members of the inner security details had all taken loyalty oaths to the Royal Family in blood and in the name of Allah, vowing to fight to the death protecting the King of Saudi Arabia, the birthplace of Islam and home to two of the holiest shrines in all of Islam. They and their families were handsomely rewarded, even by Saudi standards. They enjoyed special privileges and access to the finest ancillary services and facilities the military had to offer. It was as close to living as a royal as possible. So how could this happen?

When that call would come, "Why" didn't really matter to Geno. He would be vitally interested in "how" it happened because that would be the key to the success of the mission, which would surely be assigned to SEAL Team 6. Well into his career, Geno had been promoted to warrant officer and was now a team leader. He was the guts and brains of an operation that he knew would soon be under way. He would have his orders with real-time communication provided by satellite feeds, but he would still be making the crucial decisions on the ground.

The eighteen-day Egyptian revolution that led to the fall of Hosni Mubarak had emboldened a splinter group of Hezbollah operating from Yemen. If Egypt— the jewel of the Nile and the heart of the Arab world— could be toppled, why couldn't Saudi Arabia; a country with a small population and vast oil reserves, which fueled evil capitalists of the West, especially The Great Satan, the United States of America.

Most might think America was the prize for these Yemeni-based Hezbollah operatives, but the real prize was Israel. America was only a means for getting to Israel. They planned to cripple the West and throw it into panic and shock, choke it off at the spigot, and then hold Israel hostage. As with most Islamic hostages, there was only one choice in dealing with the infidel: he must be put under the sword. Killing Israel—not destroying it in the military fashion, but killing and destroying the Jewish race in Israel—would settle scores dating back to Jacob and Esau of the Old Testament and the Torah.

The destruction of Israel and crippling of the West would put the establishment of a worldwide Caliphate within the grasp of Islam, and Sharia law could be imposed throughout the Judeo-Christian West. Coupled with existing radical Muslim movements in the Philippines, Indonesia, and other parts of Asia, Turkey, the underbelly of Russia, China, and the Muslims migrating into Europe, the goal of the greatest jihad was within grasp.

The twenty-year investment of sleeper cells throughout America and Western Europe would bear fruit as the chaos of the oil spigot turnoff could then be coordinated by launching spectacular bombings of high profile targets and assassinations to further incite fear throughout the West. Strategic stores of anthrax, sarin gas, pesticides, and other biological weapons could be turned loose on public transportation, buildings, and the general population. Municipal water supplies, many of which were simply huge unguarded reservoirs, could be poisoned. The terror would be beyond anything the world had ever seen in its long history, and Allah would reign supreme throughout the world. Islam would assume its place as the rightful religion for the entire world to practice and live by. Those nations and people that were stragglers and latecomers could be dealt with in a methodical fashion on a timetable determined by Allah's will.

Surely, Allah willed success, because not only was

the Middle East in turmoil, but the West was also. They had spent themselves into oblivion with huge deficits to fuel their hedonistic lives. The events of 9/11 had delivered a financial gut punch to the West because, in its aftermath, the West had spent trillions of dollars in wars and prevention of other terrorist events. The West took the bait from al Qaeda, and got deeply involved in the post-9/11 war in Iraq and conflict that now involved fighting in Afghanistan.

Al Qaeda had studied the path of public opinion during the Vietnam War. They knew that the only way the American government could continue their desecration of Arab soil was for the government to maintain the soft and easy living of Americans while their puppet soldiers bled and died on the battleground. Weapons as simple as the IED had fueled America into a massive spending splurge on armaments to defend itself. These events seemed as if they were a gift from Allah and they emboldened thoughts of success for al Qaeda.

Since 9/11, al Qaeda had been following the playbook of bleeding the West dry of its most plentiful resource: money! Every resource has its limits, and the money was running out in all the capitals of the West. The printing presses had been running nearly 24/7 to float debt. This "Ponzi" scheme was now stretched to its limits and even the capitalists themselves had strong doubts that they could carry it on much longer. Still they kept marching forward with the hope and wink of an eye of a lying capitalist. The real money had been hoarded away by the elite in gold throughout the world in secret bank vaults. Those vaults too would come to Allah. The turmoil of world financial panics that would be brought on by the fall of Saudi Arabia would be the knockout blow following the gut punch of 9/11. "Allah be praised!"

Imran Ali Hamza was a thirty-year-old Arab. The name *Imran* is translated as the "greatest and most powerful". Imran had grown up in a Palestinian refugee camp, which he referred to as a giant cage for cur-dogs. It was a fenced-in desert prisonlike encampment with poor toilet facilities and rotten scraps of bread to eat, something fit only for a dog. He vowed that if he ever got out of there, he would fight Zionist Jews and their ally, America, a country that the Zionists controlled. Hezbollah and Hamas were deeply influential in a deliberate effort to radicalize young men like Imran throughout Palestine. The long arm of Hezbollah effected Imran deeply in his youth, something he carried with him the rest of his life.

Imran knew that the American money machine that fueled Zionism and put the ancestral owners of the lands of the Middle East like him in cages must be killed so that such an abomination would never again take place in the land of Islam. Imran had honed his courage and determination by throwing rocks at Israeli soldiers and facing them down against all odds. If he could just kill one Israeli, he could offer it up as a sacrifice to Allah.

There were hundreds of thousands of Imrans throughout the camps of Palestine. Imran knew that they would all come together someday and have their revenge with Allah on their side. Zionism was no match for Islam. The great Saladin proved that in 1187, in his victory over the mighty forces of the West and their "Crusades". Allah was and is supreme.

Thanks to Saladin, Islam had captured Jerusalem. Treaties were signed by the Christians and Muslims in 1187 that put Jerusalem under Muslim control, with Christians free to come and go within the city and live peacefully among Muslims. Saladin then went on a great building campaign in Jerusalem, putting the Muslim seal on it once and forever. The British had recognized the Muslim interest in Jerusalem during World War I. When that war was over, the British betrayed the Muslims by claiming Jerusalem and ruling over it from 1917 to 1948.

Then, after World War II, Britain conspired with America to find a new home for the Jews. They raped the Palestinians of their land and turned it over to the Jews. Imran hated the British too. The elders and imams who passed on the oral tradition of the rape of Palestine found willing ears in the thousands of boys like Imran, and the seeds of fanaticism were planted in those camps. The Americans and the British had to pay with blood. They would, if Imran and his fellow Palestinian soldiers of Allah had their way.

Sixty years of hatred can fuel the desire for a lot of bloodshed when that hate is turned loose. Unaware of Imran's hatred, Geno may have met his match with Imran.

Geno knew that he was about to receive a serious assignment when Admiral Gates *himself* called from DEVGRU in Virginia. It was 3:00 a.m. Eastern Standard Time in Virginia. Geno realized that something must be really hot for the "old man" to be up at three in the morning.

"Geno, Admiral Gates here. There's a jet on stand-by for you right now at Ellington Field. I want you to get your ass back here to Virginia immediately. We'll talk on a secure line when you're in the air. Get moving right now. Oh by the way, damn good job on the bin Laden raid."

"Yes, sir," was Geno's crisp response. They both hung up the phone and Geno could only imagine what was about to go down. He had been monitoring reports from Houston, but for Gates himself to call?

CHAPTER 6

LITTLE CREEK,
HERE WE COME

GENO'S MOTHER, DOLLY, HAD SUFFERED A MILD HEART ATTACK
in the aftermath of the bin Laden raid and had asked if
her son, Gregory, could come home. Geno had cleared
it with his superior officers and had been back in
Houston for only thirty-six hours when Admiral Gates
called. Hanging up the phone, he felt torn, but Dolly
was stable and not in a life-threatening condition. The
doctors had gotten to her within the "golden hour" of
heart attacks when heart damage could be controlled. He
also knew that if Admiral Gates was calling personally
that he'd better get back to Virginia immediately.

Geno had been instructed to get to Ellington Field
ASAP to pick up a Navy plane flown in from Virginia.
Ellington was fifteen miles south of Houston and
approximately thirty miles from his mother and father's
home. He quickly grabbed his things and was on his
way in the rental car. He guessed that the military
would get the rental car back to its location for him.

Ellington is a joint use civil/military airport ac-
quired by the city of Houston in 1984. In addition

to civil aircraft, the airport also services NASA and United Parcel Services. Ellington was too good of a cover to pass up for the Department of Defense. It was right out in the open, with access to both military and UPS. The armed services anti-terror efforts coordinated by the FBI were also housed in the "cardboard box", a name used by locals who thought the brown rectangular building was a plain-label hangout for some of the locals from the very large flying clubs in Texas, but it was much more. The cardboard box was a FBI/DOD task force center. Geno went there to meet his contacts and get on his flight back to Virginia.

It was now 4:00 a.m. local time. Geno was patched through to Admiral Gates' office on a secure hookup shortly after takeoff from Ellington and upon reaching flight altitude. "Geno, we've got a hell of a mess on our hands! Reliable reports are coming in that something big is going on in Saudi Arabia. We need to get you and Team 6 in there to secure our interests, the Royal Family and oil fields could be in serious danger."

What? Geno thought.

"Now listen, I want you to assemble whatever you need to get in and take care of this if it is true. Secure assets and get the hell out of Dodge without a trace. Typical Black Ops; we don't want anybody to know we were involved. Pick who you want and what you need. I'll have more details when you arrive back in Virginia."

Geno started thinking immediately about who and what. He knew he wouldn't need any Zodiacs for this one. He'd need to get in under the cover of darkness most likely, and he needed his old buddy Fats Walker. Fats may not be a waterman, but he was a desert cockroach. He could survive anywhere and knew what it took to be deadly quiet and lethally effective. Only one problem for Geno: Fats had mustered out of the SEALs a year earlier and was now a consultant in the lucrative security protections services for high-value targets such as diplomats and high-dollar business-people. Surely, Fats' wife, Dorothy, would understand and not stand in Fats' way to serve his country in such extreme need?

Perhaps he could convince Admiral Gates to contract with Fats at an amount that Dorothy wouldn't be able to refuse. A million-dollar contract was chicken feed under these circumstances, and there was the government-guaranteed lifetime annuity for Dorothy and free college for the kids if something happened to Fats. One of the benefits of Black Ops was that no one knew about these deals and a flag officer could approve them without going up the chain of command to the Chief of Naval Operations, the White House, or any nosy congressional committees. Like any other Special Forces units or the CIA, they presented line-item budgets without details, which covered miscellaneous expenditures such as Fats. Everybody that needed to know was in on the "wink and blink" budget process, thank God!

The phone rang for a long time before Dorothy answered. "Is Frank there, Dorothy?" Geno called Fats "Frank" because Dorothy thought that Fats was a demeaning name for her hubby. She had come up with Frank as a nickname for Fats' given name, Francis. When they married, Dorothy made Fats promise that he would be called Frank, not Fats.

All of his SEAL buddies used the nickname Fats; Dorothy didn't like it and corrected them whenever they were together: "You mean Frank, don't you? His name is Frank." Oh well, frankness could be a pain in the ass sometimes, so the SEALs simply avoided Dorothy when they could.

"Yes, Frank is here, but Geno, it's four-thirty in the morning."

"Yeah, I know Dottie. I need to talk to Frank." *What a pain. Did she really think I was calling for the hell of it?* She handed the phone to Frank.

"Geno, what in the hell do you want? Are you in jail somewhere? Couldn't you wait until morning to call for bail? Where are you?"

"Fats, listen real carefully. There's a serious situation brewing back at DEVGRU. I'm on a jet flying from Houston, where my mother is recovering from a heart attack, and on my way back to Virginia. I can't talk too much because your line isn't secure. I need you. Can you meet me in Virginia right away?"

"Geno, for God's sake, you gotta be kidding me! I'm out of the SEALs and in private business now."

"Fats, I know all that, but the old man called me himself and I need you."

"The old man? Holy shit, what's going on?"

"Fats, I can't talk, can you meet me in Virginia?"

"Geno, you SOB, I can't just drop and run."

"Fats, remember that time I saved your ass off the beach in Coronado?"

"Geno, that's reaching pretty far back, and you've used that trick many times before. C'mon, what's up?"

"Can't talk, can you meet me in Virginia? I need you...now!"

"Geno, you son of a bitch!"

"Good!" Geno replied. He knew that was a yes. "Tell Dottie I give her my best and tell her you'll be home in one piece. There will be a jet waiting for you at seven-thirty at Ellington. No need to pack much, bring a toothbrush and Uncle Sam will fill in the rest."

"OK, Geno, but this better be good. I guess 'the only easy day was yesterday,'" a phrase SEALs learn to embrace through BUD/S.

"Thanks, Fats. See you in Virginia." Geno settled back and caught some z's because he knew a full day awaited him in Virginia.

Geno's jet covered the twelve hundred miles from Houston to Little Creek in a little more than four hours and set down at 9:28 a.m. local time. Admiral Gates' aide and two shore patrol met him on the tarmac. "What's up, Clark?" Geno asked.

"The old man will fill you in when you get to his office. Are you ready, Geno?"

"Yes," he replied. He had done a swabbie cleaning of himself on the plane, shaved, and changed into a uniform brought for him on the plane. He would have liked some eggs and hash browns, but breakfasted on the fruits and toast on the plane, so he was ready for the day.

Geno made the trip across base towards DEVGRU headquarters, where he noticed an abnormal amount of hustle going on. "Clark, what's with all the hubbub?"

"You'll find out. Haven't you been following the news?" Clark answered rather condescendingly.

"Well, you know with my mother having had a heart attack I didn't exactly have time to glue myself to CNN," Geno replied with an equal amount of sarcasm and spite in his voice.

Clark was like all the other captains who had enough scrambled eggs on their hats to feel superior and powerful, but not enough accomplishments or skill to make the jump to flag officer. *Flip little bastard,* Geno thought.

It looked like a lot of equipment was being loaded, mostly desert equipment. *Hmmm, must be something really big brewing in Saudi,* Geno thought. *An assignment is an assignment, ours is not to question why…*

Geno squared away his uniform while Clark announced him to Admiral Gates. Clark opened the door and the old man quickly said, "C'mon in, Geno, I've got some hot stuff for you."

"Yes, sir," Geno said.

"Thank you, Geno, but let's do away with the formalities and get down to business. Coffee?"

"No, sir, I had my fill on the plane."

"Good, Clark, get him a cup of coffee, hot and black, I suppose?"

"Yes, sir, Admiral." *Thing about the brass is that they all seem hard of hearing!* Geno thought.

"Geno, you may not know this, with your mother and all, but this thing is spreading like wildfire throughout the Arab world. There are protests in Yemen, Jordan, Libya, Bahrain, Syria, Algeria, and even Saudi Arabia. The protestors are gearing up in Iran also. This thing caught the CIA, State Department, and National Security Agency by surprise and now we have to go in and protect our assets in that region. There's a lot at stake here with oil, al Qaeda and all. The Muslim Brotherhood is pussyfooting in the wings, waiting to see where their opportunities are and Hezbollah is always in the shadows. The CIA thinks the biggest risks of an event are in the smaller, less-educated, and repressed potentates of the region, Bahrain, UAE, and Saudi Arabia."

"Sir," Geno said, "Saudi Arabia may have its problems, but the Army and national security forces are armed to the teeth and loyal as hell. They also have billions of dollars to shower on the population, to buy time."

"Geno, I know that, but we follow orders from DOD and the White House. We've got teams fanning out in the region. We're going to cover this thing as best as possible, what with our activities in Afghanistan, Iraq, and Yemen already."

Jesus, Geno thought, *what do these jackasses think, you just turn SEALs and other Special Ops people off some damn assembly line?*

"You're going to Saudi Arabia; there are some credible threats on the Royal Family. We need you in there to protect our interests, Clark will fill you in," Admiral Gates said. "Anything you need for your mission is yours, and I mean that. Clark, see that Geno gets whatever he needs, got me?"

"Yes, sir, Admiral!" Clark replied.

"Ah, Admiral," Geno said before squaring around

to leave the room, "there is one thing you might have to approve."

"What's that?" Gates said.

"I need to bring a key asset in as a contractor on this mission," Geno said.

"Key asset contractor?" the old man barked. "You know we don't do contractors on missions, Goddamn it! We've got the mission, the Black Ops of the mission, the men, possible casualties, for Christ's sake. What are you thinking, man?"

"Admiral, if you want this mission to succeed, I need Frank 'Fats' Walker along with us as a contractor on the mission, and I'm making an official request to you." Geno knew how to play the game also; he had the old man boxed in.

"All right, but don't screw this up or you're out of the Navy. Clark, do the paperwork for this Fats guy!"

Geno smiled inwardly as he thanked the Admiral, turned on his heels quickly, and exited the room. Outside the Admiral's office, he addressed Clark. "Fats is already under way. Should be here by late afternoon at the latest. You'll have the paperwork ready when he gets here?"

"Yes, Geno, but my God!"

"Thanks, Clark. Where do I set up shop while I get this thing organized?"

"Right down the hall here. You've got Team 6," Clark said. "Anybody else you need besides this Fats guy?" he asked rather sarcastically.

You're a lucky man you little SOB, Geno thought as he contemplated teaching Clark a little SEAL respect, but he knew this was not the time or place. "No, Clark, that's it for now." *Get the hell out of here!* he thought. "I want to study some maps, call Ops, and find out what the insertion plans are. I'll call 6 Chief Smittee and tell him to get the guys to start getting ready to saddle up."

Saddling up meant packing gear, personal items, and weapons which normally included a favorite knife or pistol. Geno felt for his Saint Christopher medal under his shirt, gave it a rub, and thought about his mother. Things were happening pretty fast, but she'd understand. He even said a Hail Mary for her. He didn't know if he was scared for his mother or for himself, but she'd be OK with the doctors and he'd be OK with Saint Chris.

CHAPTER 7

THE DARK SIDE

Home again in Saudi Arabia after a three-month healing period for back surgery in New York, King Abdullah announced $37 billion of benefits to Saudis to officially help offset inflation and unemployment and to afford family housing for many of Saudi Arabia's underclass. That was the official reasoning; the reality was far more practical: the King had been away from the country convalescing while the Arab neighborhood he ruled was crumbling and burning down, and he wanted to buy time and favors for his people.

The Royal Family pulled out all the stops for the king to give the impression that all was well and that his people still loved him. Hundreds of men dressed in white robes performed a traditional Bedouin sword dance on carpets that had been laid out for the King's arrival. The King of Bahrain, King Hamad bin Isa, was also on the tarmac to greet the elderly and sickly King Abdullah. King Hamad had freed 250 political prisoners just a few days ago to show the Bahrain people that he too was "getting it". Bringing in King Hamad was intended to show Saudi citizens that along with the $37 billion—shall we say stimulus plan— King Abdullah and the other ruling elites were on the "cutting edge" of reform in the region also.

The problem for Saudi Arabia was that Imran Ali didn't see it that way. He was planning to strike at the heart of stability and the heart of The Great Satan polluting Mecca, the United States of America. How despicable and sacrilegious was it for King Abdullah to let these infidels linger on holy ground! He knew that King Abdullah and his aging brothers were remnants of a bygone era. Islam, through the ever-sacred Allah, had gained much power in the world compared to the out-of-touch royals. Allah had blessed the Arab world with the "poppy juice" that the West was so addicted to: oil! Oil, a divine gift from God, Allah be praised! Allah would now use Imran Ali as his sacred instrument to strike at the infidels of the West by returning Sharia law to the Middle East and the rest of the world as it slowly died of thirst without its precious cocktails of oil and gasoline. Allah be praised again!

The changes in the Middle East were set in motion in early February, shortly after the fall of Mubarak in Egypt. That fall was so stunning, so twenty-first-century textbook, so successful, that it emboldened a group to form the Umma Islamic Party to officially challenge the Saudi ruling party and government.

To understand the audacity of this move, one must realize that in Saudi Arabia political parties, elected parliament, and public dissent are not allowed. Representatives of Umma told King Abdullah that he knew well what political developments and improvements of freedom and human rights were currently happening in the Islamic world. To stand up to the Saudi government was an astounding act by Umma. Their demonstration of will could mean trouble ahead for the Royal Family.

The Umma group stated that it was time to bring this reform to the kingdom of Saudi Arabia. One of the founders of the party even went so far as to say, "You cannot just have the royal party governing the country. We want to raise this issue with government officials and persuade them to step down or move aside."

These words, statements, and deeds were a glaring example of how much freedom the citizens of the Arab nations were gaining. A few months earlier such demands would not have been tolerated publicly at all; heads would have rolled, literally, after intense and brutal interrogation sessions to see what else, or whom else, these traitors might know. Instead, twenty-first-century communication technology was causing these kingdoms to fall like giant dominos, and the dissidents were unknown. Leaders of the Umma party were placed under 24/7 state police surveillance by the Saudi security forces, but the masses could not be tracked.

At the appropriate time, when this "democracy fever" subsided, the Ummas could be dealt with appropriately by the Royals. If there was a true security threat, there were many places out in the desert where dissidents would disappear and never be heard from again. The blessing of a mullah was essential for any new political movement to proceed and for its followers to achieve paradise if killed in pursuit of change. The Saudi Arabian mullahs were not going to give that approval. The Royals expected the movement to gain little traction because there was no approval by the mullahs.

How powerful was the Arab Spring movement? While not recognized as such by the West, the inventors of technology, it actually was immensely powerful. Sixty five percent of the population of Middle Eastern and North African countries was less than thirty years old. The kings and princes, the despots and henchmen, might not know a twitter from a tweet, a Facebook post from a face on a wanted poster, or a YouTube from a piece of black tubing to beat a dissident with, but these young people, sure as Allah gave it to them, they knew! Iran had introduced Islam as a political force in the Middle East over thirty years ago, but now, for the first time, conversations, strategies, and directions could be heard and transmitted in digital, real-time, moving conversations. Political and religious ideas could be driven by the common people rather than those in the ruling classes. Some used these methods for democratic success while others promoted radical agendas.

The revolution was at a crossroads: a choice was going to be made for either some form of democracy driven by the younger population or a continuance of the Islamic fundamentalism that began after the 1979 Iranian Revolution. Iran had invested heavily in the fundamentalist movement the past three decades by exporting Arab extremism, radical fanaticism, terrorism, and anti-Israel/anti-American venom. The venom had served as a galvanizing force for Hezbollah, Hamas, the Islamic Revolutionary Guard, al Qaeda, and the Taliban, to name a few. The latter drifted in and out of Iran's sphere of influence, but never that far away from its money. The others were "rock-solid franchises of mayhem", claiming victims in blood and maiming them by the thousands, as well as creating paranoia in the West by the millions. But the young techno-savvy crowd was not buying into the radical agenda.

The general aim of terrorism is not necessarily the body count, but the aftershocks of fear that ring through a society. Fear, paranoia, and bankrupting corrupt democracies like the U.S. were the goals of terrorism. For instance, Geno's mother would not fly overseas because she was afraid a terrorist might hijack her, and if they found out her son was a SEAL, she would be subject to an immediate "separation" for interrogation, torture, and probable death.

Imran Ali was determined to bring this Middle East revolution down squarely on the side of Islamic fundamentalism governed by Sharia law before the young modernists gained traction. There would be no more trips to Paris, London, New York, or even Bahrain to bathe in the waters of the infidels' wine and liquor for the elites. There would be no more pale-skinned concubines with satanic red lipstick and body piercings in these faraway capitals of Satan! Possibly someday, when the infidels were conquered or put to the sword, and these capitals were in the hands of Allah, there would be travel to them, but not now or for the sins of hedonism.

The West had allowed millions of Arabs to immigrate to Europe, Canada (ideal launching base for terror cells operating in the USA), and even the United States of America, with student visas being the green card to eventual jihad. Did America even know that green was the color of Arab dominance and fanaticism? These Americans were truly stupid! At least the leaders of Western Europe in France, Germany, and England had said that political correctness and multiculturalism did not work. Whereas, American politicians tried to address the jihad cause with words, because they feared a real solution would label them as politically incorrect fanatics themselves.

The beauty of democracy for a terrorist is that

the terrorist always knows the democrat's views and moves because corrupt politicians have to disclose them publicly to get elected. *What a stupid system,* Imran thought. Allah certainly had the wisdom of God when he revealed Sharia law and governance to the great Prophet Muhammad by the angel Jibril (Gabriel). This permitted Islam to prosper without democratic meddling.

Bringing the revolution to Western Europe through the hulls of oil tankers from the Gulf would come just in time to stop the European ethnic hardliners from gaining traction in their efforts to compartmentalize the infiltration Islam had made in Europe over the past thirty years. The industrialized West's population was literally dying through the generations. Importing guest workers from former colonies in the Middle East had served two purposes for Europe: it brought in a much-needed lower-caste working class to do the jobs that the heavily unionized populations would not do, and it provided a social absolution for enslaving former colonists. Open and free immigration from former colonial capitals was doing for the former muslims what they could have never imagined fifty to one hundred years ago: A successful invasion and takeover of Europe. The Moors, the great Saladin, and countless other great Arab leaders had been rebuffed from accomplishing this invasion for hundreds, if not thousands, of years! Now the open immigration policies were putting Arab domination of Europe within reach.

Everything was coming together for Imran Ali and the believers of Sharia Islam, everything! Change was sweeping the Arab world faster than the ill-prepared West was able to comprehend. Bastions of corruption in Egypt, Tunisia, Libya, Bahrain, Jordan, and even Saudi Arabia had been challenged or toppled. Opportunities for fundamentalism were ripe. The rise of Red China was making natural resources and oil supplies very tight for the world and the prices were skyrocketing. There was little or no room for stoppages or slowdowns of these needed transfusions for the West. Western Europe had allowed the camel's nose into the tent by not reproducing their population. Instead, they had opted for the selfish one- or two-child lure of self-indulgence, while Imran's Arab brothers were flooding the world with offspring.

Surely, Allah had a direct hand in this, and Imran knew that Allah must be served immediately, lest he, Imran, fall into a snare. Imran must move with prudent haste. He had been trained his whole life for this mission. He had heard the oral traditions of the older ones passed down in the "dog jails" of Palestine. He had learned to read the Quran. He spent his youth battling Jewish soldiers on the West Bank. He graduated to training camps in Libya in the old days and was now in Yemen. He reveled in events of

9/11 and relished seeing soft Americans being blown to bits, as they deserved, in the cities and deserts of Iraq and the mountains of Afghanistan. It was now time for him, Imran Ali, to serve Allah on this most important mission. Allah Akbar! God is Great!

CHAPTER 8

THE MOVE

IMRAN BEGAN PREPARING FOR HIS MISSION IN SAUDI ARABIA as quickly as was prudent. Coming from his Hezbollah background, he had also established contacts through the Muslim Brotherhood in Egypt. The Brothers, as the West referred to them, were patiently standing on the sidelines in Egypt biding their time, letting events unfold, making appropriate influences, and waiting. Clearly, they had already won a key political foothold in the new Egypt when the American President had said that all—yes, *all*—political parties should be included in the new government, including the Muslim Brotherhood if chosen by the representatives of the people.

Patient politics had served Hezbollah, translated as "Party of God", well in Lebanon. After running the Americans out of Beirut in 1983 with the bombing of the U.S. Marine barracks, the largest nonnuclear explosion the world had seen up to that time, Hezbollah gained a political foothold. Elected in certified open and free elections in the 2000's, it assumed effective veto power in control of the Lebanese parliament under the Doha Agreement of May 21, 2008. Financial backing by Iran had allowed Hezbollah to accumulate strategic assets such as broadcast media, extensive social services to win the hearts and minds of the population, as well as thousands of rockets to pepper Israel such that Israel sheepishly ceased military operations against Hezbollah. Hezbollah had declared this a victory in Lebanon and throughout the Arab world in 2006.

Hezbollah became an organizational model for al Qaeda and Osama bin Laden. Their governance began with Allah and ended with groups on the ground. Hezbollah as a political force was branching out its funding reach as most political causes do. The reach of Hezbollah's funding was now reported to be as diverse as individuals and organizations in the United States, Paraguay, Argentina, and Brazil, with new suspicions arising about Bolivia, as well as the tried-and-true Iranians. Reports indicated that in the past, Hezbollah received $200 million to $400 million in funding annually from Iran. As of late, Venezuela had lent political support, if not financial. The CIA was also investigating if the NARCO terrorists of Central America were providing funding support. Hezbollah was obviously well financed from many different sources around the world. Hezbollah and the radical Arabs saw this as another act of Allah working in their favor.

Geno, Navy SEALs, and other Special Forces were well versed in the workings and organization of Hezbollah because, as it served as a template for al Qaeda and other terror groups, it also served as a manual for terrorist elimination by Special Forces and the CIA. Working together outside the boundaries of the United States, Special Forces and the CIA had been successful in eliminating various key terrorists through the years, but it seemed to be an endless job!

Reports were circulating that agents of Iran had been infiltrating the United States through illegal immigration along the Mexican-U.S. border, which is as porous as a sieve. Hezbollah and al Qaeda had long been known to be enemies of sorts, but with the U.S. military involved against both, perhaps the old Arab adage was true: "An enemy of my enemy is my friend". Despite the public discrepancies of any links between al Qaeda and Hezbollah, one had to remember that the primary sponsor of terrorism was Iran, and Iran called the shots when they focused on any given outcome. They were all one bloody family working for the downfall of Israel and the West.

In short, Hezbollah was a formidable and long-standing organized force that Imran had worked himself into. He was ready for something big, and they were too. A very critical point was that members of Hezbollah saw themselves as an evolving governing political force. The success of Hezbollah and al Qaeda through the years had taught them that fighting the enemy on a guerilla warfront was the way to achieve victory, as opposed to open warfare, which they realized they could not match. They viewed the West, particularly America, as a "Gulliver-type" giant. Someone they could tie into knots and disable through a crafted policy of bogging America down in large-scale military actions such as Iraq and Afghanistan, coupled with strategic and highly effective terror hits such as in Bali, Jerusalem, London, Lisbon, Amsterdam, and Fort Hood, Texas. Soon they would again have their way on American airliners over American soil. They had been caught in Detroit and in New York's Times Square, but it was only a matter of time before the sleeper cells of America would achieve success.

The time was right for all jihadists. Gulliver was becoming so entwined that he could not respond to the most earthshaking events in the Arab world since the takeover of the American Embassy in Tehran in 1979. Even that act, brazen as it was, was proof that America would wilt under pressure rather than risk spilling the blood of its spies in a large metropolitan center. The Black Hawk incident in Somalia in 1993 reinforced this belief as President Clinton withdrew American forces from an ill-equipped Somalia. America further reinforced this belief by adopting a hands-off policy during the Green Revolution of 2009. As the American hostages in Tehran were left spinning in a web of degradation in 1979, so were millions of Iranian protestors who took to the streets in the summer of 2009. America was no longer the feisty fighter of its revolutionary days, fighting for freedom at all costs.

America was like Britain of the 1700's—fighting wars on all fronts, going bankrupt and growing weary in the process. America had fought well in traditional military settings with its vast powers, but this era and urban warfare style were different. Bombing and strafing "innocent civilians" was not America's style of warfare, and Hezbollah was banking on this fact.

Riyadh is a city of nearly seven million people that presented many complications for the West. Forty percent of its population are guest workers from Pakistan, India, Bangladesh, the Philippines, Yemen, and Sudan. These people were from key allied nations of America that it had to consider if a wholesale military operation was launched. Another complication in considering a Saudi operation was that, its oil fields lay mostly in the east, home to primarily a Shi'ite population, a population that Radicals could easily count on to disrupt or destroy the flow of oil to the West.

The unthinkable was thinkable and was now possible. Jihadists could take Saudi Arabia. Coordination by the Jihadist Movement would be the key.

Imran's contacts within the Brotherhood and Hezbollah landed him safely in Riyadh, the capital of Saudi Arabia and home of King Abdullah. Yemen adjoins Saudi Arabia on the south. Riyadh is located in central Saudi Arabia, slightly to the north and to the east. Imran had many routes available. He was instructed to travel overland because the screenings at the airports were on heightened alert. He was able to travel from Aden on the south of Yemen to Najran on the border, then north along the inner route of the Red Sea into Saudi Arabia by way of Abha, Al Bahah, and Al Taif. At Al Taif, he traveled east on the great highway through Zalim, Halaban, and Ad Dawadmi to Riyadh. He posed as a migrant worker from Yemen with all the proper papers, but he really hadn't needed them except for his border crossing.

Once in Riyadh, Imran was directed to a safe house in the southern, less-populated section of the city. The weather at that time of the year in early summer was a warm eighty-five degrees Fahrenheit at night and reached a hundred and ten during the day. The city itself was an amalgam of shining steel skyscrapers, old palaces, affluent neighborhoods, and poor ghettos where many of the guest workers and lower-caste Saudis were forced to live. Recently the city's sewer system had flooded in those parts of the city, sparking protest marches and cries of reform.

The pot of dissent and rebellion boiled below the

surface, and circumstances were not what the Royal Family and the West had proclaimed. However, needing oil, the West—like any junkie—was willing to overlook many human rights violations, strong-arm tactics, and the like. The mantra of the West and its Arab suppliers seemed to be "Don't disrupt the oil flow with any big crackdowns and be careful how you loosen the governing grip because we are mutually addicted, you as the supplier and us as the user."

Imran could not grasp this logic in dealing with a sworn friend of Israel and therefore an enemy of Arabia. Sharia law would no longer tolerate this abomination by Saudis on the holy ground of Arabia.

While Imran was on the move, Geno wasn't wasting any daylight himself. He was on the move also. DEVGRU was in high gear, as was the entire Little Creek complex.

Little Creek is the largest base of its kind in the world. It is the major operating station for the amphibious forces of the United States Atlantic Fleet. Little Creek's mission is to provide support and services to operating forces and shore commands. Today the complex includes nine thousand acres of land and fifteen thousand military and civilian employees. There are sixty-one piers surrounding Little Creek with docking facilities for thirty naval ships. The channel has a twenty-two-foot depth, and ships of up to a twenty-foot draft traverse in and out of the channel. SEAL teams two, four, eight, and ten are based and operate from the Little Creek complex along with other amphibious forces like explosive ordinance disposal units and amphibious assault ships.

Streamlining the War on Terror efforts in 2005, various commands were consolidated into Little Creek. The new command structure alignment resulted in various Space Warfare Systems—SPAWAR— commands coming together to form SPAWAR Atlantic in Little Creek. The goal of these consolidations was to create multidisciplinary and multifunctional centers of excellence (nice terminology for the taxpayers, especially the academic and corporate crowd— and who said the military wasn't sensitive or adept at public relations!). Another goal was to reduce the timeline to bring new weapon systems to the Special Forces.

SEALs and other Special Forces were moving closer to virtualization and real time, with electronic capabilities incomprehensible to anyone except for an MIT grad student perhaps. All of this happened without a peep from Congress. It was brilliant because it was done under the guise of "trimming back the military".

Under normal circumstances there was a lot more going on at Little Creek than met the eye. However, these were heightened times in the summer of 2011 because of the ever-increasing activities of the Arab

Spring. Geno noticed that everything that could move was moving. They were stretched to the limits, as all Special Ops were, even with the vast growth of the Special Forces in the 2000 decade. All hands appeared to be moving on deck!

There was one other strategic twist: DEVGRU command was supposedly located at Little Creek along with the other SEAL teams. In reality, it was never located there; the true location was at Dam Neck, Virginia—close by, but not at Little Creek, and there was a very big reason for that. SEAL Team 6 operated in its own secret world, exempt from normal scrutiny. Furthermore, SEAL Team 6 "is not subject to the provisions of Chapter 71 of Title 5 of the United States Code and those provisions cannot be applied to the group and organization in a manner consistent with national security requirements and consideration."

In other words, when on assignment outside of the borders of the United States, the Federal Labor-Management Relations Program does not apply to anyone involved in DEVGRU. This little-noticed executive order, issued in November 1979, which no one paid attention to or really even saw, put a dark cloak around all operations and personnel.

Furthermore, "It is stated that DEVGRU has a primary function of intelligence, counter-intelligence, investigative, and national security work", making

DEVGRU one of a few units permitted to conduct preemptive strikes against terrorists and terrorist facilities. DEVGRU often teamed with U.S. Army Delta Force on missions. Whatever the mission, the outcome was never in question with these guys, especially with Geno.

Obviously, Geno was in a group that was ultra deep, ultra dark, and ultra lethal. Geno was now so skilled and trustworthy that he was part of a world that no one knew about. He had come a long way from his youth in Houston, Texas.

Imran didn't know who would be coming for him, should he succeed, only that *somebody* would come for him. He would soon find out *who* that who was. Imran, Hezbollah, Geno, and DEVGRU were on a collision course!

CHAPTER 9

ZULU TIME

AT MIDNIGHT GENO AND TEAM 6 LOADED INTO A SPECIALLY equipped Navy C-40B, a plane normally reserved for combatant commanders. The C-40B has 27,000 pounds of thrust in each of its two engines, flies at mach 0.8, 530 mph, and has a flight range of 4,500 to 5,000 nautical miles. They landed in Rota Naval Air Station in Spain for a quick refueling that lasted less than an hour before they were on their way again.

It was a gut-buster of a trip, taking sixteen hours in all to cover the seven thousand flight miles. They quickly caught some z's on their way, with lights out within an hour of takeoff. After a six-hour sleep break, it was up and at 'em with communications from Virginia, appropriate planning and mapping with the crew, and equipment list checking, but unlike the movies, no letters back home. Every SEAL family knew that their loved ones could be called up at a minute's notice, be gone for days or months on end, and would in all probability come back home in one piece, but families knew that sometimes they didn't. It was part of the territory in SEAL life. Somehow, the families dealt with it. Divorce was very common. Not because the men didn't love their wives, but because they just loved the SEAL life more.

Geno and the team played some gin and pitch during the flight to break the monotony, but they also focused on the mental preparation of the mission. SEALs had long ago adopted the mental training technique of Olympic athletes: quiet mental visualization of tasks to be performed. It was true they could perform their duties virtually in their sleep, as they visualized them countless times until they became second nature. The quiet mental visualization was coupled with thousands of hours of physical preparation and practice drills. The SEAL goal was to get in and out without anyone knowing you were there.

Geno and the team had switched to Zulu Time, Greenwich Mean Time, and the universal clock of military operations. This allowed all military to be on the same time for communication and execution purposes all around the world. Zulu Time made the team realize that they were in mission mode.

Departure was really just a process of gathering the crew together because they would pick up all their combat equipment at the Royal Saudi Air Force base within Prince Sultan Air Base, a base the U.S. military had transferred to the Saudis after a ferocious backlash from the Arab world in 2003. Arabs were incited —at the prompting of Hezbollah, Hamas, and all surrogates available—to pressure the Saudis to remove all U.S. troops from Saudi soil, the home of Mecca. The Americans and their hedonistic ways were not welcome, even though America had gone to great lengths to forbid the usage of alcohol and other Western vices; women had to be fully covered if off base.

It wasn't really about Western ways for the fundamentalists; it was about removing a strong Western force within the heart of Islam, particularly radical Islam. When the bases were transferred, an enemy of Islam was removed and the deterrence to radical Islam was removed as well. Or so the fanatics thought.

Although the Americans lost their bases in Saudi Arabia, they gained a huge military complex at Qatar, which was a short 150 miles up the highway from Riyadh. Qatar was strategically located in the heart of the Persian Gulf through which much of the world's oil flows. It wasn't really a bad trade. The Americans could fly in and out of Saudi Royal Air Force facilities at Sultan on a regular basis after the 2003 transfer. During an "irregular" basis such as this, they were hot-shotted into the Prince Sultan Air Base, where equipment for Team 6 would be waiting for them. Any other equipment could be hot-shotted in from Kuwait. Old Uncle Sam knew there was more than one way to skin a cat!

The *Golden Child* mission, as this mission was designated, harkened back to the original roots of Team 6; the guys were jacked about going into the heart of Riyadh. Among other assignments, SEALs were originally trained to covertly infiltrate hot spots to conduct recon or security assessments. They would secure King Abdullah and eliminate the opposition with all deadly force necessary. This was a "take no prisoners" operation unless they could be bound, drugged, or whisked away without danger to the squad for further interrogation at a "friendly facility", since the President was no longer registering guests at Guantanamo.

Geno was leading a platoon of twenty, including himself. Each man had a specific role, although all were cross-trained in the event of "adversity". The team had a traditional military command structure. There was an officer in charge, an 0-2 assistant officer in charge, a platoon chief (E-7), an operations leading petty officer (E-6), as well as the other personnel assigned to the team. The leadership of the team revolved around the officer in charge and the senior noncommissioned officer. Geno, a noncommissioned officer, was the heart and soul leader of Team 6. Everyone, including the Senior Officer, knew about his talents, abilities, and instincts, so they trusted his judgment and allowed him to call the shots for the team. Geno could call upon the full capabilities of the platoon, including: snipers, breachers, communicators, engineers, corpsmen, navigators, interrogators, explosive specialists, technical surveillance operators, and other advanced Special Ops men.

Equipment? Not to worry; Uncle Sam doesn't send his best without the best. The preferred weapons of choice: the M4 carbine, a converted M16 semiautomatic rifle, which came equipped with laser scopes, night vision equipment, and grenade launcher options. If that was not enough, there were other options including a shorter 10.5 inch barrel. The shorter barrel created a better kill factor for close-in combat. Sawed-off shotguns were another option that were effective in close-in combat with mass devastation. The SEAL submachine gun was also multi equipped and came with a special Navy trigger mechanism that could fire single shots or fully automatic.

They say you don't take a knife to a gun fight; well, SEALs do. It is said that the real Navy SEAL knife is whatever knife a SEAL has on him at the time, and many times it boils down to a matter of personal choice from the weapons store and what you are accustomed to for effectiveness and abilities. Remember, in a knife fight, you're not taking a prisoner. It is life or death for you or the other guy. Geno preferred a traditional SEAL knife dating back to the Vietnam era. He liked having serrated edges on both sides of the blade. "If one side of the blade doesn't get you, the other one will," was his motto. You could also cut cord and wire with either side if you were in a pinch.

Ropes? Technology had replaced traditional ropes with ultra-strong plastic and nylon blends. High-strength plastic? Ideal for securing prisoners in the "cuff version". Guy wires and stringers? Of course—haven't you seen any Rambo movies? And of course, communication gear! Communications had become so sophisticated that mission operations could be monitored or modified in real time from Virginia. Mission modifications came as a result of changing conditions or new information from spy satellites ringing the globe. Technology and resolution had become so advanced that a satellite could read a license plate from outer space.

Geno didn't mind modifications while on a mission if they were pertinent. However, he didn't like some lieutenant junior grade joy stick operator back in Virginia messing with his mission, and he had gained such a reputation. There would be ass-chewing when he got back to base if some JG had been thinking he was playing combat video games on Geno's mission.

On a mission, unless overridden from Virginia by a senior officer, what Geno said was the law. He had earned this privilege long ago in Panama, the drug cartel wars in Guatemala, and the Philippines. Geno seemed to have some sixth sense about where danger lurked, an ability to assess it and deal with it.

He prided himself, as he should, on the fact that he had lost very few men in combat, and every one that he lost came home to a proper burial with loved ones. He hated those parts of the mission.

"Flight number BA 9000, you're cleared for landing." So far so good. The 9000 sequence number indicated a ferry flight of an aircraft devoid of passengers or cargo. It was simply a shuttle of an aircraft from point A to point B. As far as anyone knew, the unmarked C40 was a shuttle within the Saudi air force. It was midnight in Riyadh, make that 0000 Zulu, ideal timing with the cover of darkness. They would have close to six hours of time to gather their gear, get mobile, and get on mission. *Golden Child* was now officially boots on ground.

Imran wasn't sitting, wasting his time, either. He was coordinating with his handlers, beading in on the King's location and routines. The security troop routines had to be gone over and over again. He had done much of this in Yemen while he was hatching his plot and running it up the flagpole. If anything, the Saudi security forces could be counted upon for their routine, discipline, and a certain lack of spontaneity. Imran and his team would use these traits to their advantage. They were not as trained, well equipped, or disciplined as the SEALs or Saudi security forces, but they had fervor, ardor, emotion, and Allah on their side. Things Imran knew the American and Saudi heathens did not have.

CHAPTER 10

HOT TIME
IN THE CITY

Hot Town Summer In The City
Back Of My Neck Getting Dirt And Gritty
Been Down, Isn't It A Pity
Doesn't Seem To Be A Shadow In The City
All Around People Looking Half Dead
Walking On The Sidewalk Hotter Than A Match Head

– MARK SEBASTIAN, *Lovin' Spoonful, 1966*

THOUGH IT WAS WRITTEN AND BECAME A TOP TEN HIT OF THE 1960's, it was still on the playlists as Geno was growing up. The tune popped into his head that first night in Riyadh because things were definitely heating up all around Riyadh. There were increasing protests all around, even in Iraq, where his brothers and sisters in arms had paid the ultimate price for Iraqi freedom.

That was not Geno's concern. He was mission-focused as always. SEALs are capable of blocking out past events and were "in the moment", particularly on a mission. In this particular moment, things were heating to the point where the Saudis were now monitoring as many social network exchanges in the region as often as possible, particularly in country. The governing body was intent on staying ahead of the curve.

The Libyan and Syrian situations had greatly alarmed King Abdullah, particularly when Colonel Gaddafi bombed rebel bases and Assad killed hundreds of protestors in his country. He was more convinced than ever that the two were insane, going off the deep end, and, most importantly, risking civil war throughout the region.

King Abdullah was also worried about the West becoming more involved militarily. Would they get more deeply involved with a direct military intervention? Would they do something more than enforce a no-fly zone? The stakes were very high in the Arab world. Such actions would roil Arab feelings to a fever pitch. The disenfranchised Arabs would see this as a deceitful opportunity from the West to have another base of operations in the region. The Americans were already in Iraq and Afghanistan. If NATO landed in Libya or Syria on a "rescue mission" they would undoubtedly stay for months, if not years, if invited by the new regime to do so.

Although friendly to the Americans, Abdullah didn't want to become a victim of circumstances in the reshuffling of the deck in the region. As an aging ruler, other than personal safety, his primary concern was transitioning governance and all of the benefits of governing the kingdom to his family and maintaining that wealth and power for them.

Furthermore, the more militant Shi'ite Arabs of Iraq, Syria, Lebanon, and Iran were increasingly encircling Saudi Arabia. The King had pleaded in a secret meeting with General Petraeus in 2008 to "cut off the head of the snake", Iran. This was a bold and dangerous move for the King to make, but it was a strong sign of how increasingly worried the Saudis were becoming over Muslim fanaticism fueled by Iran.

Ruling in Saudi Arabia came with "work", much as it did for the Royal Family of Britain. The load wasn't as heavy as it was in Britain, but it was a more dangerous load in this part of the world. The per capita ownership or access to weapons in the Middle East was off the charts compared to Europe. Any encounter could potentially turn deadly on any given day if security had not properly screened fanatics. Also, there were required monthly public forums where any citizen could come forward with a request or grievance for a governor or member of the Royal Family.

These meetings reminded Geno of a scene out of *The Godfather*, his favorite movie, when Don Corleone would meet with one of his subjects to hear their request. Of course, the recipient was obligated for life to perform any duty that the Don would ask of him. In fact, he was obligated not just to "officially" return that one favor at any point in time, but was forever indebted to the Don. It was like selling your soul. The Saudi government kept meticulous records of all people who came forward at the public meetings. The citizen could be friend or foe now or at a future date. Coming forward showed a certain boldness that they needed to monitor, and they did. With all the wealth and power of the Royal Family, there was certain vulnerability for them also.

Geno was also a history buff and a fan of The History Channel. The History Channel had recently carried a program about the privileges of being President of the United States. Although hardened extensively since 9/11, the program reported there had been ninety-one breaches of presidential security over the past thirty years. *Amazing,* Geno thought, recalling the incident in 2009, when Tareq and Michaele Salahi crashed a White House state dinner and met the President, Vice President, and other high-level officials face-to-face in person without any weapons check. They could have fired a shot at the President or anyone else in attendance at the dinner.

It also reminded him of the time in November 2005 when his daredevil friend John jumped into the security detail of Prince Charles and Duchess Camilla at the Mark Hopkins Hotel on the first day of their visit in San Francisco. John had regaled him about how easy it was and how he had been part of the security detail at the Hopkins for their entire four-day stay. In fact, the security detail became so comfortable with John that he was allowed to be in charge of the exit doors of the hotel on the morning of final departure. Geno thought this was another "Big John Tale" until John produced pictures. He even had a picture of him and Prince Charles shaking hands on the Prince's return to the hotel from a charity dinner one evening. Security organizations like the Secret Service and others all liked to talk about the invincibility of their protection, but Geno knew that any bubble could be penetrated if planning, timing, and skill were involved. After all, that was his job!

Out of the blue, there was an unexpected satellite connect from DEVGRU command. "Golden" was the call.

"Read you, Zeke. Golden here," Geno said in code.

"In addition to the possible situation with the Royal Family there are reports of large numbers of tanks moving into Bahrain from the corral (code for Saudi Arabia)."

"Copy, Zeke."

An extremely unusual notation followed: "Itinerary subject to change, will inform. Do not proceed unless contacted, sit tight." This stopped Geno is his tracks.

Holy shit, Geno thought. *That's unusual for a team that's already been inserted.* The only thing that made sense to him was the relatively easy access to Saudi's Sultan Air Base if they needed to deploy elsewhere. Other than that, they were in Riyadh with equipment, gear, personnel, and a mission. Missions don't just happen; everything has to be in place with as much planning as possible. There are no second-place finishes in this game. It takes days, weeks, or months of practice. Something big was going on in Bahrain for the Saudis to make such a bold move in such a heated time in the region.

In fact, there *was* something hot going on in Bahrain. Like all the countries and kingdoms in the region, Bahrain had a long and convoluted history intertwined with British political maneuvers in the early twentieth century. The long and short of it: Bahrain is an archipelago of three islands, with the largest being Bahrain Island. Bahrain Island is a bit larger than Manhattan, about thirty-four miles long and fifteen miles wide. The island, fifteen miles offshore from Saudi Arabia, is connected to Saudi Arabia via the King Fahd Causeway. The population of Bahrain is about 1.25 million, with half of the total being nonnational guest workers. The loyalty to the crown was 25 percent of the population at best.

To further complicate matters in Bahrain, the British had encouraged tribal wars between the 70 percent dominant Shi'ites and the 30 percent minority Sunnis, of which the ruling family was a member, in the late 1920's and early 1930's. Also, Iran has attempted to seize Bahrain on many occasions because of its historical ties to the Persian Empire. In 1927 the Shah of Iran demanded the return of Bahrain and in 1957 the Iranian parliament passed a bill annexing Bahrain as the fourteenth province of Iran. In the 1950's, as a final act of political insanity, the British decided to "de-Iranize" Bahrain by importing large numbers of other Arab tribes from other British colonies as laborers to Bahrain. Adding to the messy history of Bahrain, oil was discovered there in 1932!

The ingredients of disaster had long been in place for Bahrain, but, since the oil boom of the 1970's, the Al-Khalfia ruling family had been proactive in further diversifying Bahrain's economy, expanding its natural role as a major port stop on maritime shipping routes dating back to the Persians and before. Things were on a rapid modernization track of quasi democratization when King Hamad ibn Isa Al Khalfia ascended the throne after his father in 1999. He instituted elections for the lower house of parliament, granted voting rights to women, and released all political prisoners at that time. However, the upper house of parliament, the Shura Council, remained appointed by the King and held veto power over the lower house. The elections of 2006 though, presented Islamists with a large victory in the lower house of parliament, and pressures began building for a more fundamentalist Islamic society in Bahrain.

Americans take our freedoms for granted, but Islamic law prohibits many of the freedoms we have. So far, the events of 2011 were presenting perfect cover for radical Islamists, Iran, Hezbollah, and other interested parties to make a play for the back door of Saudi Arabia, Bahrain. Once you get Bahrain, Saudi Arabia is next.

Then, to top it off for Team 6, a good old-fashioned Arabian sandstorm blew across the desert into Riyadh. *Geez*, Geno thought, *it ain't summer yet, but the back of my neck is getting dirty and gritty! Thank God, Fats, the desert rat, is under contract. Who knows where in the hell this is going! It's going to hell fast!*

CHAPTER 11

BOILING BLOOD

IMRAN FOUND THAT HIS HANDLERS HAD SECURED "AGENTS of Allah" within both Saudi security forces and the personal bodyguard forces of the Royal Family, and with the turmoil roiling throughout the Middle East, the time for a shocking event had arrived. The final strike of the sword against the common Arab within Saudi Arabia had come when the royal government reaffirmed a ban on assembly and dissent after the Libyan uprising. The ruling monarchy was quite adept at using events within the region as conditions to tighten its rule, which it had politically loosened at other times. The ultimate Saudi principle was that the monarchy and all of its privileges would never be forgone in the interests of true political reform.

The monarchy was excellent at using the carrot and stick approach to their advantage. The carrot being massive welfare programs for the common people, to the point where most Saudis held meaningless bureaucratic jobs within air-conditioned offices, received a fair wage, city services, roads, utilities, and everything common to civilized life. After all, they were only three to four generations removed from when most were Bedouins roaming the desert sands at will without any civilized amenities. The stick was repression of individual freedoms, means of organizing, or coming together to effect change for the common population.

Groups from Hezbollah, the Muslim Brotherhood, Iran, al Qaeda, Shi'ite radical clerics, and countless other organizations had been seeding dissent for over a generation in Saudi Arabia. They further stoked the fires when America, under the cover of a weakened coalition from the first Gulf War, had invaded Iraq in 2003. All of the radical groups had seized this event as a public relations tool that the West had bestowed upon them with their invasion of Iraq. The call of action for the radicals was based upon simple Arab logic: do we want control of the immense oil wealth of Arabia or do we want it in the hands of the West and their Zionist allies when they tire of the puppet regime in Riyadh? Ultimate invasion and takeover of Arabia was not a question in the minds of the radicals. The only question was when.

The gathering of the ruling council of Saudi Arabia was the opportunity Imran and his backers had been waiting for. The events in Bahrain had provided the perfect opportunity for Imran and his forces to strike. The focus of Saudi Arabia's government and military was divided.

The Saudi military had long been looking to flex its muscles. Though they were equipped with some of the finest weaponry the West had to offer, most of its Air Force had been trained to a razor's edge by Americans, and they had Patriot Missile System protection against an Iranian attack. What had the military spent time doing? Sitting on its hands, conducting flyovers, and staging training operations out in the desert comprised the scope of their "military action". They were like eunuchs sitting at the beck and call of the royals, armed and strong but not able to function as true men.

Emasculation is the ultimate insult to an Arab male, and the Saudi military was about as emasculated as one could get. Their Arab brothers in Syria and Iran got to flex their muscles once in a while by harassing Israel, the American Fifth Fleet, or an occasional tanker ship off the coastline. But no, the Saudis were the neutered camels of the entire region. They looked good, they looked strong on the surface, but never got involved out of fear they would alienate their "Western friends". These so-called friends became anxious over their beloved oil and started applying the anxiety of the "play by our rules or your kingdom will fall" mantra. The West would also play the "Mecca and Medina card": Let us help you keep Mecca and Medina safe for all Arabs. The ground that they rest on is sacred. Let us help you keep it out of the hands of radicals that will kill all those that do not adhere to their radical creed—this was a lie the West put out there also. The West had no limits to its falsehood promises to the Arabs.

What about Muhammad and the Arab claim to Jerusalem? How long were they going to allow Jerusalem and the holy sites of Islam located in Jerusalem to be in the hands of Jews? If the royals were true brothers of Islam, and if Arabia was a true servant of Allah, such sacrileges should not be tolerated. It was time to put America, Jews, and the House of Fahd to the sword; they were not compliant to the Quran! It was time for Imran to take action in the name of Allah.

Imran and his band were waved through designated security checkpoints leading to the Saudi Royal meeting hall. They were armed and dressed in Saudi military uniforms. As they slipped into the inner sanctum of the palace, the team sprang into action, quickly spraying the hallway to the secure meeting hall with a large hail of bullets, killing and mortally wounding twenty-plus security forces guarding the entrance. Imran and his team quickly used a set of golden decorator poles in the foyer as battering rams to force open the gold-trimmed mahogany doors. As they broke inside, they immediately sprayed the secure room with their AK-47s for effect as Imran hit the security button that turned the meeting hall into the ultimate safe room.

Once inside the room, they quickly fanned out and eliminated the Saudi security guards. Blood and bullets were everywhere. The King had been knocked to the floor by his personal bodyguards who were shielding him with their bodies. The same was true for the crown prince designate and other key members of the Royal Family, which made them easy to identify. They were quickly separated as AKs barked more bullets at anyone that moved; Imran and his forces had secured the room.

Allah be praised! He had provided a Ruby of the West as an additional gift! The American Secretary of State had been delayed in Riyadh by the sandstorm, and she was meeting with the Saudis trying to implore restraint in the move to fortify Bahrain with tanks and weaponry. Ah, Allah be praised! There were more than enough bargaining chips here to change Arabia forever!

Imran gave orders to communicate the report to outside allies. He was not worried about the security of the communication, because the sooner the communications leaked out and the broader their reach, the more incitement for other bold protests, defections, and actions would follow. In addition to the royals, the battle over the oil fields in Shi'ite-dominated eastern Arabia could begin! Damage or destruction was not a worry; it was a goal! Any disruption or destruction would throw the West into an economic depression. If the West attacked, that would be OK as well because

Iran and other true Islamists would counterattack, and Israel could be in play also! Oil would soon be $250 a barrel, on its way to $500, then $1,000 and then none available for Israel and the West! "Allah Akbar!"

The American Secretary of State looked up from the floor into Imran's eyes; steel met steel.

Geno arrived back at King Al Khalid Airbase as events were exploding and early word was leaking out that an attack had occurred at the Royal Palace and a high ranking U.S. government official may have been involved. My God, if his mother were here, she'd be praying to Saint Jude. Geno wasn't praying to Saint Jude or anyone, but he did have a big gulp in his throat. This was big, really big, the biggest thing he had ever been on. He was glad he wasn't making the call on this one; that would probably come directly from the President through the Secretary of Defense and other admirals and generals with a lot more stars and bars on their uniforms than he ever dreamt of having. This was pretty heavy.

My God! Geno slapped himself into reality. Though events had jarred him pretty heavily, he began mentally zoning about the possibilities and probabilities. *My God, my God, my God! A lot of people are going to die! How could he keep his men safe in such a pot of boiling blood?*

CHAPTER 12

COMING TOGETHER
TO BREAK UP

GENO AND THE TEAM LISTENED TO THE REPORTS THAT CAME peppering into Riyadh's Sultan Field. In fact, the United States had so many covert assets at the airbase that it was nicknamed "Little Creek East". In addition, the Fifth Fleet was headquartered out of Bahrain with a full complement of aircraft carriers, destroyers, communication vessels, anti-aircraft and anti-missile ships, hundreds of aircraft, and the SEAL teams that were commonly assigned to a carrier battlegroup. Also, Special Forces were in operation throughout Afghanistan and western Pakistan, as well as those assigned in Iraq and stationed as far away as American bases in Italy and Spain.

The structure and strategy of twenty-first-century conflicts had changed so much that, while the standing military had remained stable throughout the 2000 decade, the smashing success of Special Forces in Afghanistan in bringing the Taliban down in early 2002 had dramatically increased the demand for Special Forces troops. All branches of the military, including and especially the U.S. Navy, had and were further ramping up Special Forces training. There were caches of equipment and resources available in key locations around the world. Bahrain and Saudi were strategically located for these purposes.

The monitoring and surveillance assets of the CIA and National Security Administration were widely dispersed throughout the region and directly overhead. The events in Tunisia, Egypt, Syria, and Libya had brought things to a fever pitch. Communications were being monitored intensely that day. Everything had been pointing to Riyadh, the Royal Family, and an event of great magnitude. The early report came in that an attack had been mounted but was repulsed. Later reports came in that there was an attack with unknown casualties. Finally, within several excruciating minutes, reports came in about the actual attack, the casualties, and, most importantly, the hostages. It became clear that the American Secretary of State was a hostage. This was any government's worst nightmare, as it was a clear violation of international law to take a neutral party, such as the American Secretary of State, as a hostage and threaten or injure as such. The offended country would be forced to take action or lose face throughout the world.

American forces worldwide were placed on full military alert. NATO quickly followed, as did SEATO in the Far East, as well as the Russians and Chinese, though more for self-protection measures for themselves. In their case, they never knew what kind of a dogfight was going to break out with so much firepower, so many antsy triggers and agendas once forgotten but now remembered, and with everybody armed to the teeth! Russia and China did not want to risk being attacked by anyone, particularly the United States or its surrogates or a wild splintered force such as the rebels in Chechnya.

Geno and 6 were notified they were being reassigned to the Secretary of State rescue. *Golden Child* now became *Strong Eagle.* Team 6 was the logical choice given their training, individual distinctions, and especially their black cover from government inquiry. They were expected to take care of business under these circumstances regardless of how messy the business was, and this had the possibility of getting messy within the Arab world.

Imran and his band quickly separated the captives within the room into four small groups. Each group was given its own "high value" member. Prince Naef, who had chaired cabinet meetings during Abdullah's deteriorating health in 2010, was in one group. Prince Mutaib, son of King Abdullah and head of the Saudi National Guard, was in a different group. Khalid bin Sultan, Assistant Minister of Defense and leader of Saudi military forces in Gulf War I, was in a third group, and Bandar bin Sultan, long-time ambassador to the United States and close friend of the Bush family, was in the fourth group. Each group was then given two important but less-valuable personages as members. King Abdullah and the American Secretary of State, Kathryn Kurtz, were held individually.

The terrorists were employing the "divide and conquer" strategy. Although it had required more planning and carried more risk of detection and capture, the plan was to take the four groups to separate locations and to then act individually from those locations. The rationale was that it was like having four wasp nests to contend with instead of one giant nest. If the giant nest was captured or destroyed, all of the wasps would be killed and unable to fly throughout the region, inflicting the stings of rebellion and restoration of the "True Islam". But if the wasps were dispersed in four nests, one or two or even three could be lost, as long as one nest survived to spread the Islamic fatwa and establish a worldwide caliph in the newly cleansed Holy Land of Saudi.

Time was of the essence; action plans had to be implemented quickly before the defending military and security forces had time to react in full force. As in any safe room around the world, there was also a safe exit route. The four bands hit the safety exit and were soon in the secure transport facilities within the bowels of the building, where more guards were stopped by the threat of harm to the hostages (who wants to be saddled with the guilt of being responsible for getting one of the king's own family killed?). This strategy was the terrorists' "get out of Riyadh free card". They played it to a T and sprayed the guards down with AKs for mayhem and its effect. Then they dispersed in four directions in the royals' armor-plated, bullet- and bomb-proof vehicles to remote desert locations.

King Abdullah was too sick and elderly to risk such a trip. He would not survive, and keeping him alive as a bargaining chip was essential. Imran left him behind at the security hall safe room with Josef Alami, a young, trusted Islamic zealot. Josef and Abdullah were handcuffed and ankle-cuffed to each other. Each was strapped with C4 plastique explosive, set to detonate upon Josef's trigger, or if the wiring device between the two of them became disrupted in any way by rescuers. In effect, the King was dead and Josef would share eternal bliss in paradise for eternity with seventy-two houri virgins if the plastique were triggered.

The King was old, the kingdom was morally bankrupt to Islam, Arabia was being returned to holiness, and the West was being destroyed by its own oil addiction. The King was useful only as a high-profile target of the oncoming Islamic inquisition, in which all Islamists would be judged and dealt with as the Spanish had done in the late 1400's when they cleansed their kingdom of "Jews in Christian clothing". The list of inquisition was long and included all high-profile Arabs that had been part of the sham of the West, as it had corrupted Islam with bribes of oil spoils and decadent morals in the cities of sin through-out the capitals of Europe.

The alcohol and pollution of the Arab male in the cesspools of infidel harlots throughout the Western dens of iniquity would be dealt with harshly in the inquisition. The Arab royalty that had become slaves to the West would be dethroned and dismembered while the true followers of the Quran from the repressed street level would be elevated. "Allah Akbar!"

The American Secretary of State presented her own opportunities for Imran's agents of Allah. She was valuable, she was dangerous, but she was expendable. She needed to be exploited in every way possible to further humiliate the "great" United States of America. Her capture could lead to a declaration of war by the United States, but upon whom—a brigade of Arab zealots? Wasn't there already a declared war on terror? Wouldn't it be "double foolish" to declare war again on an unknown, undisclosed, undocumented force?

No, the apologetic American President could be counted on to fire a few cruise missiles, launch some drones, rattle swords, and rant in the United Nations, but there would be no war. The Secretary of State would be mourned in the West. She would get her portrait placed in a prominent location at the State Department lobby if killed. Upon her death, she would be given a high honor medal and possibly become the first female Secretary of State of the "Great Satan State" to be buried at their sacred Arlington Cemetery.

Killing Kurtz would be a last resort though, her exploitation would be a great tool for Imran's cause in inciting further action by his brothers. She would be taken to a remote desert location where she could be hidden but exploited much like America did to the great Osama bin Laden. Now Muslims in America would have their very own "American bin Laden" as she preached in her burka about the greatness of Islam and the lies of the West that she was forced to carry around the globe. She could be a great asset for the Muslims—or she could be put to the sword.

"Fats, saddle up! We're goin' to the desert! We gotta rescue none other than the Secretary of State, she's counting on us," barked Geno.

CHAPTER 13

DEAD OR ALIVE?

FATS ORDERED THE SQUADRON, "GEAR UP." THEY WERE heading into the desert south of Riyadh, the location where reconnaissance satellites, Saudi and American flyovers, boots on the ground, and spies in the city all seemed to indicate that Secretary Kurtz was being taken. The Team would be ferried out by choppers. In addition to the equipment that was standard issue in this type of mission—lighter-weight desert camo, guns, knives, state-of-the-art communication, appropriate food and water stocks—they would also have their DPVs (desert patrol vehicles) to travel across the desert.

The DPV Rat Rods packed quite a punch, with a few custom extras the street boys back home did not have. The DPV Rat-Rod had a sealed bottom, two mounted M60 machine guns, a mounted .50-caliber Browning machine gun, two anti-tank missile launchers, held three personnel, and could travel across desert terrain at speeds of up to eighty miles per hour. Machine guns and missile launchers were frequently changed in and out to suit the mission. Travel distance range was 210 miles, but special fuel bladder tanks could create travel ranges of up to one thousand miles. At a sticker price of $250,000–$500,000 each, this was not your grandfather's SEAL vehicle!

SEAL 6 and their equipment were transported in by their buddies from Seventy-fifth Ranger Regiment, First Special Operational Detachment, U.S. Army, Delta Force. SEAL 6 and elements of Delta Force had been assigned the job of capturing Saddam Hussein, as well as other "High Value Targets" throughout Iraq and Afghanistan including bin Laden. Delta and 6 were the first to infiltrate Baghdad to provide recon for airstrikes in the 2003 Operation Iraqi Freedom. The Delta pilots brought them through the sandstorm to land near Layla, in the Ar Riyadh Province. Layla was about two hundred miles primarily south and a bit east of Riyadh.

Layla was believed to have been named after a seventh-century woman immortalized in the poetry of her lover, Qays ibn Al-Mulawwah. Qays and Layla represented one of the most famous romances in Saudi literature, but that was not why Imran selected a location near Layla for his female Secretary of State captive. The CIA and all the intelligence powers also zeroed in on Layla right away as a hideaway because of one strategic asset that the region around Layla possessed and not seen in most of Arabia—caves!

A drying Lake Layla provided caves throughout the locale. Caves would get Imran and his "guest", as well as his band of fanatics, below ground and out of the scan of aircraft and satellites. As a bonus, it would be a little cooler in the caves. The temperature in the Layla region was hotter than Riyadh. Daytime temps were already up into the low 100's, feeling like 130, and night-time lows were typical of a desert, cooler at 70.

Secretary of State Kurtz was coping as well as anyone could that had just witnessed the bloody slaughter of twenty or more troops and officials—within arm's reach in some cases. She had coped with being blindfolded and hooded, as well as having her hands and feet bound with ropes. She wasn't assaulted in a personal manner, but in the hustle of speed, she had been groped in private parts of her body, and she had coped with that too. Getting inadvertently groped was the least of her worries; she was focused on four things: survival, where she was going, how she was being transported, and how long it would take that transport to get her there. Tracking these four elements would help Kurtz calculate her own escape if possible. That was Kathryn Kurtz: logic, organization, depersonalization when necessary, cold calculations, all with a warm smile.

Every Ambassador or Secretary of State has a warm smile; it's part of the uniform. Kurtz was raised in spartan surroundings and modest expectations, but she had drive and was smart; mostly street smart in the rough-and-tumble world of politics. She was known to be a bare-knuckle brawler when necessary. She had come up through the ranks in the traditional manner of working and sponsoring the right political horses. Kurtz had worked for President Carter, where human rights were the central element of his foreign policy. Then she became a Fellow at the Center for American Progress, a liberal think tank. She later worked in the Clinton Administration as a State Department Undersecretary, focusing on human rights.

An attractively plain-looking woman, Kathryn reminded many of Queen Elizabeth in her looks: medium height, curly white hair, a firm look on her face, a forced smile when needed, a clutch of the purse, and a steady forward march. Retreat was not in her vocabulary, unless it was to circle back around for what she really wanted. She was known to be good with a head-fake. Geno and Fats thought it was too bad she hadn't bobbed and weaved out of the hall before Imran got there.

Kathryn Kurtz was called into service as the Secretary of State nominee by the new Democratic President, who also wanted to make human rights the centerpiece of his foreign policy. However, the political right had called him "too apologetic" for sins he felt America had committed as a world leader. Even Kurtz herself felt that he went too far in the first year of his presidency. Kurtz understood that in many parts of the world where human rights are most violated, cojones and testosterone are more respected than apologies. In fact, for many brutal dictators, apologies are a sign of weakness.

Kurtz and the President's new Chief of Staff, along with the loss of the House and near loss of the Senate during the recent midterm elections, convinced the President to throttle back the apologies and get on the offensive. Though it seemed against his inner will and upbringing, he was willing to do it if it meant a better chance of getting reelected in 2012.

Kurtz was getting a new hands-on lesson in diplomacy, desert style, where the gun and ammo you had access to were the best calling card you could have. Maybe she would have to rethink the human rights thing, she thought to herself as she was forced facedown on the backseat floor of the large SUV she had been thrown into. *She would make it, she would make it,* she kept telling herself. *Kick into survival gear, kick into gear.* The Army, Navy, Air Force, Marines, CIA, somebody would track her and find her. The question even in her own mind was would they find her dead or alive?

CHAPTER 14

PARTWAY THERE

GENO AND THE TEAM ALONG WITH THEIR EQUIPMENT WERE
helicoptered into the desert by Delta Force UH-60
Black Hawk helicopters and CH-47D Chinooks.
The equipment, including the DPVs, was in the
Chinooks and the team was in the Black Hawks.
They landed about one hundred clicks north of the
reported location of Secretary of State Kurtz.
The landing was "routinely safe" compared to the
Delta Force landing in the Iranian desert in April 1980,
when President Carter authorized the ill-fated rescue
attempt of the American hostages from the American
Embassy in Tehran. Iranian revolutionaries had taken
the entire American consulate staff captive in November
1979. Eight American soldiers died in that rescue mission
through a series of miscommunications, equipment
failures, and weather conditions—the crews had never
been briefed about how to navigate in a haboob, a fine
dust storm—and Murphy's Law prevailed to the
Nth degree.

The 1979 mission was in planning stages for nearly
five months, but no haboob training! This very

complicated mission had actually reached meeting locations in Tehran. Iranians and others were picked up and brought to the desert for extraction with the hostages that were also to be brought to the desert. After getting back to the rendezvous point, one of the choppers flew into another, setting off a chain reaction fireball that encompassed a tanker truck, killing the eight men and injuring four others. The entire rendezvous point soon came under Iranian attack and within twenty minutes President Carter aborted the mission.

Some of the helicopters left on the ground were not sanitized for records, and consequently, names of Iranians working for the United States government fell into the hands of the revolutionary government. Some Americans were also rumored to have fallen into the hands of the revolutionaries. This entire debacle was an ultimate embarrassment to the United States of America, the American presidency, and the United States Army. The U.S. Special Operations Command was formed shortly after the failed rescue, and Jimmy Carter was not reelected President. The following Presidents took note of that history lesson and ramped up all desert training. The Vietnam military style died in that desert debacle making way for current methods and training.

The Layla landing was perfect, unlike 1979. Thirty years of training had paid off.

The team unloaded, setting up a defensive perimeter around their position, allowing the equipment to be unloaded safely. Geno put Fats in charge of the DPV brigade. Fats would have come back to the SEALs and mission just for the DPVs if he had known. The million-dollar "consulting fee" was just a bonus now.

Fats quietly and quickly organized the men and equipment of the six DPVs. They would demo any excess equipment prior to rendezvous departure if necessary or along the way as they saw fit. Fats had the team and equipment unloaded from the choppers and organized in the DPVs within a twenty-minute window. Each man was well trained in his assignment, so there was no barking of orders. SEAL silence was the only order of the day. Each DPV had a driver, a gunner, and a marksman. They took out the maps they had been studying on their flight to Layla and planned their route.

It was now dusk and SEALs own the night. They were downright comfortable in the dark. The plan was to fan out so that they would not be one individual target, but not so far as to stray away and get lost in the haboob. Night vision goggles and thin facial scarves were a complement to their desert camo ninja-like outerwear. They wore their lightweight combat body armor vests beneath their camos and their crossover tactical vests on the outerwear.

Everything was specially designed for Special Forces protection, durability, flexibility, and ease of access to fire weapons and use knives and garrotes. The live fire weapons were equipped with silencers. If given the opportunity, SEALs and other Special Forces were trained to avoid conflicts, focus on the successful conclusion of the mission objective, and kill silently where necessary. Hence, garrotes and knives were favored kill weapons. With Geno and Fats at the wheel, 6 got under way.

Even though the DPVs had speed potential up to 80 mph, they proceeded with more reasonable speed. SEALs don't swoop in like John Wayne and the Seventh Calvary. The first element of success is to not be discovered. They also realized that it would be very likely that Imran and his supporters had set up two or three rings of perimeter defenses. The rings could be five to ten klicks out or as much as twenty to thirty, though they doubted the latter. They were unable to count on usually reliable airborne surveillance because of the sandstorm conditions. Light pollution was not a problem in the deep of the desert, and the darkness made the night vision goggles more effective. Team 6 was in its element.

Things proceeded well for the first thirty klicks, with no contact. The team members rode silently through the night, exchanging glances, mentally checking their routines, engaging in limited talk about the equipment and the mission; but not too much because an enemy could pop up at any time and the whole mission would be compromised. Team 6 was zoning in on the mission and procedures.

They travelled in a V formation of sorts. Geno was in the lead vehicle. Fats was a wingman to the left and Ozzie was wing to the right. Marco and Artie were outer wings. Mad Mike and J'effie (pronounced heff-eh) were trailers. It bugged the hell out of Mad Mike that he was a trailer, but Geno knew he had to keep him under control. Mad Mike was their balls-to-the-wall interior combat guy.

Mike grew up in a hunting environment and was excellent with a knife. J'effie was sort of the party boy of the team, but he was a fanatic with details and precision. He loved head and heart shots. Marco and Artie were as different as they were alike. Marco was a worrier and a strategist and a big talker, Artie was a reliable mule type. Steady, steady, steady, hard working, conscientious, very quiet, but deep as a well. He didn't say much, but when he did, it was worthwhile. The mule had carried a wounded comrade ten miles to safety in the initial covert surge into Afghanistan in the aftermath of 9/11.

Charlie, Joe, Steve, Matt, Harley, and Joe Miggs filled in 6. Charlie was the youngest of the team, still sort of wet behind the ears by SEAL Team 6 standards. Joe was midcareer. Steve was sort of tall and lanky; not what you'd picture a SEAL to be. Matt and Harley were smaller versions of Fats, husky and muscular. Joe Miggs was the smallest of the team, but as the team knew, "nobody messes with Mr. Miggs!" They had seen him in action in the Swiss Alps on a covert rescue mission. Let's just say it was "mission accomplished" with no questions of Mr. Miggs when the Swiss Ski Border Patrol finally arrived for a little mop-up action.

The team was set and under way. They were partway there, but the real action lay just ahead.

CHAPTER 15

WE'VE GOT COMPANY

THE SEQUENCE OF EVENTS UNFOLDING AT LIGHT SPEED WAS accelerating everything for everybody. The hostage taking of King Abdullah and other members of the ruling council—with the King being held in the secure hall and the other groups fanning out in four different directions—had hell breaking loose all over. Not to miss an opportunity, Imran's Yemeni contacts were in action also. Imran had sent a member of his party forward at high speed via car to alert the Yemeni contacts while he formulated a plan and waited for further instructions regarding Kathryn Kurtz. The taking of this prized hostage necessitated the creation of a new plan.

Upon crossing the border, the group sent ahead arrived at a safe house and was able to access their network. Yemeni terrorist leadership then sent a new group of reinforcements to Layla in the new camels of the desert, Toyota pickup trucks. Geno and everyone had become accustomed to the sight: a ragtag group of bearded fanatics racing through the countryside in pickups laden with men, guns, and mortars in the back of the truck.

Four such trucks with twenty-five to thirty men were racing back to Layla at breakneck speed to join up with Imran. They also carried new orders to Imran: the Secretary of State was not to be killed or harmed in any mortal way. She too had a new mission, she was to be taken to a safe house in Yemen for transport to western Pakistan. She would be featured in new propaganda videos from bin Laden's lieutenants. Using hostage indoctrination techniques, she would become the twenty-first-century "al Qaeda Jane", if you will. "Allah be praised to think of such a cunning strategy!"

Hearing the news, Imran was nearly beside himself with pride to think that Allah and his soldiers would deem his mission to be of such importance and opportunity. He would surely be trusted with some of the most important plans and operations of the future because of this honor. Allah himself was promoting him. The only greater honor he could achieve would be that he could give his life to martyrdom during the completion of his mission. He had come a long way from the cur-dog cages of Palestine lobbing rocks at Jewish soldiers as a youngster. Surely, his mother and father would be proud of him also and would share the fruits of Islam as part of a reward for leading such a mission if he was killed.

Quickly gathering his thoughts as any good

commander would do, Imran ordered half of the new reinforcements out to the perimeter defenses. He also immediately began preparations for the move to Yemen with the remainder of the group. There was no point in staying in Layla now, cave protection or not the hostage must be moved.

Geno and 6 were now halfway to the target zone without encountering any resistance. He hand-signaled, pointing two fingers at his eye goggles and then straight ahead to the team to be extra alert. They were now closing in on the twenty-klick marker and action could begin anytime. He actually slowed the team down. Though equipped with state-of-the-art muffler devices, there was still increasing danger of being detected as they got closer to the target.

Moving through the twenty-klick radius, Geno brought 6 to a halt. They could not linger long, but he sent Matt, Harley, and Andrew's DPVs ahead for recon. They moved forward and Geno ordered the rest of 6 to set up in a defensive position. Moving along in a zigzag maneuver, the three ahead detected nothing for about the first fifteen minutes. They were now within range of the ten-klick marker.

Scanning the desert with their night vision goggles and scopes, they spotted movement. Off to the left, a group of four trucks was parked in its own defensive position. The recon team moved slowly, very slowly forward to get a better look through the sandstorm.

The storm was letting up, but not enough to get an exact head count and position alignment.

They moved to within about a thousand meters of the encampment. They detected a small fire, Bedouin style, behind a V of two trucks. This fire would become the guiding star for 6's attack on the group. They detected twelve targets. They also noted the topography—virtually flat—the small amount of moonlight, the location of the moon in the sky, the weapons the group had in their position, and the physical build of all the members of the group. They were all slight of build, had AKs and rocket launchers for weapons. They were not particularly military disciplined, and there didn't appear to be a command structure for the group, fortunately. They were twelve Islamic radicals out in the desert with deadly weapons if used properly. The SEALs completed their recon within twenty minutes and quietly slipped back to the main group for report.

Upon getting the recon report, Geno ordered a take-out-before-detection order. That is, kill everyone before being detected. They did not want any of the rebels to get any shots off that might alert the rest of the group farther ahead at Layla. Code words for completion of various elements of the attack were gone over again. "Communication earpieces in place?" Geno checked. Nods of the head.

6 would move forward in their V formation and then split into two groups, surrounding the camp on foot. Orders were given to the team to be aware of any additional defensive perimeters that might be on the back side of the target. If there were additional perimeter defenses, "Pincer" was the code word for "move in as in a pincer maneuver" to crush the target between the two sides of the vise.

Moving like cobras in the night, slithering across the sand in the haboob, 6 completed the encirclement. "Circled" came the word from the back side. Later, "Circle in three" came the word to all from Geno, meaning that the circle should begin to tighten in three minutes and all were to stop in place one hundred meters out.

"Hold at one hundred" said Geno.

"Engage in sixty" came the call as Geno indicated a move to attack the camp in sixty seconds.

With the team crouched and creeping forward, Geno kissed his Saint Christopher medal, and tucked it back into his camo. "Don't let me down now pal," under his breath, "Acquire target," Geno said aloud. "On my mark, five, four, three, two, one."

Years and years of training took over as if it was an involuntary muscle reflex action. Most of the enemy band was felled with the SEAL double-tap head shots from submachine guns with silencers on semi-automatic mode. As his man spun around, lifting up his AK, Geno was able to grab him, put him in a neck breaker hold, and slit his throat with the top side of his serrated knife before the guy could let out a breath. He threw him down to bleed out on the sand.

The group quickly came together, did a 360 scan for more terrorists, but found none. So far so good, but more to come. They re-conned any materials the group had with them: maps, communiqués, Qurans, whatever might have the slightest bit of information that would be useful for the source of the group, who they were, where they came from, where they might be going, who they were working with, anything.

They found a map that had a pen-marked route from the border crossing of Narjan, where Imran had crossed the Yemen-Saudi border. The route was also marked from Narjan, south to Sana and farther south to Aden on the coast.

Were they coming or going? Geno wondered and asked Fats.

"Hell, I don't know," Fats responded. "You know these fanatics, anything is possible."

Yes, Geno thought, *anything is possible*. But the mission lay dead ahead a short ten klicks away. Maybe they could get some answers there.

They quietly got back on the DPVs and moved forward again. Imran was also making preparations to move again. Without knowing it, between he and Geno, the race was on.

CHAPTER 16

LIVE FIRE

MOTORING INTO THE CAVE AREA, ALL WAS QUIET IN TEAM 6.
The real mission was now at hand, the rescue of
Secretary of State Kathryn Kurtz. Imran had his own
mission to accomplish. Diametrically opposed to 6's
mission was Imran's to speed Kurtz out of the country.
The race was indeed on.

Imran had split his remaining forces into two
groups. Half were to stay behind as a decoy for forces
he knew would come while he escaped across the
desert to Yemen. Aden was his target. There was a team
waiting in Aden to smuggle Kurtz into western
Pakistan. He ordered his forces to deploy in and
around the caves of Lake Layla. They were more than
willing to follow his order to fight to the death to stop
the American forces. They were left with AKs, ample
ammunition, RPGs, and cluster bomb grenades. Imran
was willing to travel lighter on the guns and ammo
supply to make sure the Layla group would be
successful. Their success was key to his success.
Even a major time delay from an extended firefight at
Lake Layla would nearly assure his escape.

Creeping along at five to seven miles per hour—speed was not paramount, surprise was—6 moved forward in the zigzag again.

Imran ordered Kurtz into the SUV and ordered his security detail into two pickup trucks brought up from the south. Rather they were intercepted at Layla or along the way to Aden, Imran knew that the Americans would not use deadly force with Kurtz under capture. She was a precious gift to them from Allah. He also knew that even though the Americans espoused a no negotiation public policy with freedom fighters and soldiers of Islam, behind the scenes it was totally different. The higher the profile of the target, the more willing they were to negotiate.

The ultimate example of this was President Reagan's Arms for Hostages deal in the 1980's. That deal nearly cost Reagan his presidency until he faced the American people as any true actor would and fell on his sword, saying that, unbeknownst to him, members of his administration had traded arms for hostages, but he knew nothing about it. *Maybe he didn't,* thought Imran. *He was an old warrior by that time and his lieutenants had probably outmaneuvered him, silly old man. Americans always seemed to come up with an excuse when things didn't go their way. Is that how a mighty power acts?* thought Imran. *They are weak. They have proven it over and over again. The current President is willing to let Libya and Syria burn.*

They will never risk killing Kurtz. He knew this and made it part of his plans.

As Imran was getting ready to pull out of the Layla cave complex, 6 was within range. The noise of loading everyone into the trucks and the SUV, along with the noise of setting up their resistance positions, had given the group away to 6. Using whisper communications through the earpiece communicators and with hand signals, 6 dismounted and fanned out. It appeared to 6 that some type of move was indeed under way. Geno figured it involved Kurtz. She was the prize for both sides. He knew they wouldn't risk losing her back to the Americans.

Team 6 scanned the horizon in the predawn light looking for Kurtz. Geno didn't want a firefight to break out until they located her. Kurtz's survival was vital. The military aspect of the maneuver by the terrorists would be no match for the SEAL team. This would be men against boys.

"Where in the hell is she? Scan until you locate her!"

J'effie spotted her through his binocs. "They're loading her into the SUV," he whispered over the earphones.

"Damn!" Geno said audibly over the earphones. "Miggs and Mad Mike, I want you to work your way to the back side as quickly as possible, and whatever you do, don't let that SUV get out of here! But, Mike, don't kill the Secretary in the process! Fats and Artie, we're going up the middle. Matt and Harley, you go right with Andrew. Joe and Steve, you go left and cover Mike and Miggs. J'effie, get yourself between Mike and Miggs and the caves. Fire down from the top of the caves. Charlie, stick with Fats and me. Don't be getting your ass shot off. We aren't taking that home to your mother, rookie.

"This is it. Surprise is key. I want you flankers to fire into the middle and kill as many as possible. Fats and I will come up the middle and make our move from there. Any questions?" asked Geno.

"Yes, sir," replied Charlie. "What do you want me to do?"

"Don't shoot me in the ass." Geno chuckled. "Seriously, provide cover fire for Fats and me, then break for the SUV. Don't shoot the Secretary. Move, move, flankers! Miggs and Mike, move and react on my count."

Fats, Charlie, and Geno crawled forward ever so slowly while the others got into position. Miggs and Mike had the farthest to go for their backstop. Within a few minutes, everyone reported in on the earphones. "In position," came the word, group after group. Then Geno gave the order: "Team 6, on my mark, five-four-three-two-one, mark!"

All hell broke loose. Imran's head came up like a rocket, looking for the source of the commotion.

"Allah Akbar, Allah Akbar, God is Great!" Imran shouted as a fight to the death command. He shoved Kurtz into the backseat of the SUV and jumped in next to her with his AK pointed directly at her head. Hassan jumped in behind the wheel and Imran gave him orders to speed out of there. Of course, there was the matter of Mad Mike and Miggs blocking their path.

Joe and Steve began firing into the cave area from the left; same for Matt, Harley, and Andrew from the right. J'effie was spraying down from the top side. Fats, Charlie, and Geno moved up the middle. "Charlie, get the grenade launchers fired into those caves in the bank! Cover Fats and me! Grenades, grenades NOW, Charlie, NOW!"

Whisshh, whisshh, whisshh, whisshh as the RPGs slammed into the caves.

"Fat's, let's move, NOW!"

They ran forward in a crouched position, firing their machine guns as they went. *Zing, zing, zing* sounded all around them as they moved forward.

Four of the cave fighters came running out of the smoke- and confusion-filled caves, firing as rapidly as their AKs would allow. They sprayed left, right, and up the middle. "Allah Akbar!" they shouted as they sprayed. J'effie and the pincer teams cut them down.

"Charlie, get up here and cover the wings as they

come in, fire directly ahead! Wings in. Fire for kill and effect, fire! Joe and Steve, get in those caves and take out any survivors! J'effie, stay up top and cover. Matt, Harley, and Andrew cover with Charlie."

Geno and Fats broke for the SUV. One of the cavers within the entrance to the cave fired off an RPG slightly to the center right. Matt and Andrew were hit with shrapnel. J'effie cut the shooter to ribbons as he came out. Joe and Steve crawled into the caves that were more like dugouts. Single shots rang out. Joe and Steve came out. All those inside the caves were dead. The battle had lasted less than three minutes.

Imran was speeding away in the black SUV with Secretary of State Kurtz. Mike and Miggs fired at the tires and the radiator as best they could, but were not willing to risk the life of Kurtz.

"Damn!" Geno muttered. "Regroup, regroup quickly! Anybody hurt?"

"Yes, sir. Matt and Andrew took shrapnel from a grenade."

"How bad is it?"

"Matt has a flesh wound, but Andrew's been hit pretty bad."

Geno and Fats raced over to Andrew. "Andy, how bad is it?" Geno asked as he looked him over.

"Not bad, Geno, I'll be OK. Leave me here and I'll be OK."

"Sailor, you know we don't do that. You're coming with us. Steve, get a look here and see what you can do to get him fixed up so we can get moving!"

The adrenaline of battle was still running through everyone's veins. Geno knew that Andrew was gravely wounded. Shrapnel to the gut, with blood oozing out of his mouth. He was likely ripped to shreds inside.

Steve came over to his side. "It's not good, sir."

"I know that, Steve, do the best you can and we'll figure something out."

"Yes, sir."

"Geno, we're going to have to leave him," Fats said.

"Goddamn it, Fats! Have you been off the team long enough to forget we don't leave men behind, dead or alive! What the hell's wrong with you?"

"Geno, it's going to jeopardize the entire mission. Andrew is gut shot and he's not going to make it. We gotta move on. They're on the run. We don't have any time to waste."

"Waste? That man has nearly as many commendations as you had, and he's part of our team. We don't leave anybody behind."

"I know, sir, but Andrew would say the same thing as me."

"Fats, we've been friends for a long time. We've been through plenty of scrapes together. Maybe I shouldn't have 'wasted' my time on your fat ass on the beach at Diego. Don't push me here." Geno glared at Fats with a look of cold steel.

Fats knew it was time to back off. Running back to the group, Geno barked, "Steve, get Andy stabilized and get him loaded into my DPV. You come with us. I want you to do everything possible."

"Yes, sir. I will, sir. You can count on that."

"I know I can. Photograph all the KIAs to get them into the Intel files. Saddle up. We're gonna catch these bastards."

Steve did the best he could. Andrew McMahon died in the belly of a DPV somewhere in the desert of Arabia between Layla and Narjan. An American Navy SEAL, the best that America had to offer. Years and years of training, a member of a special "Band of Brothers", a family back home. Few back home in America would know that he had died. His family would mourn, but they wouldn't know how or where he died. That's just the way it was in SEAL Team 6.

It really ate at Geno to lose a man under his command. That's what made him as good as he was.

CHAPTER 17

BAND ON THE RUN

KURTZ, HASSAN, IMRAN, AND TWO TRAILING TOYOTA pickups roared out of the Layla Lake and cave complex with Team 6 fully engaged. They were lucky to get out at all, let alone alive! The second truck took significant fire, the only survivor was the driver. He was on the far side of the shooting, and his passenger, Tariq, acted as a shield from the flying bullets. The two in the back were shot to hell, with guts and brains all over the bed of the truck.

Hakeem, the driver, had soiled himself from fright during the escape. He was so rattled that he couldn't tell for sure if the right-side tires had been shot out or not. The right rear tire was leaking and he was falling behind.

"Allah, Allah, please save me from these blood-thirsty Americans, but if it be your will, allow me to kill as many for you as possible." Falling farther behind, he turned his truck back toward the Americans. He would launch his grenades and fire his machine gun until he dropped.

On the horizon, 6 saw him coming and was ready for him. "Mike, take the bastard out," Geno commanded. With that, Mad Mike fired off a rocket-propelled grenade and Hakeem and his Toyota became an orange ball of fire. "Good job, Mike."

"My pleasure, Skipper."

One down and two to go, thought Geno.

Imran made a rapid-fire petrol stop in the city of Layla. It was four hundred miles to Narjan. The vehicles could make it to Narjan with full fuel tanks and petrol cans in the back of the truck. Imran ordered Kurtz to the floor with a gun to the back of her head, covered her with a blanket, and feigned sleep himself. The riders in the back of the truck feigned sleep also. They posed as migrant workers heading out of Saudi Arabia and all its live-fire problems, seeking safety. Fortunately, both vehicles carried Yemeni ID tags and papers, since both had originated there in the first place, before coming up to Saudi for their mission.

Amazing, Imran thought, *we're posing as migrant workers on both ends of the trip, in and out of Saudi. Oh well, it worked.* They were quickly on their way with ample petrol supplies for the trip to Narjan. He allowed Kurtz to get up off the floor of the SUV.

The sun was coming up and it was getting hot very quickly. "Dates, Madam Secretary?" he signaled to her, speaking Arabic and using hand gestures. "We must keep you alive," he said without Kurtz understanding him.

She quickly grabbed the handful of dates and water bottle Imran offered. It had been nearly twenty-four hours since she had eaten or drank. She worked at being in shape, but she was sixty-four years old. Fortunately for her, she had no real medical issues.

Kurtz had told herself all she had to do was survive. Special Forces, conventional forces, the U.S. Air Force, CIA, FBI, all resources would be focused on finding and rescuing her. She was such a strong-willed, determined, bullheaded, opinionated woman that she didn't look at herself as needing rescue. She looked at it as if the terrorists were captured! Besides, she was no babe in the woods. She had been round the world a time or two herself.

She busied herself contemplating negotiation tactics and strategies. She had been well trained in body language techniques to overcome language barriers. She was busy plotting her release and Imran's "surrender". Stockholm syndrome was not in her vocabulary. She picked up the word "Aden" in the lingo back and forth between her captors during the escape from the gun battle. She knew, as sure as she knew anything, that they had encountered Special Forces in the firefight. She didn't know who, what, or how many, but she knew. With that knowledge, she also knew that they would not be far behind, so she had to be ready for whatever was coming her way.

With a gracious look on her face, she signaled a "thank you" back to Imran. She would win him with sugar and sympathy or sting him like a black widow if she had to. *His choice,* she thought.

Imran ordered Hassan to drive as fast as possible. He hoped to make it to Narjan well before nightfall. It was hot and risky to travel by day, but they had no choice. They knew it was likely the Americans were following. They just had to stay ahead of them, get safely into Narjan, and then travel to Aden under the cover of darkness. Imran made up his mind that, if captured, he would kill Kurtz. She deserved to die for perpetuating the American double-talk with the Arabs on behalf of Israel. Israel, Jews, Americans, all profanities to Allah. They must all die; the Quran plainly stated that all infidels must be put to the sword unless they submitted to Islam and Sharia law. Oh, he longed for Allah to allow him to see the day of victory, but if he must die and go to paradise, Allah be praised.

Geno and 6 were under way after caring for and loading Andrew into Geno's DPV. They also re-conned all maps and papers they could find. Not much there, other than the important map indicating the group had originated most likely out of Aden. Geno had told Steve and Joe to sanitize the place—that is, torch and burn everything.

They were all down from their adrenaline high and they were sober over the thought of Andrew. They bore down across the sand and down the road. Everyone was quiet. Geno ordered MREs for all and power naps for the riders. He knew it would take an hour or two to get close to the caravan ahead of them. They were not concerned about fuel because they had filled the extra fuel bladders and now had a range of nearly a thousand miles. They were alone out in the desert as the sun moved higher during the day. It was getting hot, but the breeze of the open ride kept them cool.

"Keep yourselves hydrated," he belted into the earphones. "I don't need any wilting violets when we catch these bastards."

Geno wasn't worried about the daytime travel. The only air forces they would see, if any, would be friendlies, either Saudis or Americans. What's more, he knew they would not likely see anyone because they would all be focused on events in Riyadh and King Abdullah or on the other members of the kidnapped party and whatever was going on in Bahrain.

God Almighty, he thought, *you couldn't ask for more action than this! Pick of the litter for adrenaline rushes!* He quickly brought himself back into focus from his musing. His orders gave him full latitude to be successful in finding and securing Secretary of State Kurtz. The only question he had was, should he break communication silence to radio in what had taken place and report where he thought the mission was likely headed? He opted not to, for now.

He needed more confirmation of where this band on the run was heading. Aden was a very likely location, but Sana, Damar, and Tiaz were also other jumping-off possibilities. They could also cut from Narjan to the east toward the small port town of Al Mukalla. Al Mukalla would be just as close as Aden, away from the hustle of Aden, and away from U.S. Navy refueling stations off-port of Aden. The Navy had stopped refueling in the Port of Aden after the *Cole* bombing, but still fueled off-coast. There would be significant Naval forces in and around Aden if the terrorists had illusions of taking Kurtz east toward Iran. Imran knew Iran would not likely touch Kurtz with a ten-foot pole. Better for Iran to have surrogates do that. They would eventually travel east if they were thinking of ungoverned western Pakistan, and Iran might secretly help along the way.

Thoughts were rolling through Imran's head. They could very well go to Aden, or stop short of Aden along the coast of the Red Sea and cross the narrow channel to Somalia. They could disguise themselves as fishermen out of Somalia, hug the coast of Yemen, not come close to any merchant ships, lest they be targeted as pirates, and sail east or go west down the coast of Somalia to Mozambique to catch some type of transport to an ultimate destination.

Geno recalled training that highlighted Arab terror tactics in the 1970's. They would hijack a jetliner and then fly from airport to airport in the Middle East until they got what they wanted. If need be, they would kill a hostage to prove a point. There were scores of such hijackings, but only one stuck out for all SEALs. Twenty-three-year-old Navy Petty Officer Robert Stetham was aboard TWA flight 847 in June 1985 when Hezbollah terrorists hijacked it and held it captive for seventeen days.

Growing up in Virginia Beach near DEVGRU Command and Little Creek SEAL Command, Stetham always wanted to follow his father and grandfather into the Navy. He did and became a diver, as SEALs are also trained. Terrorists on the plane targeted Stetham when they found his identity card. The terrorists beat and tortured Stetham when their demands were not met. They then shot Stetham dead and dumped his body out of the plane like a piece of trash on the tarmac below. *That would never happen to Kurtz on Geno's watch!* God, such actions really got his motor running.

Hell hath no fury like a SEAL hot on the trail of terrorists, especially those with an American hostage. Mission first, blood second, but if blood comes with the mission, so be it!

CHAPTER 18

IN THE HEAT
OF THE DESERT

SHAKING OFF THE STETHAM THOUGHTS AND FOCUSING ON where this Imran character might split to, Geno and 6 were in hot pursuit. They pushed as hard as they could, motoring sixty-plus miles per hour. He knew that the band ahead would have to fuel again some-where, Narjan was a likely place to stop for fuel and hopefully 6 could intercept them there. He strategized that his team would circle around to the south side of the town. The planned interception point was in the desert outside Narjan. This would cut off any of Imran's escape options.

Narjan was crucial point on the map because of the optional escape routes the terrorists would have once they cleared Narjan. Geno radioed out the plan to the platoon. "Keep pushin' till we get near Narjan. We'll circle around to the south side of town, where we'll set up a blocking and capture point. We're about two hours out by my calc."

"Roger" came back the replies.

About thirty minutes later, Miggs radioed in. "Skip,

we got a problem. We're losin' power over here. The temp and generator numbers are fine, but something's goin' on. We're stalling out pretty fast. We're gonna have to stop."

"Damn it! Sir, we're dead in the water over here," Miggs said as his rig died on the spot and coasted to a stop.

"All right, everybody circle back around to Miggs and let's see what's going on. Artie, check it out."

Artie was the designated and trained mechanic of the platoon. He had had some auto mechanics in high school, did motor pool maintenance before getting accepted into the SEAL program, and then trained on DPVs as part of his specialized training.

Damn it! This is going to cost precious time, Geno thought. If it was anything major, they would have to double up and abandon the vehicle. "Artie, get over there and get that thing checked out. We're losing major time."

"Yes, sir." Artie crawled over the engine. Even though cooled by the open air, the engine was hotter than Hades. "All your gauges fine, Miggs?"

"Yeah."

"Hmm, I wonder. Let me check the air filter to the engine. With all the sand we plowed through, we might have a blockage...Yup, looks like the air filter is blocked. The engine can't get any combustion if it doesn't get air in the cylinders. I think we can knock the sand out of this one, but let me check supply in the back to see if they gave us a spare…Nope, they didn't, sir. I think we can just knock this one out and we'll be fine. Take me just a few minutes, sir."

"OK, Artie. Do it quickly so we can get rolling."

Ten minutes later, Artie had the filter clean and the air breather cap back on. "Start 'er up, Miggs." Boom, she turned right over!

"Good job, Artie. Saddle up, boys, we gotta burn!" They were under way, but nearly twenty minutes had been lost to the band ahead.

Imran and his crew were sailing along smoothly in the SUV and truck. It was getting hot, about 115 degrees during midafternoon. The air-conditioner in the SUV was barely working. Kurtz seized upon the opportunity; that's the kind of woman she was: snatching victory from the jaws of defeat.

"Imran." She pointed.

He looked at her with a "What?"

She indicated that she was faint, her stomach was rumbling, and she was going to vomit or go the other way with it. He looked at her with a "what do you want me to do about it" look on his face. She cramped over and moaned very loudly, grabbing herself from behind as if she was trying to keep something messy from occurring inside of the car. Then she let out a loud "Oh, God" and clutched herself tightly again.

"Pull over," Imran told Hassan. Hassan looked at him, somewhat astonished. "Pull over, now!"

Hassan did and Kurtz rolled out of the car into the desert. She knew she could not escape, but she could delay. She gave some fake dry heaves, clutched her abdomen in pain again, and motioned for the two men to give her some privacy. Knowing that she couldn't run, they did.

Kurtz went to the front of the SUV to shield herself from them and went through the motions and sounds of going to the bathroom. She kicked sand around her spot to "cover things up". She then staggered back to the side of the vehicle and fainted, dead like, on the sand.

Imran and Hassan went to her and poured some water on her face. She gradually came around and they loaded up again to get under way. Imran kept an eye on her and looked at her suspiciously. She gradually seemed to feel better, especially since she knew that she had cost their little band about fifteen minutes in the desert. It made her feel especially good that she had left a portion of her slip blowing in the breeze from the sand heap. Not likely to be spotted, but she could always hope!

Approaching Narjan, Imran began to get anxious from lack of sleep over the past thirty-six hours. He was also getting angry and aggressive. He knew he had to make the quick stop for fuel in the outer limits of Narjan. He opted for a stop on the south side because he didn't want his pursuers to intercept him on the north, knowing they were probably close behind. He would have a better escape possibility if he fueled on the south side.

Imran opted for a stop in a crowded area on the south side. He wanted a crowd around because he wanted to be able to blend in and get away in the hustle and bustle of the city. The stop was routine and fast. They grabbed some dates, nuts, and water from a bazaar nearby. Under way again!

Team 6 had lost twenty minutes in the desert, but Geno had the pedal to the metal, and 6 was gaining. Where would this Imran character stop, Narjan? They scanned the north side as they approached, looking for the black SUV.

Hmm, go through or go around? Geno pondered. "Fats, what do you think?" Geno was back on speaking terms with Fats after his blow with Fats over Andrew McMahon.

"Go through," Fats replied.

"Steve?"

"Around."

Geno thought for a minute. "We really can't go through because we might come under harassment from the locals, slowing us even more." *It's a lot more like the Wild West down here,* he thought. Making a decision, "All right, men, we're going to circle around. Fats, you take Miggs, Mike, J'effie, and Matt and go right. Steve, Marco, Charlie, and me, with the rest, will go left. Everybody keep a sharp look for the black SUV. Use your scopes and binocs. Take your time but don't go too slow. This is a pretty big city for the desert and it's going to take us close to an hour to meet up. We'll meet up halfway between the city limits and the border crossing. Use your GPS. We'll meet up at 17 29 30 North and 44 7 56 East, any questions?" Geno asked.

"Yes, sir, what if we don't find them?"

"We'll cross that bridge on the south side when we get to it. We can't just drive through a town of two hundred thousand in these rat-rods, all dressed in camo," Geno said.

"Well, sir, maybe they'll hole up in there?"

"Good point, Matt. But we can't search the town either. They're not going to stop, because they've got to get somewhere so they can transport Kurtz to a location for an escape from civilization. They're not going to stop, get a TV crew in so they can grandstand her and then all get killed in a ball of fire from F-16s.

They can do that anywhere along the line if they have to resort to that. She's far more valuable alive than dead. They know that and their handlers know that too. They'll keep her alive and keep moving. The maps indicate Aden and that's where I think they're going. The birds, satellites, and drones will be searching the deserts. We can't afford to gamble going east or west; let the birds handle the desert, we're going to go right down the pipe to Aden. That's our best resource in this game. We could be out there in the desert for months looking for her and never find a thing. Her best chance and our best chance is to move due south as we figured."

Everyone nodded in agreement.

"All right, mark time and coordinates. Meet you in sixty."

Nobody saw the black SUV and brown truck. They met on mark and coordinates. Going on instinct, Geno said, "Let's head south to Aden. We're gonna find 'em. We're on target. I can smell it."

They motored along and Geno broke radio silence. "Eagle here, do you read me?"

A young commo came back, "Eagle, copy."

"Pursuing objective, crossing over south side (indicating the border between Saudi Arabia and Yemen). Papers in order (indicating they had skirted the border crossing and were proceeding safely). Blue objective ahead (indicating they were going to Aden on the ocean)."

"Roger."

"One brave (indicating the platoon had suffered a KIA)" Geno replied.

"Oh…copy."

"Birds to the left and right?"

"Roger that."

"Eagle out."

"Copy, out."

"Let's wait thirty minutes to see if they show, and if they don't, we'll move," Geno said to the men on the ground.

And that was that. They had reported in, communicated their plan, confirmed birds were searching to the east and to the west. They were approved to proceed on plan. Thirty minutes passed. No Kurtz sightings.

"Saddle up again, boys. Drink lots of water; I don't want anybody crappin' out for the fun ahead. Better chow down on some of those delicious MREs while you're at it! Let's go!"

Once again, 6 was on the move in the heat of the desert. *Sure was different than balmy and pleasant San Diego training,* Geno thought. *This gamble going towards Aden better pay off otherwise we may have lost the Secretary for good.*

CHAPTER 19

CONTACT

THE TEAM WAS WELL OVER HALFWAY TO ADEN AFTER LEAVING Narjan when Geno determined it was time to go for broke. He broke radio silence again. Breaking radio silence was not as dangerous as it was in olden days, pre-digitalization. Communications such as his were now done via digitalized and encrypted messaging. Messages were encrypted and sped up twenty times normal speed so that those listening in could not decipher the message it contained. Upon receipt they would be slowed back to normal transmission speed for listening. However, Geno still considered using the radio somewhat dangerous because they were on such a high value mission.

Geno always worried about some traitor like the John Walker spy ring from the '80's or this Julian Assange guy from Sweden who was currently leaking classified information through Wikileaks, including many military secrets. *Why don't they execute these bastards?* But he knew the answer. They were kept around for intelligence gathering and for high-value prisoner swaps, even though the swaps were always denied publicly.

A nation like the United States needed a bank of prisoners to swap when the need arose. *God, how many prisoners will they demand for Kurtz if it comes to that? Hell, we might have to give them everybody in Gitmo and other secret prisons around the world to get her back!* He knew it was time to "go for it" because the United States could not risk a prisoner swap. That in itself would be a public spectacle and demeaning to the power image of the United States and would surely require a trade for very high-value detainees.

"Eagle here, do you copy?"

"Copy, Eagle."

"Get the senior." Geno said.

"Give me five, Eagle."

"Roger."

Five minutes later, "Eagle, Senior here, copy?"

"Copy. In pursuit, approaching blue zone. Need to have some road damage inflicted ahead. Can't win a race if camels stay on hard surface. Need to get camels off into terrain." Geno relayed.

"Copy that; will create situation north of blue zones. Security of package must stay intact. Copy that last?"

"Copy, Senior."

"Blue birds will lay eggs in the sand."

"Eagle out."

Per Geno's request, without risking the safety of Kurtz, they would use F-16 bomb drops to take out the roadway ahead of Geno and Imran. This would force the SUV carrying Kurtz and the support truck following them off the main road into the sands. Geno was betting they would be slowed or stuck there. Also, it would keep them out of Aden, a large and dangerous city.

"Fats, we're going to try to slow these guys down in the sand dunes. Any ideas for me?"

"Well, it's a good idea and I see where you're comin' from, but it won't be as easy as we think. What if they get through without much hassle? Or what if they do get bogged down? I don't think they're gonna want another firefight with us after that ass-kickin' we gave them back at Layla. They won't let the Secretary survive a second time. If they see they're goners, they'll kill her this time for sure. She's no value to them if they're dead."

"Yeah, I know, Frank."

"Frank? You don't ever call me that unless you're really worried about something! What's the matter? Don't you think we can pull this off?"

"I don't know, Frank. We've been on a wild goose

chase for over twenty-four hours now. If we're getting tired and edgy, how do you think they're doing? They're likely to do something really stupid with her."

"Geno, am I gonna have to pull your ass out of the sand this time? We train constantly to maintain our mental toughness. What's a little freezing water for an hour or two or the scorch of the desert for a day or two? What's to worry about a couple of flying carpet jockeys out here in the desert? OK, they got the big prize, but we've been here before. This ain't our first rodeo, pal! It's starting to get late again and we shine in the night. Get a grip on yourself or I'm gonna tell Dorothy what a wuss you've become! She won't let me come on any more adventures with you if that's the way you're gonna be!"

"Sorry, Frank. I guess I was thinking a little bit about my mom back home in the hospital. This damn long drive gives you too much time to think!"

"Geno, she'll be fine. She'll probably have a big kettle of pasta on for you when you get home!"

"I hope you're right," Geno said as he clutched his Saint Christopher medal again. *What the hell is wrong with me?* Geno thought. *Hell, yes! This isn't my first rodeo, and I do have Fats here.* "I'm fine Fats," he said aloud.

But Fats was a little taken aback by the whole exchange. He really hadn't seen that insecurity in

Geno before. Maybe it was time for Geno to send in his papers too. If you're not extremely confident in your skills, ability, and success of your mission, either you or your buddies are going to go home in a body bag like Andrew. Fats was determined to keep an eye on Geno and stay close by his side during any action ahead.

Meanwhile Imran and his buddies were making light of the situation. They would soon be in the safety of Aden. The mazes and alleyways in such a large and raucous city would give them the advantage. Aden was a shoot-em-up city, where the AK ruled and Americans and Europeans were not welcome. In fact, they were prime kidnapping and kill prospects.

Aden residents were particularly inflamed about their President's cozy relationship with the Americans. He was allowing them to use drones in sovereign Yemen territory to kill al Qaeda and other Yemeni freedom fighters. Protest riots occurred regularly. Hatred for the government reached a boiling point when government forces blocked off the exits to the town square and killed nearly fifty people by using snipers from rooftops. Now the President was on the run and the city was on the brink of lawlessness.

Imran and his band knew that when Yemen fell in this collapse of leaders in the region, it would fall to Iran and Hezbollah. Victory in such a choke point for the shipping lanes to America, Europe, and Asia was all part of the bigger plan for Imran and those like him!

"Allah be praised!" they chanted in unison as they drove side by side on the roadway. Kurtz lay on the floor knowing it would be very dangerous in Aden, making a rescue that much more difficult.

Imran, she gestured. *Planes and bombs with big explosions,* she gestured next. She then pointed individually to the three of them in the car and indicated with her hand *boom, splat, gone!* Then she gestured, *why?* Pointing to the three of them as a circle in a team, she gestured, *Let's be safe. We all live so that you can gain your victory. If I live and I am part of your victory, so be it.* Was she getting Stockholm like? No, she was playing a mind game with Imran. She deduced that he relished the starring role and as such would like to live for bigger and better glories. One thing she had learned in her years of diplomatic service in various offices and posts: Power is an aphrodisiac and can be used to wound an enemy.

Just what did she have up her sleeve? Imran looked at her and gave her a look that evoked a small amount of agreement from him. He didn't care if she lived or died, but he realized that keeping her alive for propaganda purposes would be much better for his resume than letting her be killed. Quite a pair, this Imran and Kurtz.

Looking ahead, Hassan saw smoke and dust on the horizon. "Imran, Imran, look, look!" Imran looked, and his face paled. Thoughts raced through his mind faster than a desert Mercedes, and they weren't all happy thoughts! *Contact! Now what?*

CHAPTER 20

SMOKE IN
THE DESERT

IMRAN BROUGHT HIS CARAVAN OF TWO TO A HALT.
The damage to the road ahead could be one of three
things: sabotage by fellow freedom fighters to cut off
troops coming down from Saudi on a mission to
rescue Kurtz, the same rebels preventing the troops
from streaming into Yemen to take part in the
evolving civil war, or it was the Americans themselves
doing something to slow Imran down and take him
out. He leaned toward the first.

The West might think Yemen was just another
Arab domino, but far from it. It was a strategic asset
for the Arab wolf pack of Iran, Hamas, Hezbollah,
al Qaeda, Taliban, and radical Shi'ite clerics who were
battling hearts and minds for Sharia law. Yemen
was strategically located on the Red Sea with close
proximity to the eastern coast of Africa, including allies
in Somalia, Ethiopia, Kenya, Tanzania, Mozambique,
and Zimbabwe. Arab causes backed by Iran were
gaining great traction to varying degrees in these
countries along the eastern African coast with access to
the valuable shipping lanes.

With Iran having access to the Straits of Hormuz and Yemen on the Red Sea, fundamentalist Arab freedom fighters would be in a position to control or cut off all oil supplies to the West. Let the French, English, and Americans have their play along the north coast of Africa. Imran and any freedom fighter worth his cottage milk knew that the atrocity being committed on Arabs in Libya, Syria, and against Hezbollah was to protect the Zionist state of Israel from attack. Iran and its surrogates like Imran, Hezbollah, and the rest were eyeing a fresh prize to the south, oil routes! Yemen would now be the new key to the Land of Allah.

Yemen is truly a godforsaken piece of the world, thought Geno. There was a sort of no-mans land between Yemen and Saudi Arabia, not even a firm border. Sand, spiders, snakes, and heat—nothing else except for some primitive cities to the north of Aden and along the coast. There were some temperate climates in the western mountains along the Red Sea, but the vast majority of this country, like two Nevadas laid end to end, was extraordinarily hot, dry, and harsh desert.

Who in the hell is interested in this piece of real estate? thought Geno. *Maybe the scorpions and snakes, but...* "Keep the binocs up and looking for any signs of smoke and plume on the horizon—most likely our boys settin' the stage for us!" he squawked in the ear jacks.

Imran and the truck slowly approached the smoke and rubble on the road. It looked like a bomb drop to Imran. "Hassan, we must get out of here as soon as possible!"

"How, my brother? The road has been bombed and we may not be able to cut across the desert to find it again!"

"Hassan, we must! We have no choice! Get the truck and bring it forward, I have a plan. Brothers," Imran said as he spoke to the group, "Allah has dealt us some misfortune to test our will and dedication. He has called us to make a great sacrifice that only some will be allowed to make. I must get this Kurtz woman to Aden where she can be handed over for humiliation and trial by Sharia law. She will undoubtedly receive the full punishment for her Zionist crimes. She will surely be stoned to death in the public square, shown live on Al Jazeera for the entire world to see. America will be humiliated. Jews will be humiliated. The world will see the weakness of The Great Satan and its master, Israel! Who will help me make this possible?"

All in the band raised their hands with short bursts from their AK-47s. "Allah Akbar! Allah's will be done! Allah, I am your servant, even to death for you! Allah, I will die for you!"

With that, Imran told Hassan and four gunners to stand with him. Speaking to the others, Imran said,

"My brothers, Allah has picked you for a great cause in his holy war. Brothers, you must stay behind, here, to slay the Americans. They are agents of Zion and Jews! They must be slaughtered and put to the sword! Can you do this great honor for Allah?"

"Allah Akbar, Allah Akbar!" they chanted, firing off AK-47s. "We will destroy the Americans in great victory for Allah! They will die here in the desert! Their blood will serve as a marker to Allah! Their rotting bodies will be consumed by vermin and vultures. Then they will know that there is no greater God than Allah!"

"My brothers standing here with me, will you also dedicate your lives to the delivery of this American Zionist to the altar of Allah, for Allah to do with her as he shows justice and power to the world? Will you too die with me to make this sacrifice to Allah possible? Will you destroy as many Zionists as possible in your lives if we should so be blessed to live, to make up for the work that our brothers we leave here in the desert will not be able to do if they are sacrificed to Allah in performing their duties to him?"

"Allah Akbar!" again and again by the smaller band.

"My brothers, let us all turn toward Mecca and offer our evening prayer, with the setting of the sun, together this one last time," Imran said, "perhaps before we all meet again in paradise. Oh, Allah!

We beseech you for help and guidance and seek your protection and believe in you and rely on you and extol you and are thankful to you and are not ungrateful to you, and we declare ourselves clear of, and forsake him who disobeys you. Oh, Allah! To you do we pray and prostrate ourselves and to you we do betake ourselves, and to obey you we are quick, and your mercy do we hope for and your punishment do we fear, for your punishment overtakes the unbelievers. Oh, Allah! Exalt our master, Muhammad, and his people and his true followers."

Imran instructed the fighters to fight at any cost to delay or kill the Americans. Josef would be commander. "Spread yourselves some distance from the bomb damage. Stay hidden, let them come in to you. Josef will signal the battle by firing a burst from his rifle. Launch rocket grenades immediately. They will kill and confuse the Americans. Leave no Satan alive. Kill them all, including the wounded. Take their vehicles and catch us as quickly as possible. They should be here soon. Your numbers are good because Allah is with you! Your courage is fortified by the strength of Allah! Your desire is pure! Allah will reward all of us in this life or in paradise. Do not allow these Americans to desecrate the land of the great Arab nations by allowing them to proceed any farther on this holy ground on which you battle for Allah. This land is Allah's land! The brothers that live on this land are children of Allah; you must defend Allah's children to the death!"

"Allah Akbar!" Josef and the band cheered loudly again while firing another round of celebratory fire.

Josef and his band took up their positions as Imran shoved Kurtz into the front seat of the truck, along with himself and Hassan, the driver. The four protectors shoved the back of the truck as Hassan worked to rock the truck back and forth to loosen it from the sand. "Brothers, come shove for Allah!" he shouted to Josef's band.

Working together, they were able to loosen the truck, get it moving up to the road, and soon it was on its way. Josef's band took up their positions again among the debris of the road, awaiting the Americans who would soon arrive.

"Smoke in the desert," J'effie called out.

"Hold up!" Geno commanded.

"Smoke at two o'clock, Cap."

"Got it, J'effie. OK, everybody listen up. Looks like the flyboys have been here and done us a favor. Let's creep up a mile or so, get off this road, and do our surveillance. Have your night vision goggles close by, sun's going down soon. That's good for us. Everybody take care of business right now if you need to. We aren't going to take piss breaks in battle; take care of it now. Check your weapons, check your gear. It's a great night to fight! Mount up in five."

Team 6 crept in slowly. The terrorists had left a major clue by leaving the SUV on the side of the road. "Jesus," Geno said aloud, "are these guys plain stupid or are they just plain dumb? Watch for claymores and other devices. Not likely, but don't get blown up before the big show!"

"Cap, I got two over here," Artie whispered.

"Roger, one here, with a rocket launcher," J'effie reported.

"Got one or two here," Marco came through.

"There could be eight to ten of them. We don't know for sure. The truck is missing. So there's probably a max of six in the truck, which might only leave six," Geno said. "Keep scanning and we'll make a decision."

"Skip, it's hard to see with all this debris."

"All right, we're going to cut the pie. Spread out in clock face formation. Everybody gets an 'hour' to cover. We'll focus on dark tactics with knives and garrotes. I don't want any gunfire until we've got this web closed in. You're going to be shooting across the clock, so let's not have anybody killed by friendly fire. Do NOT fire a weapon unless it is life or death or until I give the command. Radio check, everybody on?"

"Yes, sir," the squawks came back.

"On my mark: five-four-three-two-one, SEAL kill."

Mad Mike garroted the first one. J'effie covered the mouth of another, slit his jugular, and stabbed him in the heart for good measure. They each radioed their kills. So far so good, without a sound. Matt covered the mouth of another and snapped his neck.

This is too easy, Geno thought. "Stay alert," he whispered. Then the sound of a rock sliding. "Steady and stay in place. Let's see if we get any movement." An unfriendly crawled across Artie's space to the space of Steve, the medic.

"Steve, you got one coming into your zone."

"Roger, Artie," he whispered. With that, the un-friendly crouched up to survey the landscape and Artie nailed him in the heart with his blade. The guy squeezed off a round before he fell. Indiscriminate gunfire broke out immediately. The unfriendlies were spraying the area with their AKs. Fats got one with his M22. Marco got another. Geno did a jumping lunge and got Josef from behind. He hit him in the head with the butt of his rifle, knocked him to the ground, and took him alive, cuffing him with plastic wrist bands. Geno crammed Josef's scarf in his mouth. All was quiet again. The men of 6 continued searching their clock face, finding no others.

"Charlie, Matt, J'effie, Marco, and Steve, post up on lookout. Mike, get over here with Fats and me.

SMOKE IN THE DESERT

We've got some work to do with our friend. Pour some water on his face and wake him up."

Coming to, Josef realized he wasn't looking at the face of Allah!

"Who are you and who sent you?" Geno asked in crude Arabic. No answer. Geno asked again. No answer. "You want to do this the hard way?" Geno asked in Arabic. "Who are you and who sent you?" No answer. "Mike, check his IQ."

Mike gave him a hard right to the head. "Not much there, don't believe, Skip."

"Check again."

Nothing.

"Check his jaw to see if it's broke." Right cross to the jaw. "Talk!" Nothing.

Tie him up, hands and feet. Cover his head with a bag and load him into my DPV. I'll be driving our guest with Steve. Check recon for any papers, maps, or books. Bend the barrels of the AKs, put all the weapons in a pile and burn 'em with flares. Stack the grenades and burn them too. Photo all of the KIAs for intel purposes then destroy everything. They might think it was from the air strike, let them know we were here!"

He turned. "Mount up, gentlemen, looks like we're going to the beach. Aden's next."

CHAPTER 21

ADEN

IMRAN WAS AT THE OUTER CITY LIMITS OF ADEN. HE WAS brimming with confidence, pride, and joy. He had made it! He needed to connect with his network to find out where to take Kurtz. He hoped his brother knew that he had such a prize! He would make a cell call and let them know, get directives, and move.

He bought three disposable cell phones in a bazaar and made his call. The voice on the other end was shocked and elated, but worried too. This was the United States Secretary of State who was easily recognized in the Arab world because of all the times she had been shown on Al Jazeera television through the Middle East. "My son, come into the city, we will talk again," the shocked voice replied.

Geno called headquarters from his location, "Eagle here, do you copy?"

"Copy, Eagle."

"Approaching blue, request all available recon and resources from the fleet and in the area."

"Roger, Eagle. We've been expecting you, very busy here. Lot of hot potatoes baking in ovens around the region. Currently hot on top of the oven (Libya), red in the heartland (Saudi Arabia, Bahrain, and United Arab Emirates), going red in your house (Yemen), with more potatoes ready to go in the oven soon (Syria, Jordan, Lebanon, and Palestine). What can we do for you?"

"We've only been on holiday for a few days!" Geno said, referring to the time 6 spent in Riyadh and in their pursuit of Secretary Kurtz.

"Copy that, Eagle. The travel agency (head-quarters) has been very busy."

"Copy that, any travelers (other teams or agents) in town?"

"Copy, yes, will arrange for a tour together. Check with the travel desk again. We'll have a tour arranged for you."

DEVGRU had been monitoring satellite recon, voice communications through the NSA, intel from the CIA, paid informants on the ground, as well as Special Forces on the ground in the city from Delta and a SEAL team in the city from the Fifth Fleet. This was a "balls-to-the-wall effort" by the U.S. government to secure Kurtz's rescue and another reason why the United States was willing to hand off the Libya operation to the European Union and NATO.

"DEVGRU, we have a KIA traveling with us, McMahon." Geno somberly stated.

"Copy that, Eagle. We are aware of that from your previous check, our thoughts to you and the others. Chief McMahon will be addressed with full dignity at the earliest time available."

"Roger that, DEVGRU. We have a live detainee prisoner also."

"Wonderful, we'll also arrange for that package. We'll want to visit with him."

Aden is a city of over one million people that sits on the shores of a natural harbor. The harbor is part of an extinct volcano crater. Trading routes in and out of Aden date back to the seventh century BC under the kingdom of Aswan. The city and ports are connected to the mainland by an isthmus, much like Coronado SEAL training facilities are connected to San Diego by the "Silver Strand".

Like many Middle Eastern countries, Aden was once under British rule as part of British India. Aden was separated from British India in 1937. Aden's location made it an ideal link for connections between the Indian Ocean and Europe. Aden became a popular stopping point for sailors of all types from all countries in the region, with all the accompanying "sailor pleasures", along with coal and fresh water for both steamers and sailors. British Petroleum built a large refinery in Aden in 1952. The Brits tried to stabilize Aden in 1963 from assault by Russian-backed insurgents from the north. The Brits pulled out in 1967.

After Northern and Southern Yemen were united in 1990, al Qaeda conducted its first terrorist attack in Aden in December 1992. They bombed the Gold Mohur hotel, where servicemen from the United States had been staying en route to Somalia, of *Black Hawk Down* infamy. Al Qaeda unsuccessfully attempted to bomb the guided missile destroyer USS *The Sullivans* in the port of Aden as part of the 2000 millennium terror attacks, but were unsuccessful. Al Qaeda did succeed in bombing the USS *Cole* in October 2000, killing seventeen and injuring thirty-nine sailors.

Aden was one of the most dangerous cities in the Arab world. The Brits tried everything from guns and butter to psychological warfare, dropping leaflets, pitting one terror group against another, dropping large bombs on rebel strongholds and other tactics to secure and maintain their position. Nothing seemed to work and the Brits gave up on Yemen in 1967, and things started sliding downhill or, shall we say, into the ocean in a dramatic fashion.

Geno was headed into a tough city. Sure, there were affluent areas of town for the government officials and those on the take or making money in illicit ways, but the city was being overwhelmed with peasants and refugees from the countryside with nothing but time on their hands to brew trouble. The young men in the city were similar to Palestinian youth in that they had been deprived of freedom and the basics of life for their entire lives. They were open to rebellion, any rebellion, and the more radical the better. The present leader of Yemen, President Ali Abdullah Saleh, backed by the United States, was quickly losing power and was on the run. Barricading and having snipers shoot fifty demonstrators had not improved his recent poll numbers either. He could topple any day, making any mission—particularly one of this sensitive nature—more difficult.

Iran was licking its chops at this prospect and had infiltrated the country with thousands of protestors. They wanted to be ready for the fall of the American-backed government. Yemen, with its civil war history and oppression from many sides, was ripe for occupancy and a radical government as Lebanon was some years ago. Lebanon was now a deadly thorn in the side of Israel, and Yemen would be a thorn in the foot of American-backed oil producers of the north. Iran could couple with Yemen to wreak great disruption for the West. Iranian-backed pirates of Somalia had proven the disruption that a few dinghies could produce by capturing oil tankers and merchant ships without firing a shot. Only Allah knows what a well-armed and coordinated Yemen-Iran effort could do for chaos in the Red Sea shipping lanes and the trade routes down the east coast of Africa.

Imran called his handler on his second disposable cell phone and was told; "Brother, Muhammad has an ocean view for you near the port. Proceed to the mosque nearest the port, on the east side of the docks, and wait there. You are driving a what?"

Imran replied, "A brown Toyota truck."

"Very good, my brother. Be brave. Allah will care for you. You will be approached by a brother carrying a backpack with the colors of the Yemen flag. Wait for him and be brave. You must be brave," the voice on the other end repeated.

Meanwhile back in the United States, the National Security Administration and DEVGRU were planning.

"DEVGRU, Jones at NSA."

"Yes, sir, Norman here."

"Intel for you. We have a possible intercept on Kurtz. Inform Team 6 to proceed to the port area of Aden. Delta has a safe house in the area. Proceed to safe house area and wait for our update. We're trying to get a satellite over that area. Won't be able to do a pass-over for six hours. AWACs and other assets deployed with discretion. We don't want to tip anyone," Jones stated.

"We've got that, sir. Thank you for the intel. Admiral Gates is personally monitoring the situation with his team here in Virginia from the SEAL Team 6 recon satellite. The Secretary's life is at risk, as we all know," Norman replied.

"State Department, Joint Chiefs, and heads of House and Senate Intelligence and Defense committees are hands on up here. This is the biggest thing since Kennedy for all of us. Nobody wants any conspiracy theories floating around, given the Secretary's near miss in getting the nomination from the President. He's pretty touchy about this. Doesn't want anything laid at his doorstep," Jones volunteered.

"Yeah, I hear you. Everybody's about as nervous as the proverbial whore in church on a Sunday morning. I wish the politicians would calm down and let us do what we're trained to do," Norman replied. "How are things in the rest of the area?"

"Proceeding well, but could be a dangerous slide at any time," Jones replied.

"Look, I need to get off the line," Norman said.

"Me too, trying to keep everybody happy," said Jones.

Evidently, the stress had gotten to this pair. They were talking on lines monitored by internal security agencies. They would be relieved of their duties shortly, placed under watch, interrogated, and investigated for possible intel leaks, or worse yet, espionage, drummed out of the military and placed on a lifelong watch list by the FBI. Wars can get messy and sloppy. That's why Geno always kept his communications to a minimum and did a "gut check" for possibilities before moving in. He knew the old adage "loose lips sink ships", or in his case, "loose lips can get me and my guys killed!"

Imran drove through the city to the mosque near the eastside docks. He spotted a man wearing a backpack with the Yemeni flag on the back. They casually approached each other, sizing each other up. The "backpack man" walked to his car. Imran walked to his car and instructed Hassan to follow the other man's car. The Delta Force Special Ops surveillance team saw them both. A drive from the docks to the terrorist safe house ensued for all.

"DEVGRU, we're on location," Geno communicated.

"Roger. Eagle, pack your bags. Lodging found for you. Bring full wardrobe. Weather unknown at the present time."

"Roger, we have a full wardrobe. Please provide location."

"Copy, Eagle, proceed to blue route using appropriate detours. The concierge will take you to your lodging."

"Roger, DEVGRU," Geno said.

Geno turned to his men. "Time to see the bright lights of the city! Let's go. Strap in our passenger. We're on the move."

CHAPTER 22

HOUSEWARMING

AN IMAM GREETED IMRAN AND THE HOSTAGE. "IMRAN, my son, you have done a great thing in the eyes of Allah. Surely, you carry Allah's blessings with you. Your success tells us that you must do more yet for Allah. He has blessed you, and you have blessed our cause beyond measure. We will visit, but I would like to meet our guest first."

Seeing Kurtz, the imam thought, *she is a small woman. Her silver hair indicates years of experience. The journey has left her somewhat disheveled.* "Please follow me to your quarters, Mrs. Kurtz," the imam said in fluent English. She was then led to a window-less room.

"Please sit. Would you like to refresh yourself from the journey, Madam Ambassador?"

"Thank you, but not now," she replied. "I am Kathryn Kurtz Secretary of State of the United States of America. I am entitled to diplomatic immunity and full diplomatic rights and privileges under the Geneva Convention and the United Nations.

I demand that you release me immediately."

"I realize this, Madam Secretary, but Geneva and the UN seem to look the other way with frequency when it comes to my people. Surely, you can understand this. You will be our guest here for as long as we see fit. Please, make yourself comfortable." He turned to another man waiting at the door. "Bring the Secretary tea and food to eat. She will feel better soon. Madam, we will provide you clean clothing and water to bathe yourself. Please, rest. You must be tired from your journey."

The imam came from a wealthy Saudi family. He had been educated in London and trained in the art of diplomacy and negotiation for his family's business. He had chosen a different path after coming in contact with a radical imam in London. However, he was able to use his skills in negotiating to promote cooperation between various factions within radicalized groups of Islam. His ploy with Kurtz was to treat her with the dignity and courtesy to which she was accustomed. This approach would make her less combative and perhaps somewhat complicit. His goal was to develop a level diplomatic playing field whereby she would not feel personally threatened and would engage in "diplomatic discussions" the next morning. His goal was to "negotiate" information back and forth between them.

The Arab fundamentalists were rapidly growing

very concerned about a seismic shift away from fundamentalism to personal freedoms and some form of a more liberal Islamic governing body. The fundamentalist groups were alarmed that a significant majority of young people in these regions were choosing liberalization instead of joining in the "Islamic Cause". Young people had been the recruiting ground for Hezbollah, al Qaeda, and many other groups. Perhaps the imams and clerics had overestimated their strength among the young. The imam himself had counseled against the heavy-handed approach in Iran against the protestors in Tehran. Understanding the power of Western media technology, what he had feared had happened: The images shown on Western media of beating and killing unarmed, well-dressed young professionals had placed new thoughts into the minds of the younger generation throughout the Middle East.

The imam was one of those in the diplomatic councils of fundamentalists who did not think they could keep winning the hearts and minds of the young leadership groups by literally beating them down. They had seen on these so-called media outlets of the West, such as this Facebook, that groups could organize much easier than ever before. Al Qaeda was a great user of the Internet but had not engaged in this Facebook thing. Also, the West was turning the tables on al Qaeda and others with YouTube and other forms of social media. Al Qaeda had posted beheadings of

Daniel Pearl and others on the Internet as a recruiting and terror tool. Now the West was using YouTube to post carnage and attacks by savage groups and rulers. These YouTube videos were shocking the world as never before. The rebels in Libya had used them as a great ploy to lure NATO and even some Arab states to destroy Brother Gaddafi.

Al Qaeda and Hezbollah were interested in learning as much as possible about the plans of America in what was developing into a "new" Middle East. Perhaps the imam would detain Secretary Kurtz for an additional day or evening if their "diplomatic discussions" were going well.

Leaving the room for the lower level, the imam motioned for Imran to follow him. They entered a fortified bunker-like room. "Imran, my son, please sit," the imam indicated, switching back to Arabic. "Imran, there is great chaos in much of the Arab world that Allah has provided us. Of course, you were key in creating the great chaos in our sacred land, Saudi Arabia. I cannot tell you at this time what has transpired, but I can tell you that your journey has not ended. We will restock your men and supplies and you will journey with the Secretary to Pakistan. The Secretary will be useful to our cause from a safe haven in Pakistan. Time is short, and proper arrangements have been made. You will travel a short distance to the east where you will meet a dhow fishing vessel. The crew of the dhow will take you eastward along the Yemeni coast beyond Sayhut and Salalah, in Oman. You will be met by another fishing vessel from Iran that will provide transportation to a secure location where the Secretary will be transferred and become the guest of our people in Pakistan."

Imran was brimming with Arab pride, freedom fighter pride, martyr pride, and personal pride. "Allah's will be done," he said quietly.

"You must rest, my son. You too have had a long and dangerous journey. You have more travel ahead of you. Please, refresh yourself, eat, and then rest. Sleep with the darkness of night and be refreshed for tomorrow. There is work to be done. Allah be with you, my son."

"Allah Akbar, Imam."

Imran knew not to ask for any names. Knowledge of names was a weakness that could be exploited by the torture of the American Zionists. If he were captured, he could endure any form of torture without providing information to his captors. If Allah chose and he were not to complete his mission, he would die in full confidence of being a pure martyr, not having provided any information to the enemies of Allah. He cleansed himself ritualistically, ate some breads, drank tea and drifted off to sleep. It felt good to rest after nearly forty-eight hours without sleep. He was soon in a very deep and heavy sleep. All was well.

Geno and 6 met their contact near the waterfront. McMahon's body was transferred with full respect to another vehicle. The prisoner was also transferred. Geno and the Delta commander on the ground went over the plans of capture. They refueled the petrol bladders of the DPVs in the event there was an escape and long chase. They also restocked ammo, MREs, and water, preparing as if they might be engaged again for a long haul.

"Over-prep and overstock" was always the rule of the day when planning for these missions. The ground commander brought black "ninjas" for them to wear during the night as well as fresh desert camos.

Wow, Geno thought, *hell of a wardrobe selection!* "I know this isn't on your radar screen, but any word on my mother back in Houston?" Geno asked the ground commander.

"Sorry, I didn't know she was sick. Serious?"

"Chest discomfort, mild heart attack, sir."

"Is she in the hospital?"

"Yes, sir. I was called home to visit her."

"Sorry about that."

"Oh, she'll be fine. She's a tough one!" Geno replied.

"I can believe that after what you've endured the past forty-eight hours! Chip off the old block, huh!"

"I guess so, sir."

"OK, Genelli, you better get going. You OK?" the commander asked.

"Yes, sir, my men and I are good to go."

"All right then, get going. You have full resources at your command and Delta as backup. We're secure on the communication lines. Keep us posted on all developments. You're our eyes and ears for this. Bring her home safe," the commander said.

"Will do, sir," replied Geno. He rejoined his men and addressed them, "Time to go 6. Saddle up. Delta Force will lead and we will follow with another Delta team on our backside. Keep your eyes and ears open. Our escort and trailers will cover us. 6, DO NOT open fire on anyone en route. Leave that to Delta. Nothing should go down, but if it does, divert and regroup. Bad guys along the way are not our business, Kurtz is our only objective."

They arrived at the Delta safe house. Geno and the platoon leader of Delta exchanged pleasantries and got down to business. 6 would be leading the extraction maneuver. Delta would provide cover and transport. Delta and the Fifth Fleet had all arrangements made. Geno's job was to get in and get Kurtz out. They both wanted to move as quickly as possible with the cover of night. There would be guards and lookouts, but even terrorists had to catch some shut-eye. The timeline required that they be in and out before morning prayer at sunrise. The terrorists and the city would be awake and moving after that.

Delta provided satellite recon and topography maps. They also had a proposed floor plan of the house. The house sat on the top of a bluff surrounded by decorative trees and shrubbery. Geno called Fats over. "What do you think?"

"I like those bluffs and shrubs," Fats said.

"Me too. Let's use the shrubs for cover," Geno replied. "Let's get Artie, Miggs, and J'effie up those bluffs, they're our best climbers. You, Harley, and Charlie go to the back side. Send Joe, Matt, and Marco to the other side. I'll take the front with the rest. Delta will provide cover for all of us."

Geno gave assignments to his men, showing them on the map. "We have our typical beachside villa here. This is a map of what the floor plan should be like. The guy that owns this villa is in all likelihood affluent, probably connected to people. This is not your typical Aden housing. The walls are likely reinforced somehow. They could have an underground bunker or something like that for communication and command. We won't know for sure what we have until we get in there. The fact that they are using it and seem rather casual about it tells me they feel secure. They could have a reason for that. There could be other lookout and security units in some of the surrounding houses."

"Delta, you're going to have to cover that while we're in there. This is almost too quiet. It feels like we are being lured into a trap. Everybody, stay sharp!"

Geno reviewed the assignments and responsibilities of each team. "My team will split once inside, with one group going for the bunker to destroy all communication and command. The rest of my group will move forward in a direct route to the backside of the house where Kurtz is likely to be. She'll probably be secured somewhere deep in the house, we'll have to get in and get out quick. Radio in any exits you find; we may need them. I'd like to go in the front side, grab Kurtz, and go out the backside. It will be a straight run-through. Your respective teams must take out any security guards and be ready to create havoc from your locations. Delta will deal with the rest of these guys after we're out. SEALs don't normally say this, but we're going to cut and run after we get Kurtz out of there! Got it?"

"Yes, sirs" all around.

"Artie, Miggs, and J'effie, Delta will provide any cover you need going up the bluff."

"Yes, sir," they acknowledged, looking at Delta, who nodded also.

"Delta, you're to remain on the exterior of the house to provide cover and support. There may be other bad guys in the neighborhood. Absolutely blow them away

– 177 –

if they show. Delta, we may need firepower on the inside if we have problems, but Kurtz is to be rescued safely. Everyone understand that? SEALs and Delta have worked together before. We've done this in Afghanistan and Iraq, as well as every other hot-spot in the world. We're all cross-trained with each other in these maneuvers and techniques. We know what to do. SEAL 6 gets the insertion duty this time. Next time we could be backing up Delta. We all good on this?" Geno asked.

"No problem for Delta. We're happy to be on call to rescue you SEALs if you can't take the heat in the kitchen!" the Delta commander joked. "We've got your back," he said.

"Artie, what's your ETA to get around to the base of the cliff and climb up to the house?" Geno asked.

"Sir, I would estimate fifteen minutes," Artie replied.

"All right, we'll make it twenty to be on the safe side. That gives the rest of us plenty of time to get into our positions," Geno said. "Radio check for everyone."

"Check, check" all around.

"Check your buddy's face grease, gentlemen. We want to look pretty for the house warming! Command and control, do you read us?"

"Copy, Eagle, we have you and have all resources available to you. Black Hawk gunships in the air. F-16s armed and in the air for your call. Zodiacs and patrols offshore. Medical chopper insertion units ready if you need them. Birds stocked with marines for you. We are good to go on your count, Eagle."

"Copy that. Communication protocol in place. Communication will originate from the ground. Listen-only mode for C&C except for updates of unknown or unplanned events," Geno said.

"Roger on that one, Eagle. Communication protocol in place. Good luck to you," C&C said.

"Roger that one," from Geno.

Of course it went without saying that since Kurtz was involved, everyone from Admiral Gates in Virginia to the Chief of Naval Operations and the Secretaries of the Army, Defense Department, State Department, and those gathered in the White House situation room were all listening into the communications through a live feed. Perspiration broke out from Aden to D.C.

"Move. Zulu minus twenty." Artie and his team moved to the beachfront and began crawling to the cliff in their black ninjas, their modified M16s slung on their backs with their rucksacks. Fats and his team began moving around to the backside in a wide semi-circle maneuver. Joe and his team moved in a quarter-circle move to the side facing away from the ocean.

Geno and his group crawled forward to get in position. Delta covered each group.

"Zulu minus fifteen...Zulu minus ten...Zulu in five." Geno rubbed his Saint Christopher medal and put it back against his chest.

The team was like coiled steel, ready to strike, but as mentally calm as placid water while they lay listening to the Zulu countdown.

CHAPTER 23

TAKEDOWN

THE FINAL CHECKS CAME IN AT ZULU MINUS ONE. "BAD GUYS all around," came the calls. There were two to three lookouts and guards on each side of the villa. "Were you expecting a red carpet?" Geno asked. "Silence-only mode," he added. Silence-only mode indicated that knives and garrotes were available, of course, but also the silencer-equipped M16s and the handy P228; a military designated M11 used almost exclusively by SEALs which was also available with silencers.

"Mark your targets, go on my call. We'll storm through the front. Fats, come in the back if you can. Eliminate your targets and go with the plan," Geno issued as a final command.

"We copy you," the C&C reported from the carrier. Once the operation began, it would be done with as little chatter as possible. In and out, then away.

The entire chain of command was listening intently and feeling the stress as the mark-time approached. "This better work," the President said to his National Security Chief. I don't need a "Kennedy" is what he was thinking.

Admiral Gates was thinking his career was either going up or he was done in the Navy. He had hand-picked Geno's team for the mission. The top Senators and Representatives were thinking how they would spin the outcome for their respective purposes, regardless of the outcome. The State Department and CIA were just hoping for a success.

Geno wasn't thinking about anything like this. He was thinking about the mission tactics. He was focused. He was like an athlete that was in the zone with his mind and auto reflexes.

Helicopters and Zodiacs began moving in closer to shore.

"Zulu on my mark. Five-four-three-two-one, mark!"

Thud. Thud. Artie and Miggs took out the two guards beachside with their M11s. They dropped like sacks of potatoes without a sound. Crack! "Ughhhh." *Thud.* Joe and his team took out the three in their quadrant with a broken neck, a cover of the mouth with a serration of the throat, and a silenced M11 shot on the third.

Fats had his hands full on the back side with four bad guys. Two of his targets had heard a noise. One got zapped with a silencer as he did a rotational turn to look. The bullet entered through the forehead and blew out the back side in a bloody spray. The second was met with a laser-guided frontal shot, a double-tap to the forehead that took out the back of his head too. Gray matter painted the side of the villa.

Harley garroted his man with his eyes bulging as he died. Charlie slit his man's throat and, with typical thoroughness, gave him a direct lunge into his heart with his knife. His gloves were covered in blood.

Geno, Steve, and the rest of the assault team rushed toward the front entrance with their silencer M16s, spraying and killing the four armed sentries as they went. Those inside barely rustled from their night sleep, except for Kurtz and the imam who were each thinking about the next day and what it might bring for them. They both had a lot to gain, but their goals were vastly different.

Steve and Ozzie hit the front door with a battering ram like a SWAT team would. Geno threw a blast grenade to stun the occupants followed by a gas grenade to choke those inside. He burst in with the team in a spread formation behind him. He was on point. Leaving on his gas mask, Geno immediately began scanning for Kurtz through his night vision goggles.

Steve and the other members of the frontal assault team quickly killed four more men in the stairway. Steve took two of his men with him downstairs to the bunker where he killed a communication man sleeping on the floor. Seeing no one else, they came back up the steps and threw a hand grenade down the steps to destroy the communications equipment.

Geno had spotted two sentries standing by the bedroom doors down the hallway. One was posted outside Kurtz's room and the other was posted outside the imam's room. Kurtz and the imam were both in an alarmed state by this time, but they had little time to react because things were happening around them in a matter of seconds! The imam lunged for his door as his sentry squeezed off a burst of rounds with his AK, wounding Jase in the left thigh and lower abdomen. He began bleeding badly.

Geno fired off a quick burst of his own, killing the guard. Fortunately for her, Kurtz was frozen in a crouched position behind her bed. Her sentry had raised his AK to fire, but Geno got him with a hail of bullets from left to right. Two of the bullets went through Kurtz's bedroom door, lodging in the wall behind where she was hiding.

Fats and his group had gained entrance through a back door. They shot the hell out of the handle, locks, and holders with their M16s. Geno gave them a hand signal to check the two back bedrooms, one on each side. Fats gave it the "yes" head signal and motioned to his men to secure the rooms.

Harley fired his M16 with a massive spray of bullets

through one of the back bedroom doors, threw in a stun grenade, and found a dead terrorist on the floor. *Score one for the good guys,* Harley said to himself. He immediately turned back to Fats and both faced the other door.

"That bastard who led us across the desert and got Andrew killed could be hiding in here. With all this noise, I'm sure he's up and armed, so let's be careful here. Kick the door. I'll go low and you cover me," Fats ordered.

Harley kicked the door in and Fats followed. Fats quickly hit the deck and rolled while Harley sprayed the inside of the room to provide cover. Imran was trying to fire off his AK with limited success because his hands and body were shaking so violently. Fats knocked the AK out of Imran's hands and did a wrestling reversal on him putting Imran in a chokehold.

"Take him alive!" Geno shouted. Fats, let up on his choke hold and pinned him down while they bound and gagged him.

"Get a hood on him!" Fats barked to Harley.

Hand signaling to his team, Geno called them forward and gave the "eyes on" signal for both front bedroom doors. He motioned Steve to the right side door, while he focused on the left side. Steve broke down the door of the imam's room with a powerful lunge of his big frame. The imam began firing a 9mm as Steve hit the deck with a body roll. He completed the roll, coming up and grabbing the 9mm while the others slammed the imam to the floor.

"Cuff him! We want him alive!" Steve said angrily.

"Secretary Kurtz?" Geno shouted into the other bedroom.

"Yes!" Kurtz replied.

"Navy SEALs coming in!" Geno broke the door lock and looked in. Kurtz was frozen on the floor. "Let's go, ma'am," he said as he quickly grabbed her up. "We gotta get out of here! We've got bad guys all around, but you're safe, ma'am. Let's go!"

"Oh, thank you, thank you!" she cried.

"Quiet, ma'am," he said as he put his hand over her mouth. "Get Jase and let's get out of here!" Two men grabbed a blanket off a bed, laid Jase in it, and lifted him up. Another man pressed on his leg wound and another on his abdominal wound. He was bleeding very badly.

Amid all the chaos, Geno shouted, "Photograph as much as possible! Grab all the manuals you can and throw them in the rucksacks and let's get the hell out of here! Fats, can you get us out of here? Jase is hurt pretty bad!"

"Yea! Follow me out the back."

"Rendezvous!" Geno barked out on the radio.

"Roger," the other teams replied.

Delta was on ultra high alert outside. They had moved from defense to offense, looking for any sign of movement or disruptions nearby and on the horizon. They were locked and loaded with fingers on triggers. They scanned with both night vision goggles and scopes. C&C radioed that birds were in the air and would be landing on the hilltop nearby. The Delta captain had already ordered a squad up to the hilltop to secure it. Everything was a "go" on the outside with Delta in full offensive mode.

"Insertion team exiting the target with package and two extras," Geno radioed.

"Copy that. Birds in five."

"We're ready. One of ours wounded in the fight." Geno replied.

"Roger, will send medivac."

Fats led them to the rendezvous point with Delta. Geno trailed with Jase and Kurtz. They hurried up to the landing zone as quickly as they could. A few house lights were beginning to come on and some folks were out on their balconies but quickly took cover or scurried back into their houses as they heard the helicopters approach. Friend or foe, they did not want to be caught in any crossfire from anyone. Risking life and limb was not for the affluent. That was a job for the poverty-ridden youth in the city squares!

Artie grabbed Jase and threw him on his back and ran as quickly as he could. Geno grabbed Kurtz and threw her on his back and ran as fast as he could too. They were about a quarter mile from the landing zone. The birds were landing.

"Run, run, run!" Geno was shouting.

"Cover! Cover!" the commander shouted for Delta to provide cover fire if needed. Everyone was full of adrenaline. They reached the helicopters and scrambled on board. Artie threw Jase into the medivac helicopter and jumped in himself, but it was too late. Jase was dead.

Geno and Kurtz jumped on bird one with the helicopter door gunner providing cover. Fats and the other part of the team boarded bird two with Imran and the imam. They would be transferred to offshore secure CIA facilities for interrogation.

The helicopters lifted off for the return to the carrier. The adrenaline rush and relief of getting the mission accomplished was quickly offset with the radio call from Artie: "We lost Jase." The group was silent.

Kurtz, not wearing headphones, asked, "Is something wrong?" She didn't even know Geno's name.

"Yes, ma'am. We lost one of our men on

the mission."

"Oh," she gasped, staring at Geno with tears welling up in her eyes.

"It's OK, ma'am, we're safe," Geno said.

"I know, but that young man? It's so terrible. I feel so terrible. You did this all for me…" She trailed off.

"It's OK, ma'am. We did it for you and we did it for our country. It's a good world out there, but it has a lot of bad people in it. Our job is to deal with the bad people so that good people like you can do your job to keep us safe."

"That's very kind of you to say that. I don't even know your name. What is your name?"

"Gregory Genelli. My friends call me Geno."

"Geno, I'm very pleased to meet you. My name is Kathryn Kurtz."

"I know, ma'am. Pleased to meet you."

The helicopters headed eastward into the sunrise…

CHAPTER 24

HOMEWARD BOUND

THE SCENE ON THE DECK OF THE AIRCRAFT CARRIER USS
Ronald Reagan was like a scene from the movie *Top Gun.* F-18s circled overhead as the helicopters carrying Kurtz and Geno's team landed on board the *Reagan* just as the sun was rising. Sailors rushed forward as the helicopters landed. "Hoorahs" abounded everywhere, nearly drowning out the choppers. The captain of the *Reagan* welcomed them aboard as they climbed out of the choppers.

Kurtz did look a bit worse for wear, but the captain did not give any signals as such as he shook her extended hand and said "Welcome to the USS *Ronald Reagan*, Madam Secretary."

"Thank you, Captain. I wouldn't be here if it weren't for these brave men," she said, motioning to Geno and the rest of SEAL Team 6.

"I know, Madam Secretary. All of these men and women here are the best people in the world and the finest military force in the world. It is our honor to preserve freedom throughout the world. Allow me to escort you below deck to your quarters, if you will permit it."

"Yes, Captain. I would like to freshen up just a bit and then I need to talk to my people back at the State Department. I would like to talk to my family also."

"Of course, Madam. I'll arrange for you to speak to your family from your cabin. Please follow me." The captain motioned for stewards and security to lead him and Mrs. Kurtz to her cabin.

Geno and 6 were then rushed by the sailors on board. There were hoorahs and high fives all around. Geno looked at Fats with that look of accomplishment, and Fats returned the look. Fats rushed into the group of men and everybody hugged and cheered.

Geno broke off from the celebration to go to the medivac helicopter. Perspiration was still sitting on Jase's facial camo grease paint. Artie had taken off his headgear and covered his torso. Geno removed the blanket. Jase's clothing was soaked with blood from his two gaping wounds.

Geno touched Jase's left cheek, and then came to attention and gave Jase a somber salute. Artie was weeping with a dazed look on his face. "C'mon, Artie, let's get out of here."

As solemn as it was on board the medivac, Washington was ecstatic. "Get that man a medal!" the

President proclaimed, waiving the traditional backlog of red tape. "Talk to the Chief of Naval Operations. I want this done as part of the welcome home ceremonies."

"Yes, sir," replied the White House Chief of Staff.

Geno would be awarded the Navy's highest honor, the Navy Cross. The Navy Cross is second only to the Congressional Medal of Honor as an award for valor and courage under fire.

Kurtz talked with her family and with the President. All agreed she should return to Washington immediately. SEAL Team 6 settled into the bowels of the ship, debriefing with DEVGRU about the mission. The imam and Imran were under lock and key.

Secretary Kurtz was escorted into a C-2 Greyhound for the first phase of her trip back to Washington from aboard the *Reagan*. The morning and early afternoon had passed with conference calls and debriefings for her. She would travel from the *Reagan* to Qatar with an F-18 fighter escort and then from Qatar to Washington. She was truly looking forward to getting home to her family. She was a strong woman, but the intensity of the past seventy-two hours had been more than she wanted, and she hoped to never experience anything like that again!

"Secretary One, ready for launch" as the flight crew designated her C-2 and catapulted it from the *Reagan*.

They flew without incident to Qatar and transferred planes for the flight home to D.C. Flying from Qatar, she looked westward at the setting sun as they flew up the Persian Gulf, and went into a left banking maneuver entering Saudi, Jordanian, and Israeli airspace. Electronic jamming defenses and a fighter escort protected them. The view was serene and Kurtz was relieved to be going home. Geno would follow in the morning and would arrive in Washington one day after her. The ceremony and honors would take place the following day. The nation and the world needed a victory!

Glancing out the window at the sunset, Kurtz was happy to leave it all behind. Suddenly, out of no-where, there was a giant fireball in the sky over Israel, the likes of which she had never seen before! Her plane shook violently and then the lighting in the cabin failed. Her plane appeared to stall and the cabin was filled with the light of the fireball.

"God help us!" Kurtz cried as a plane in the distance fell out of the sky.

Part II

SEAL Team 6: bin Laden and Beyond

———————————————◾———————————————

CHAPTER 25

TRANSFORMATION

SECRETARY OF STATE KATHRYN KURTZ AND GENO GENELLI
had both returned from the rescue mission in Yemen
in which Genelli led a group of Navy SEALs across
the great expanses of southern Saudi Arabia's desert
to successfully rescue Kurtz from a group of terrorists
that had kidnapped her in Riyadh, Saudi Arabia.
It had been a terrifying chase and rescue for Kurtz.
Though it was a relatively short hostage-holding
period of only seventy hours, it seemed like a lifetime
to her. The ordeal was transforming her political and
military views with each passing day. After all, she
had come to the current administration with a
"New Age Global Vision" for the State Department.

Kurtz had pushed hard in the State Department
to abandon titles like "War on Terror", "Enemy
Combatants", "Islamic Terrorists", and others. Like
the President, she believed that if people, any group of
people, were treated in a civilized manner, they would
come to know America for its goodness and abandon
their terrorist goals and tactics in return. That view as

an approach to working with extreme groups was fading rapidly in Kurtz's mind because of the ordeal she had experienced.

Geno had come back to America very reluctantly. The Middle East appeared to be unraveling at an alarming speed and he had left his unit, SEAL 6, including friend Frank "Fats" Walker aboard the aircraft carrier USS *Ronald Reagan*. In addition, two members and friends of his team were now at Andrews Air Force Base being prepared for burial. Andrew McMahon had been killed in the desert shootout with Kurtz's captors in the Layla region of Saudi Arabia. Jase Erickson had been killed by a terrorist during the rescue of Kurtz in Aden. Geno was back in America with a heavy heart for his SEAL brothers and with the gnawing desire to get back with his men on the *Reagan*.

The thought of the coming medal presentation and planned American Patriot Day celebration was almost more than Geno could bear. He didn't mind staring down the barrel of an armed terrorist in a dark alley in some god-awful location, but the thought of his mother dealing with the media circus at home worried him immensely. Here was a man who had spent his entire Navy career in the black world of Special Ops and had done everything in his power to keep his mother in the dark to prevent her from worrying more than necessary. Geno and his secret career had been exposed by the President, but worst of all, his mother would now be in the crosshairs of the media.

The only thing that drove him forward with this political circus was that the order had come directly from the President, by way of the Chief of Naval Operations Admiral Foley. It was his duty to accept the medal, and he was a man of duty. He planned to send the medal home to his mother, Dolly, who was recovering from her heart attack. Thank God for her recovery, which was going well. *There is a ray of good news in the world,* he thought, it gave him hope.

Geno was awarded the Navy Cross. The President awarded the medal on the south lawn of the White House, in full view of the Washington Monument. Pennsylvania Avenue had been blocked off, and it was estimated that nearly a quarter of a million people filled the area south of the White House fences to the Washington Monument. Dignitaries from Congress, departments of State, Defense, and the Navy were prominently situated for television and photo opportunities.

The President performed the actual presentation, assisted by Secretary of State Kurtz, behind a large bulletproof shield. Secret Service agents were hidden nearly everywhere surrounding the presentation area. Snipers lined the roof of the White House out of view of the public. Reagan National Airport was shut down for two hours while F-16s patrolled the skies. Helicopters patrolled from afar. FBI agents, Capitol Police, Washington Metro SWAT, and special agents mingled and filtered through the crowd. Extra medical and trauma resources were also on hand, all for the possibility that a terror group may try to upstage the presentation and celebration.

Geno stoically stood at full attention in his dress white uniform, his gold SEAL trident shining brilliantly in the sun. The President pinned the Navy Cross upon his uniform, then shook Geno's hand and offered the nation's thanks to him. Geno responded with a "Thank you, Mr. President" and a crisp military salute.

Secretary Kurtz followed with a handshake and a very sincere "Thank you" with tears in her eyes. Geno smiled at her and gave her a military salute also.

The President moved to the podium to announce that he would like to say a few words in honor of Warrant Officer Genelli, and then proceeded to give a long speech.

The President began, "My fellow Americans and citizens of the world, we gather today to honor an individual whose heroic actions serve as a model for all of us throughout the world seeking peace and democracy. Warrant Officer Gregory Genelli has been awarded the Navy Cross by a grateful nation and a thankful world. Warrant Officer Genelli went far beyond the normal call of duty in leading his team on a mission of mercy that resulted in the safe return of Secretary of State Kathryn Kurtz. Warrant Officer Genelli led his team into harm's way without regard for his personal safety. Warrant Officer Genelli personally led a frontal assault into an insurgent stronghold near the city of Aden, Yemen. The successful return of Secretary Kurtz has provided the opportunity for the United States of America and the United Nations to continue peaceful pursuits against the violent actions of the few. Warrant Officer Genelli, your nation and the 'world nation' are grateful to you for your brave actions."

Geno thought that was enough to be said, but the President continued. "The world order is being transformed before our very eyes. Dictators and despots are falling to democracy. We hail this transformation but realize these matters must be resolved by the individual citizens of countries in their respective transition. Recent administrations have too quickly and freely committed the military strength of the United States of America throughout the world. We are now at a time when we must move forward with, or defer to, our allies. We must be willing to let others lead. However, let me make it perfectly clear, America stands clearly in the light of the beacon of democracy; but we cannot and we must not impose our will on other nations of the world. It is my belief that peaceful negotiation will bear more fruit than the bitter herbs of war in these matters. Madam Secretary Kurtz stands solidly with me in this matter. Negotiation instead of confrontation. Diplomacy will rule over tyranny. Might does not make right. America must treat all nations of the world as equal partners in this pursuit of peace through diplomacy."

The President continued, "We must turn our resources inward as we seek a just and fair way of life for all Americans. No longer should this nation be known as a nation that represses its own citizens because of the excesses in our economy that have been allowed to build over recent years. Every parent and every child should have access to the basic rights and dignities of life, whether it be health care accessible to all, not just the few; a dignified home in which to raise a family, not a slum dwelling; nutritional diets that develop both mind and body, not the soup kitchens of the homeless shelters; universal access to a college degree that will lift the standard of living and opportunity for all, not just the offspring of the elite. And last but not least, the right to a dignified retirement life for our senior citizens, those who worked so hard to make this country great, who seem to be willing to be cast aside by those seeking even more wealth and power for themselves. This is why men like Warrant Officer Genelli do what they do: serve whenever called to do what is necessary to preserve our ability to achieve our goals throughout the world in a peaceful manner *and* for that peaceful approach to turn our resources inward unto our nation to fulfill the destiny of a dignified life for all Americans!"

He turned. "Warrant Officer Genelli, please come forward to share this vision with me."

Thoughts were racing through Geno's mind: *Who is this man? Is he insane, or is he just that naive? Is this real or am I in another world? What in the hell is going on here?*

"Damn it!" Geno had told Admiral Gates at DEVGRU headquarters in Dam Neck, that he did not deserve any medal, and if anyone did, it was McMahon and Erickson, who had been killed in the rescue mission. He had been adamant about that, and he did not want a public spectacle as had been planned, and he was not going to tour the nation on a goodwill mission as recent Congressional Medal of Honor recipient Salvatore Giunta had done. He just wanted to get back to the *Reagan* with his men.

Geno was caught totally off guard. Should he stand? Of course, but should he shake the President's hand and sit down politely, deferring to humility—or should he speak? If he spoke, should he defer to the President or should he speak for himself and his bands of brothers serving throughout the world in harm's way?

My God, I'm not a frickin politician, I'm a warrior

for my country! Respond like a warrior, then. Show respect and humility; don't push yourself forward at the expense of others...On the other hand, you just were awarded the nation's second-highest military honor, they can't fire you... All these thoughts went through Geno's mind as he arose and moved to the podium.

"Mr. President, Madam Secretary Kurtz, Admiral Gates, honorable guests, Mom recovering at home, Dad, my family, and you, the American people, thank you very much for this great honor and privilege you have bestowed upon me. I accept this recognition in the names Andrew McMahon and Jase Erickson, two men who paid the ultimate sacrifice for their country and deserve this award far more than I. I also accept this recognition in the name of my brothers who accompanied me on this mission. And I accept this recognition in the names of all forces, especially Special Forces, serving in remote and dangerous locations around the globe."

Then Geno did something he had not planned but felt compelled to do under the circumstances. "The President has spoken with great passion of his view of America and what America can be in his view. The President is correct. The freedom to express and govern according to his views and those of the American people is why I and all others in uniform serve to protect freedom for all Americans, both at home and abroad. I have seen many areas of the world in my duties, most of which are places where these freedoms do not exist. Being Americans, living in this great bastion of freedom and democracy, sometimes we take our freedoms and liberties for granted. Please listen to me: My service to this great country has instilled the belief in me that truly, 'Freedom isn't free.' Often it comes at a great price, the blood of our American heroes serving in those remote and dangerous locations of the world of which I spoke.

"Two of the men who went off with me to rescue Secretary Kurtz, did not return. Their blood was spilled on a field of battle in a distant land. Freedom isn't free. I have served in the Balkans where genocide was the way of life in that corner of the world. We lost forces there. Freedom isn't free. We were sent to the Philippines and to the mountains of Afghanistan after 9/11 to track and eliminate al Qaeda and men were lost. Freedom isn't free. We went to Iraq and Afghanistan and suffered the loss of thousands of lives. Freedom isn't free.

"We do these things because we willingly serve the people of the United States of America. People who volunteer to be killed in the pursuit of freedom take the Constitution very seriously. In fact, we take an oath to the Constitution, just as our President, Senators, Representatives, judges, and all civil servants do. Allow me to state that oath for you: 'I do solemnly swear that I will support and defend the Constitution of the United States against all enemies, both foreign and domestic; that I will bear true faith and allegiance to the same; that I take this oath freely, without mental reservation or purpose of evasion; and that I will well and faithfully discharge the duties of the office on which I am about to enter. So help me God.'"

Geno continued, "Ladies and gentlemen, especially those of you at home, the world is a dangerous place right now. Our forces, especially our Special Forces, are stretched to the limit. Your nation needs you. The United States military needs you. The next generation of Americans needs you. Please consider serving your nation's peacekeeping forces, the United States military, as we continue this fight to defend this country and our God-given liberties. Thank you very much, America. I love this country! God bless the USA!"

My God, I knew he had 'em, but this guy really has BIG cajones! Kurtz thought as she and Geno exchanged glances as he sat down.

The President gave the master of ceremonies a hard glare. Congressmen and senators looked at each other with a degree of shock or amusement, depending upon their political views. The admirals and generals wondered if heads would roll over this event. The public chanted "USA! USA! USA!" The master of ceremonies thanked all for coming and quickly concluded the ceremony.

The President gave the crowds and TV cameras a big wave and smiles all around before he turned on his heel and glared straight ahead to the political refuge of the White House.

Geno thought, *Maybe I crossed the line, but that was for Andrew and Jase and everybody else that has been KIA. Demote me, fire me, send me to the brig, or better yet, send me back to the* Reagan *and then you won't have to deal with me. Transformation? I don't think so. USA number one, baby!*

Geno wasn't busted, fired, or sent to the brig. Secretary Kurtz intervened with the President and the DOD on his behalf and he was sent back to the *Reagan* with his men. *God, he's got guts,* thought Kurtz. This, coming from a woman who had fallen just short of winning the presidential nomination herself. She had the experience factor and her name working in her favor, but the President had charisma working for him. He was now in over his head and she would be waiting in the wings for her party's call. There could be a major transition in the next election cycle...

CHAPTER 26

GIVE IT A REST

TEAM 6 HAD REMAINED ABOARD THE *REAGAN* WHILE GENO
was back in Washington for his Navy Cross presentation and the public celebration attached to it.
They had heard snips of information about his speech
that had incensed the President. What they did not
know was how close Geno had come to being "retired"
from the Navy. When Secretary of State Kurtz had
said that she would be forever indebted to Geno, she
assumed he would not be calling in his chit within
forty-eight hours!

Actually, he did not call in any chit; Kurtz
voluntarily gave it to him without his asking.
Furthermore, they didn't know this grandmotherly
looking white-haired lady that reminded many of
Queen Elizabeth with her ever present purse on her
wrist, possibly had even bigger plans for her man
Geno. They had observed her under fire, literally,
and they knew she had *big brass*, but they didn't
know she was such a devotee of others with *big brass*.
Her experience of kill or be killed had altered her view

of how foreign and military powers could work together for the same outcomes.

True warriors fight and kill only as a last resort. They would rather let the diplomats have their sway for a peaceful outcome if possible. True diplomats negotiate and compromise to avert wars for the military. Everybody with any degree of sanity doesn't wake up and say, "I want to get myself killed today! I think I'll start a war."

Kurtz had realized in her recent personal experience that there are factions in the world that want no part of diplomacy. They actually *do* wake up and say to themselves, "I want to get killed today if I can kill many others for my cause." Kurtz was coming to realize that there was no negotiation possible with those factions, but if they could be dealt with in a military fashion, it would open the doors of peace to rational peoples and their diplomats. Maybe the generals and ambassadors could work together, each playing to their strengths for a common good.

Team 6 spent the better part of the first twenty-four hours on board the *Reagan* in debriefs with DEVGRU in Dam Neck. They had uploaded all their films of Layla and Aden, points along the way, and all their captures and kills. It was a mild treasure trove, but DEVGRU was very happy to have the imam and Imran alive, plus the films of the Aden safe house and its neighborhood. Imran and the imam were being processed at a non-USA interrogation center. The CIA and their teams would "mine" those two for all they were worth. Too bad they were not going on an excursion to Guantanamo, but other facilities had been ramped up to state of the art interrogation centers.

Fats took over as de facto leader of 6's daily training and preparation during Geno's time in D.C. There were mission drills to be practiced. Equipment had to be restocked: guns, ammo, nylon ropes, garrotes, knives, plastic cuff devices, everything they had used in their firefights at Layla and Aden. "Three squares" with plenty of protein had to be consumed to build their depleted bodies back up to fighting readiness. Physical fitness drills had to be done throughout the day. These consisted primarily of stamina exercises and martial arts emphasizing leverage, disabling and kill moves, and the ever necessary stealth of all their tactics. Finally, incoming intelligence was a paramount concern. To the best of their ability through DEVGRU at Dam Neck, they had to be aware of what was going on in the world of the bad guys so that they could be aware of any call to a future mission.

Geno arrived back aboard the *Reagan* within forty-eight hours of his citation presentation and speech in Washington. He had to pass through Dam Neck for a good old-fashioned "come to Jesus" lecture by Admiral Gates' staff. Gates himself was still in D.C. smoothing things over, mostly for his own benefit.

Somebody would take the fall for the White House; Gates just wanted to make sure it wasn't him.

Gates was also briefing the White House on all of the dire revolution situations of the Middle East and selling how important continuity was during these times. He had thirty-plus years in the field of Special Ops, dark ops, and political preservation and destabilization. He was the acknowledged go-to expert in this area. He pledged his loyalty to the White House and the President and gently suggested that more time in vetting Genelli may have prevented such an outcome.

There was a very slight nod of the head by White House Chief of Staff Smrow on that point. He knew the President was very anxious to honor Kurtz and celebrate her safety because of their heated presidential primary contest.

Gates took the nod as a "You're gonna make it" statement. He did not show it, but he was extremely relieved by that nod. He thought about giving a wink back, but that would be an over-the-top presumptive. He knew he had to stay on the hot seat a bit longer. Six months is what he calculated.

Geno arrived with two new men to replace Andrew and Jase. They were younger vets handed picked from Team 1, stationed out of Coronado. Nick Vee was a handsome, black-haired, thirtyish man from Seattle. He had eyes so brown and sunken that they looked black. He was about six feet tall and was lanky-muscular. He had built his reputation in demolition and takedowns. He was known to be a bit gloomy and moody at times, but as loyal to the unit as loyal could be. He relished in going "black".

Louis Henry was another Iowa farm boy. He was also about six feet tall, but had a large, bony frame that he was still filling in at age twenty-six. He had very dark brown hair and green eyes. He was prone to mischief and known as Lou by his friends. He amused his friends by telling tall tales late at night. He enjoyed whittling with his knives and horse-back riding. Lou was a raw-boned SEAL with brute strength that appealed very much to Geno. Geno saw a bit of himself in this new man. Quiet, except for his late-night tales, into physical fitness and strength, good core values, and no woman in his life. Lou would fit in well. Both of them would.

"Geno, any word for us? Any idea of what's next?" Fats asked.

"Nope."

"Did you get your tail feathers clipped pretty good by the brass?"

"Yup."

"You gonna make it?"

"Hope so, but I'm not gonna worry about it,"

Geno replied.

"What now?" Fats asked again.

"Fats, like I told you, I don't know. I'm goin' below. What are you so worried about? Ain't you ever stared down the barrel of an M16 before? That's child's play for guys like us. The gig for the guys up top is shaking hands and kissing babies, we've got bad guys to kill. Relax and we'll find out 'what now' soon enough! For God's sake give it a rest!" Geno replied.

They did.

CHAPTER 27

IT'S A
BEAUTIFUL SHIP!

THE USS *RONALD REAGAN* WAS A BEAUTIFUL SHIP. "PEACE
Through Strength" was the official motto of the ship.
The motto reflected the view of its namesake,
Ronald Reagan, the 40th President of the United
States of America. As President of the United States,
Reagan shoved all the chips to the center of the world
poker table and challenged the Soviet Union to
match him. They tried, but they spent themselves
out of an empire. On June 12th, 1987, Reagan even had
the audacity to stand at the Brandenburg Gate of the
Berlin Wall, the symbol Communism, and challenge
Soviet General Secretary Gorbachev to "Tear down
this wall!"

His exact words being blared into East Berlin by
the CIA were, "General Secretary Gorbachev, if you
seek peace, if you seek prosperity for the Soviet Union
and Eastern Europe, if you seek liberation, come here to
this gate! Mr. Gorbachev, open this gate! Mr. Gorbachev,
tear down this wall!"

Two years, four months, and twenty-nine days later,

attaining peace through strength and without firing a shot, the Soviet Union stood by as the people of East and West Berlin tore down that wall. *An aircraft carrier and an airport are nice namesakes*, Geno thought, *but Reagan ought to be on Mount Rushmore! How beautiful is this ship?* Geno rhetorically thought. *Not only beautiful, but it's big!*

The *Reagan* was a Nimitz-class nuclear-powered super carrier, christened in 2001 and outfitted with all of the latest technology and comforts at sea. The *Reagan* was assigned to the Pacific Fleet as a tribute to President Reagan's love of and service to his adopted home state of California. Being a world-class asset of deterrence, the *Reagan* began earning a reputation on her maiden deployment to support Operation Iraqi Freedom and Operation Enduring Freedom in February 2006. Even though the ship was a "young one", the *Reagan* had battle condition experiences on her pedigree well before Geno and Team 6 came aboard.

Size does matter, so they say. The *Reagan* had an overall length of 1,092 feet and beam width of 252 feet, both of which were essential to launching and landing its ninety fixed-wing aircraft and helicopters. The ship had a draft of thirty-seven feet into the ocean below. There were 2,480 air wing personnel assigned to the ship and 3,200 operation and support crew. SEAL teams were also assigned when appropriate.

Geno was also happy to be on the *Reagan* because of the reputation of the crew. The crew had one of the most envied set of crew awards since the ship had entered active service in 2006. The *Reagan* was awarded the 2009 Chief of Naval Operations Afloat Safety "S" Award. In 2010, the ship was also awarded the Pacific Fleet Battle "E" Award for combat efficiency. This was the vessel's third Battle Efficiency "E" award in four years. This was a sharp crew that performed with efficiency, safety, and excellence—traits that reflected the SEALs themselves. Geno was impressed and delighted to be aboard!

Down below, Geno had settled in with his personal gear. "I wouldn't get too comfortable," Fats said as he popped his head in Geno's door.

"Why?"

"My God, man, you know why! This part of the world is lit up like a lighthouse in the fog! What's the matter, Gates take the starch out of you?"

"Give it a rest, Fats. I've had a grueling seventy-two hours. Damn near got whacked in D.C., been on a round trip halfway around the world and back, spilled my guts out in Saudi, and lost two good men. What do you want me to say, Fats, it's been wonderful, great, fantastic, amazing?" Veins bulged in Geno's neck.

"Whoa, big fella," Fats responded. "You think you're the only one that went through what we all went through in grabbing Kurtz? You think you're the only one hurting over Andrew and Jase? Huh? Give me a frickin' break, pal! You're the one that shot your mouth off to the President, not us, that's on you!" Fats shouted back to Geno. "Artie's got the latest intel report, if you're interested. If not, I'll tell the men that you're indisposed from your long trip." Fats was officially pissed at Geno.

"Screw you, Fats!" Geno shoved Fats out of his quarters and slammed the door shut. He collapsed in his bunk.

Geno fell into a fitful sleep. His dreams were whirling around like desert haboob. He dreamed of the rescue mission, the deaths of Andrew and Jase, the trip to D.C. and back, the speech, the roar of the crowd, and the chants of USA, USA, grabbing Kurtz and throwing her over his shoulder, running for the helicopter and putting Kurtz into it. He awoke in a sweat when he saw a vision of his mother, Dolly, waiting for him inside of Kurtz's rescue helicopter.

This had never happened to Geno. He never had nightmares before. He was stressed for the first time in his career as a SEAL. Anxiety swept over him as he thought about the possibility of another high-risk mission. Could he command? Could he lead? Would he lose more men? Was he fit for service? Should he tell Fats of his experience so that at least he would know about it if something went wrong with him?

Then, a calm spirit came over him. *Gregory, why are you afraid? I am with you always, wherever you go. You know that. I am at your side always.* Geno didn't know if it was God or his mother, but he kissed his Saint Christopher medal and got down on his knees to say an Our Father, Hail Mary, and Glory Be for the first time in years.

He got up from his knees and went looking for Fats. Geno was now back in the game.

CHAPTER 28

HERE WE GO AGAIN

"ANYBODY SEEN FATS?" GENO ASKED STEVE AND MATT as he ducked his head into the crew's mess.

"He's down in the PT center blowing off some steam, he was pissed about something." Matt replied.

Geno headed straight for the ship's fitness facility. The gym aboard a ship, especially a giant ship like the *Reagan,* with six thousand testosterone- and hormone-producing units, was as important as any weapon. There was a lot of tension and stress to work out. It was not uncommon to be on an assignment away from any port for up to six months. That's a long time to spend with six thousand people on any island, especially one that is only 1,100 feet by 250 feet. The ship got smaller and smaller after a few weeks at sea, let alone several months.

"Skip, I think you need to hear this," Artie relayed to Geno from the Intel room as Geno was walking down the passageway to the gym to make amends with Fats. This was the second time in less than a week that Fats had to slap him upside the head verbally to get him back in the game. The other guys knew that Geno had a relationship with Fats that went as deep as their missions together, but Geno was a withdrawn guy who didn't want to show a lot of feelings and emotions to others. Therefore, you didn't get a "deep" look into his personality or emotions. He didn't even have a steady squeeze, for God's sake!

Fats was the only guy able to cut through Geno's protective layers and get to the heart of an issue. Let's face it, not too many Navy SEALs or other Special Forces get too touchy-feely with anybody except their gal. So Fats getting through to Geno was a bit unusual; maybe that's why Geno had talked him into signing up for the mission. Regardless, you would think that Geno would be the dominant personality in the relationship between him and Fats and that Fats would be the lesser because Geno saved Fats from the ocean during BUD/S training so many years ago. Remembering the rescue offshore Coronado you would think Fats would defer to this alpha male.

Here is what the guys had figured: Geno was the dominant leader in all things military, especially on a mission or while training for one. Fats wasn't a leader; he was a supporter. Fats was always there to support Geno. Geno knew it. Fats knew it. They knew they could count on each other, and Fats knew that part of his support role for Geno was to keep him from "flying too close to the ground" when things built up in him, as they had the past week. Geno knew this. This was the reason that Geno insisted that Fats come on the mission; not because Fats was a great sand rat, demo expert, or anything else. The real reason Fats was on the mission was because Geno needed him by his side in the rescue of Kurtz or in whatever else would come their way. Geno "needed" Fats and had missed him on the Team for the year that he had been away. Now Fats was stuck out in the middle of the Indian Ocean with no way home! Geno thought about Fats being trapped and he let out a ferocious laugh. The stress of the past week was still coming out of Geno and the laugh was a good sign.

"Skipper, are you OK?" Artie asked Geno.

"Yes, I'm OK. I was just thinking and laughing out loud about poor old Fats. He signs up for a mission and gets trapped with us here in the middle of the ocean, and he can't get home. He's like a POW of his own government in an undeclared war. That is frickin' hilarious!"

"Skip, that's not funny," Artie said.

"I know it, Artie, but it really is." And Geno chuckled again.

"That Navy Cross mess with your head, Skip? You OK?" Artie asked.

"I'm fine. Relax. Don't worry about me. I'm battle

tested, fit and ready, full of piss and vinegar! Whatcha got for me?"

"Well, we've been getting lots of live feeds while you were away," Artie said. "Things are getting pretty dicey in the neighborhood, real dicey, as a matter of fact. I think we're going to get another mission real quick-like," Artie said.

"Yeah, I figured when that El Al flight blew up over Israel on Kurtz's way back to D.C. that the Israelis would be jumping into the fray somehow. They're not going to sit back and take that. I'm sure Kurtz and the President are working overtime to keep Israel's finger off the trigger," Geno said. "I'm glad I'm a warrior and not a diplomat. That talkin' round and round would get old in a hurry. Then, after all that talkin', you still don't know if you have a deal or not. Not for me, Artie. Give me a mission where I can get in, get out, and see the results after I'm done. That's what I like. Why don't we dial up Dam Neck and get a briefing?" Geno asked, and Artie nodded.

Artie had the ship's communication officer contact Dam Neck. DEVGRU responded that they wanted Geno and the rest of 6 assembled in the ship's video conference center for a live feed at 2100 Zulu, which was in less than three hours.

The video feed came in on a secured video conference system aboard the ship. All of Team 6 had assembled, along with the captain of the *Reagan*, his executive officer, and the command master chief, as well as the battle tactical staff officer and the supporting staff officers. It was a large group, but that was what DEVGRU had ordered. The information was extremely delicate and DEVGRU wanted the key leadership assembled for a full presentation. DEVGRU did not want any loose cannons or second-guessers.

Here we go again! 6 thought.

CHAPTER 29

AHH . . . TTENTION!

CAMERAS WERE CLICKING AS IF A HAILSTORM WAS FALLING on a tin roof when Secretary of State Kathryn Kurtz stepped to the podium to give a major address directed by the White House. The address was being made at the White House to underscore the seriousness the administration placed upon the address. The presentation was done by Secretary of State Kurtz because of her role as chief diplomatic spokesperson for the United States of America. The President reserved his media time for press conferences and political addresses to the nation. Kurtz was speaking to the world community. She began:

"The United States of America is a peaceful nation seeking only peace for the world community. The United States of America has invested trillions of dollars throughout the world community to upgrade living conditions and basic human expectations for billions of people throughout its history. Currently we are bringing water and sanitary services to many nations throughout the world that do not enjoy these basic human services most of us take for granted as part of our daily lives.

"We are also making inroads on the scourge of AIDS throughout much of Africa. Our ships and aircraft carriers have delivered food and water to the earthquake-ravaged areas of Haiti, Chile, and now Japan. We are assisting African countries to build roads and bridges through primitive areas of their countryside. We provide millions of tons of food to poor nations of the world through our USA Aid program, to name some of the things we as a caring nation provide to the world. We do these things freely as a nation because Americans understand their role as a bountiful nation within the world community.

"America has never asked for any reimbursement or repayment of these actions. We assisted our allies after World War II through the Marshall Plan, which led to the successful rebuilding of Western Europe, again as an act of peace by our nation. We also assisted our allies in Japan and Asia in the rebuilding of their countries after World War II. We did much of the same after World War I and other wars. As you can see, our history goes very deep in matters of peace and compassion. We always seek peace and compassion throughout the world and have tried to lead by example. This is the 'American diplomacy' we practice and have practiced for our 235-year history."

Kurtz continued, "War and violence is not the method of diplomacy we choose as a nation. Throughout history, our enemies have often chosen violence and war as a means of diplomacy to bring change in the world, not us. The United States of America does not and will not consider such actions as an act of diplomacy. Quite the contrary; the United States of America has considered and will continue to consider these types of actions as acts of aggression and warfare. In these instances, the United States of America has and will continue to seek peaceful methods to end these acts of aggression in the world community. However, throughout our history, we have been and are now prepared to engage in a more forceful diplomacy against these aggressors to bring about the end of their aggression and to restore peace by using military might if necessary.

"At the present time, the United States of America stands shoulder to shoulder with the nation of Israel against the hostile actions of aggressors in the recent downing of El Al Flight 4 and the deaths of 189 innocent civilians on board. In conjunction with our allies, the United States of America will use all of the options at its disposal to subdue this common enemy and restore peace to the Middle East. Again, we do not choose warfare as a form of diplomacy, but our enemies have. As a result of their deliberate choice, I have been instructed by the President to deliver this message to these aggressors: 'We seek peace. We come in peace. We ask you in peace to voluntarily surrender those individuals responsible for the actions that killed 189 innocent civilians on El Al Flight 4 to the appropriate authorities to the United Nations or to the World Court of Justice in The Hague. We know who is responsible for this action. We peacefully seek resolution of this matter with those responsible. We desire no further bloodshed.' Thank you very much."

"Madam Secretary, Madam Secretary!" the reporters shouted.

"No questions at this time," the White House press secretary stated. Secretary Kurtz and her entourage immediately left for Andrews Air Force Base to board flights to Tel Aviv and other capitals throughout the Middle East to begin their diplomatic efforts. Meanwhile at Dam Neck and aboard the USS *Reagan*...

"Attention on deck!" from Captain Smart as Admiral Gates walked to the podium at Dam Neck, Virginia, DEVGRU Headquarters. The assembled group in Dam Neck rose to full attention. The men assembled on board the *Reagan* sat up in an erect posture.

"At ease," Gates said. "Men, DEVGRU has been ordered by the White House and DOD to engage in a serious and delicate mission. I don't need to tell all of you how serious the world situation is at this very moment. Oil flows from the Middle East, particularly Saudi Arabia, are in jeopardy, which in itself is a matter of national security. Libya is still up for grabs! Syria is in chaos! Israel is going to pull the trigger any minute if we don't address the downing of that El Al flight over Israel. Our government is exerting every ounce of diplomacy we have at our disposal to keep the Israelis in check at this moment. I know that you men have just completed a successful but stressful mission to bring Secretary of State Kurtz home safely. My sincerest congratulations to you for accomplishing that mission. The President personally asked me to thank you on his behalf for your heroic actions in rescuing Secretary Kurtz."

Gates continued, "Men, your last mission was incredibly important to the power and prestige of the United States throughout the entire world, but if we are going to survive in this world as we have come to know it, the mission ahead is of even greater importance. We *must* be successful in this next mission. There is no other option. Events in the Middle East are on the verge of going nuclear if we don't stop them. I want to emphasize again, for myself and for the President, the success of this mission is extremely important to everyone, everyone in the world. Men, this mission is for all the marbles. Do you understand? Captain Smart will present the details."

The reaction on board the *Reagan* was very somber.

Not a word was spoken by anyone in the room.

Captain Smart began, "Men, CIA and DOD both confirm that elements within Iran are responsible for El Al being downed over Israel four days ago." There was a collective groan in the video conference room aboard the *Reagan*. "Team 6, your capture of the Imam of Aden during the Kurtz mission was critical in confirming this information. Obviously, I cannot go into details about the sources of our information or how it was obtained, nor how it was confirmed, but the White House, DOD, and CIA are all confident about the accuracy and reliability of this information. We would not act if there was considerable doubt.

"DEVGRU has received orders and SEAL Team 6 has been assigned a mission that will strike directly at the elements involved in planning and executing this act of war against Israel and her allies, including us. We experienced as a nation the horrors of such an act when Mummar Gaddafi ordered the downing of Pan Am 103 over Lockerbie, Scotland. Men, your mission must be swift, it must be successful in its outcome, and it must help ensure that this type of terrorist warfare is not engaged in again. The White House wants a very noticeable public retribution for the Iranian action. The White House and Israel will accept nothing less. Am I clear on this so far?"

Heads nodded and a collective "Yes, sir" was

communicated back to Captain Smart from the *Reagan.*

"Good, let us proceed," Smart said. "Secretary of State Kurtz has been dispatched to Tel Aviv for intense lobbying with the Israelis. She is also conducting a shuttle diplomacy with other Arab states in the region as best as possible given the current unrest in Saudi Arabia, Bahrain, Syria, and Libya. This environment has made it extremely difficult and dangerous to travel throughout the region. However, as you men from 6 know, this woman has courage of a lioness and she will not be deterred. She will, by the nature of her office, try her very best to reach a diplomatic solution to this situation. However, in an official speech yesterday she put those responsible on notice that 'forceful diplomacy' is coming their way soon if they do not cooperate."

Good for her! Geno thought. *Good for her! I knew I liked her!* Geno had come to respect Kurtz nearly as much as he respected and loved his mother. Here was a woman who was circling the globe, smiling and shaking hands while making cutthroat deals on the side. Meanwhile, his mother, his anchor, was at home cooking pasta and saying the rosary for him.

Smart filled in the initial details of the mission. "Men, you are being assigned to a covert drop into Iran. The *Reagan* and other elements of the Fifth Fleet will do a head fake to divert attention from your drop.

Mossad and other Israeli forces will not, I repeat will not, be involved in this mission for obvious reasons. We do not want to risk any further acts of aggression by Iran or other Arab states against Israel, nor do we want Israel in a position where it feels it must counterattack if there is a second set of incidents against them.

"Men, we are 'taking one for the team' on this one. Captain Kelly, you will be briefed at 0600 Zulu by Fifth Fleet command for the *Reagan*'s role in this mission. Team 6, you are to report back at 0700 Zulu for your briefing. Are there any questions, gentlemen?"

"Not at this time," was the collective answer.

"Fine," Smart said, "6 will convene again at 0700. Meeting dismissed!" Everyone at DEVGRU rose to attention again Smart nodded his head and walked out of the room. The group on board the *Reagan* also stood at attention as he left. The formality and serious tone of the meeting had the desired effect DEVGRU had wished for. Everyone took the meeting quite seriously.

"My God," said Lou, the new guy, as they walked out the door.

"What do ya mean, kid?" Geno said.

"Well pardon me, sir. I'm new to the crew and of course...of course, I don't have near the experience you do, sir, but, but..."

"But what?" Geno toyed with him.

"Well, sir," Lou said. "I'm not sure if they have a clue yet of where we're going, or what we're going to do, sir…"

"You're pretty savvy for a rookie. They don't," Geno replied.

CHAPTER 30

PREPARATIONS

DURING THE GREEN REVOLUTION OF 2009 IN IRAN, THE USAGE of Facebook, Twitter, YouTube, and Internet e-mail proved successful and set the stage for current events for protagonists throughout the Middle East. The CIA and intelligence groups from around the world quickly saw the opportunity to monitor, communicate with, and feed ideas and tactics to those seeking to overthrow repressive regimes. It was as if the "networks" of these organizations literally went viral in size. In effect, the internet gave the CIA thousands of de facto agents on the ground throughout the entire region. They dutifully reported breaking news on incidents of brutality and oppression to Western media.

Demographics also played a key role in the Arab Spring movement. The population of the Middle East and in Iran in particular had become extremely youthful, and the younger population was very anxious for change. They were also extremely proficient in the usage of these communication technologies, whereas the older, established leadership was not.

They were entrenched in their vertical communication and governing style, whereas the younger people had gone horizontal in communication and distribution of information.

The younger generation informed far more people in a far shorter time than the older generation could imagine. This phenomenon was probably the best illustration of Thomas Friedman's concept of "The World Is Flat". The world was now flat for communication. The young people "got it"; the fifty- to seventy-year-old leadership groups did not. The door of change was open and the young people were running through it by the millions.

The President had been highly criticized for not helping the young people of the Green Revolution in Iran in 2009. Critics felt that the West had missed an opportunity to topple the Iranian government. The administration felt that the risks were too great and, as a new administration, they did not want to risk a long and deadly war in Iran. However, as the administration gained seasoning, especially at Kurtz's prodding, and as events continued to unfold, they were more open to becoming involved in events as they unfolded.

Afghanistan, Libya, and Yemen were examples of a new hardened policy. The administration had substantially increased targeting of militants in

Afghanistan, Yemen and Western Pakistan, with the use of drones through its "Kill-Capture" program. An estimated twelve thousand Taliban and al Qaeda operatives were killed by drone attacks in the past two years alone.

Without notifying Congress, and with heavy influence from Kurtz, America was heavily involved in a no-fly zone in Libya under a United Nations resolution and the NATO umbrella. The President did not want to be seen on the Middle East political stage as the leader of that operation. Through 2009, 2010 and the first months of 2011, preparations for contingencies throughout the Middle East, including Iran, had intensified. With presidential elections coming in a year, the President wanted to avoid a weak or pacifist image heading into the election season.

The CIA had been working through back channels to investigate the strength of the backing that President Kharmini of Iran had from the ruling clerics. The clerics had publicly given their support to Kharmini in the summer of 2009 during his crackdown on the Green Revolution. Rumors of unhappiness by the clerics at that time were not substantiated. Reliable reports now circulated that the ruling clerics were unhappy about Kharmini's near constant radical statements directed at Israel including threatening to "wipe Israel off the face of the earth." It was becoming dangerously unclear to the world if this was an official government policy or political rhetoric by Kharmini geared to maintaining the backing for him from the Iranian establishment.

Despite years of trade sanctions, vast pockets of established Iranians, particularly in Tehran and other major cities of Iran, enjoyed a very comfortable lifestyle through highly inflated prices for many of the modern accoutrements of the West, including fashion and consumer goods. There was no uproar in rural areas either because these peoples were still leading ancient traditional Iranian life-styles practiced over the past hundred years or more. They were not politically tuned in and were living in their own world.

Iran would be a military challenge for an enemy in an all-out war. The talking heads of the Western media typically did not take into account the vast size of Iran. Iran is nearly three times the size of the state of Texas. Neither do these talking heads comprehend the natural defenses Iran enjoys against attack from any foreign sources. Iran is protected throughout its entire northern and western borders by significant mountain ranges.

Tehran, the capital of Iran, is nestled near the northern mountain ranges in north central Iran. The eastern border is joined by Afghanistan and Pakistan, and those borders are heavily fortified. The southern border along the Arabian Sea is protected by the Mesopotamian marshes that Sadam Hussein found so deadly in the Iran-Iraq War of 1980–1988.

All professional military leaders know that invading Iran is a near prohibitive action. If it were to be done, it would require a massive bombing campaign eventually followed up with hundreds of thousands of ground troops. The West was not up for this. What to do with a regime that was so entrenched politically, militarily, and geographically was the question.

Also, the West had been concerned about Iran's nuclear weapons program for years. There was no doubt that the program was well under way and making steady progress toward the development of a nuclear bomb. The West appeared to have significantly delayed the progress by invading Iran's nuclear development computer network with a virus called The Worm. The Worm virus was undetectable by the Iranian's at first as it slowly but gradually invaded and ate away at software programs. The West gauged that The Worm had set the Iranian nuclear effort back three to five years. It was apparent that western spy and intelligence agencies had been busy in Iran the past several years. Hopefully, this could bear other fruit as time passed.

The downing of the El Al flight now forced the hand of the West. It was time to call in all resources to come up with a plan to make Iran pay for its action. Israel had invested vast sums of money and personnel spying in Iran since Kharmini had been chosen as President and had unleashed his rhetoric against Israel. Israel took such comments with grave seriousness because of the Holocaust. America would need to call on the full knowledge of Israel's gathered intelligence to devise a plan of action.

Not being able to put boots on the ground or to engage in any military strikes at this time, the Israelis were willing to share state-held secrets about Iran with America. They were willing to give America one chance to strike a retaliatory blow, but if America was not successful, Israel was prepared to launch their own nuclear missiles against Iran.

The American plan was focused on what they called the "Iranian Solution", but was built knowing the reality of events in Libya, Syria, and particularly Saudi Arabia because of the capture of King Abdullah. The Saudi crisis would be used as a diversionary ploy for the Iranian operation. The *Reagan* Battle Group, with its full complement of air power, destroyers, and guided missile cruisers, would turn from the central Arabian Sea back toward the Gulf of Aden and the Red Sea, indicating military support would be headed for Saudi Arabia and Israel.

This show of support would demonstrate to

everyone in the region—especially Iran—that the U.S. was taking the threat to Saudi Arabia and Israel very seriously. Sending the *Reagan* through the Red Sea and narrow Suez Canal was such a great risk that it would surely convince the Iranians that the US's focus was elsewhere.

To further deceive Iran, twenty-five hundred U.S. Marines were launched from Camp Lejeune, North Carolina, in troop carriers bound for the eastern Mediterranean Sea, and a second deployment of twenty-five hundred more marines was publicly announced for the same destination. The U.S. Naval and Air Force bases in Italy and Spain were publicly alerted to be at the ready for possible offensive duty in the Mediterranean beyond their assignments in Libya. France, England, Italy, and Spain agreed to make similar announcements. Their inclusion was intended to signal to the region that other Western powers took serious note of the threat to Israel and the Saudi Arabian oil fields and it would not be tolerated. U.S. government officials were sure this decoy would succeed in throwing off the Iranians. After all, the concentration of forces was nearly 1,000 miles away from the Iranian capitol.

The public announcement from the United States and its allies read: "Given events in Israel and Saudi Arabia, it is imperative that the oil resources of the Middle East region be guaranteed a free, stable, and safe flow to the world so that the basics of human life are available to all. We will not engage in any offensive actions that would endanger any nation's sovereignty or its right to govern itself. These actions are designed solely for defensive humanitarian efforts. These actions will be disengaged as rapidly as events permit."

The USA had long enjoyed a somewhat mysterious relationship with Saudi Arabia. Saudi Arabia had both oil and al Qaeda. The United States seemed to allow one to exist within Saudi Arabia to get the other. However, the U.S. knew that at some point in time, it might have to intervene in Saudi Arabia if the government and oil fields fell into the hands of extremists. Perhaps now was that time. They asked Saudi Arabia to officially "request" military assistance, and they did. They were reeling because of the terror attack on the Royal Palace and the capture of King Abdullah. Like the USA with the Kurtz capture, Saudi Arabia was open to any and all solutions to secure their King.

The marines and elements of the Fifth Fleet, out of Bahrain, as well as the air power from bases in Italy and Spain were heading to Saudi Arabia to protect the oil fields "at the request of the Saudis". Secretly, the United States placed all missile defense systems on the highest state of alert. Allies and other key world players such as Russia, China, and Japan would be secretly informed at the last possible minute by

Secretary Kurtz of this alert.

It was now 0700 aboard the *Reagan,* and time for Team 6 to assemble in the video conferencing room to see what their mission would be. Preparations had been made for all involved.

Extraordinary times demand extraordinary solutions.

CHAPTER 31

GETTING FROM HERE TO THERE

GENO AND THE REST OF 6 GATHERED IN THE *REAGAN* VIDEO conference center for their 0700 briefing from Dam Neck. It was a bit like the briefing scenes from *Memphis Belle* and other World War II movies. Some of the guys were cutting up with each other, some were quite serious, some exchanged nervous glances, and some were taking it as "another day at the office" prior to the feed from DEVGRU.

"Team 6," Captain Smart began as he spoke over the video link, "you will be proceeding to Iran for a black insertion. Working with the CIA, the goal of that insertion will be to detain President Kharmini."

Everyone, everyone, stared intently at Captain Smart when he stated the mission goal. "You want us to detain the President of Iran?" Geno asked in a clarifying tone.

"That is correct," Smart replied.

"How?" Geno asked.

"The CIA will have that call," Smart replied.

"Your mission will be to protect CIA assets at all costs, while they secure Kharmini."

"OK...?" Geno replied, somewhat questioningly again.

"Look, I know this is asking a lot, but you are going to have to trust us in this effort," Smart replied. "We have our best intelligence assets working on this. The Israelis are sharing any and all intel with us that they have. The CIA has been very active in Tehran since the Green Revolution of 2009. A number of reliable Iranian personnel assets within the government have been secured the past couple of years. Let me just say, without elaborating, we are not flying in blind with this, nor are we unprepared. Your departure from the *Reagan* will be at 1200. There will be two stops along the way where you will pick up your equipment and be further informed. If there are no further questions at this time, you are dismissed. Genelli, stay behind for a minute if you would, please. The rest of you are dismissed," Smart commanded.

The rumble in the hall and in the quarters was a variety of incredulousness, shock, and, yes, awe. "This could be a suicide mission. How in the hell are we going to do this? You've got to be frickin' kidding me!"

"Hey, we're SEALs, goddamn it! This is what we do, the impossible! Get hold of yourself! Man up and gear up!" Fats was pissed with the attitude of the men.

Artie nodded in agreement. "Skip'll get us through this just like he did in Aden and Layla and every other mission."

"Maybe we'll get one of those Navy Crosses," Lou Henry said.

"Shut up, kid," Matt joked at him. The tension had been broken and the unit started focusing on the business of gathering their personal weapons and gear.

"Geno," Smart said. "I know you probably have some questions, not the least of which is 'Do you expect us to be successful' or 'What happens if we're not?' The answers are 'Yes, we expect you to be successful' and 'We can't guarantee anything if you're not.' Geno, you know the Admiral and JSOC (Joint Special Operations Command) have Delta Force, the PJs (Air Force 24th Special Tactics Squadron), and SEAL Team 6 at their discretion for a mission like this, but 6 is the best unit for this particular mission. You *will* be successful, we'll cross the other bridge if we get there, but we're not expecting that. You will go underground with the CIA once you are dropped in country until we can get all of you out of there. Your contact with the CIA will be 'Cardinal.' That is all you need to know at this time. Everything is being siloed for security reasons, so that if any of you are captured, the rest of the operation and our assets on the ground will not be endangered. Do you understand, or do you have any questions?" Smart asked.

"Not at this time," Geno said.

"Good luck and God speed to you and the men," Smart said as the conference screen soon went dark.

The team departed the deck of the *Reagan* in two aircraft bound for Fifth Fleet headquarters in Manama, Bahrain. From Bahrain, they flew to Baghdad and on to a military base near Baku, Azerbaijan, a new highly subsidized "ally" of the West after dissolution of the Soviet Union. They arrived in Azerbaijan in the wee hours of the morning local time.

"Warrant Officer Genelli?"

"Yes, right here." Geno raised his hand.

"There's a message waiting for you at HQ," said a young lieutenant that greeted them on the tarmac. "This way." Geno followed him.

The lieutenant led Geno into an office. "We've been expecting you," the captain said as he handed Geno an envelope. Geno opened the envelope and saw a paper with a simple message on it: "Welcome to Cardinal Country. Wait for further directions." Geno smiled to himself. *So this is how the CIA operates…*

Aloud he said, "Lieutenant, I'm going with my men to get some chow and sack out for a while. I'm sure you'll contact me if I receive any further messages?"

"You can count on that." the lieutenant replied.

"Do you get many cowboys through here like us, sir?" Geno asked.

"More than you think. I'll let you know anything as soon as I get it."

"Thanks, Lieutenant," Geno said, and then headed for the mess hall.

Everybody chowed down and then sacked out. There was a knock on Geno's door about 1500, and Geno came out of his nap.

"You have a message over at HQ, sir." Geno got out of his rack, splashed some water on his face, and followed the young enlisted man to HQ, grabbing a cup of coffee on his way into the captain's office.

"There is going to be a download at 1600 for eyes only," the captain said, meaning that the message was for Geno only and that there would not be a paper communiqué.

This was the information he had been waiting for. Geno stretched, took a walk around the building, clearing his mind and sharpening his focus. He went back inside at 1545 and was taken to a secure room loaded with communication equipment.

"You need to put this headset on. The message will appear on the communication screen and there will be a verbal accompaniment with it. Do not take any paper notes. This information will be totally black and off the books. I doubt you'll get a long feed. At least that's the normal procedure for guys that process through here," the captain said.

Geno nodded, and sat and waited for the feed.

"Cardinal here," came the communication.

"Copy, this is Falcon," Geno replied.

Cardinal continued, "You will depart under cover of darkness at 2000, fly in Black Ops aircraft across the Caspian Sea, over the Elburn Mountains, and be dropped in for rendezvous with a team waiting for you. Your gear has been arranged for you and will be dropped with you. Do you copy, Falcon?"

"Falcon copies," Geno replied. The feed went silent and Geno got up from his chair and went back to quarters.

"Gentlemen, let's rise and shine! Grab some chow again. Get lots of protein in those bellies! Get organized and be here at 1900 sharp!" Geno barked with enthusiasm. "We've got a night flight to catch. Duty calls!"

"Hoorahs!" all around was the reply from the unit. Geno loved his men.

CHAPTER 32

COMING AND GOING, TWISTING AND SPINNING

GENO AND THE TEAM LOADED INTO A BLACK OPS MC-130W flown in from Kuwait. The 130W was painted a flat black for maximum stealth appearance, capable of carrying the team and their equipment. The "Ws" climbed higher and faster than previous models and could take off and land in shorter distances. The mission of the MC-130W Combat Spear was to conduct infiltration, extraction, and resupply of Special Operations forces in theater. The flight range of 1,200-plus miles would allow the flight crew to comfortably fly a round trip from Baku. The flight plan through the passes of the Elburz Mountains of northern Iran would take them through largely uninhabited regions and through areas of Iran that did not have an elaborate air defense system. Normally the 590-mile chain of steep mountain peaks did the job. Landing in the desert to the east of Tehran, along with the electronic jamming capability of the 130W, would help avoid detection. The CIA would be waiting at the drop site with GPS markers, similar to the markers used to guide smart bombs with pinpoint accuracy. The markers would guide the cargo bundles to their location. The team would then parachute to the meeting point.

Secretary of State Kurtz had been very busy using "shuttle and stall" diplomacy while Geno was preparing for his mission aboard the *Reagan* and in the period since. Geno didn't know it, but his mission was already in motion by the time he had given his speech on the White House south lawn. Kurtz, hardened by her experience in Saudi Arabia and the harrowing but successful rescue by her man Geno, was thinking out of the box by everyone's standards. She had learned through her experience with Geno that sometimes the only diplomacy is military diplomacy. Kurtz was not willing to risk an all-out war with Iran to keep Israel out of the fray, but she feared the war that would result if they were not kept at bay. The kidnapping of King Abdullah and members of the ruling Royal Family had provided her with an extra strategic element that might let everything come together for a solution acceptable to all. She would need to use her diplomatic skills *par excellence* with Israel, Saudi Arabia, Syria, and Iran. She had her work cut out for her, but she was up to the task.

Within the U. S. government, the military was the easiest group for Kurtz to convince. The State Department posed no problem because she could simply overrule the staffers as their superior. The

COMING AND GOING, TWISTING AND SPINNING

President and the executive branch were the difficult parties, this was where she placed her focus. Kurtz pointed out to the President and key members of his cabinet and his chief of staff, essentially his reelection committee, that his focus on the domestic agenda and his tactics of keeping-his-options-open approach to the Middle East and the "domestication" of the war on terror were taking a toll on his poll numbers the past two years. In fact, she pointed out to the President, his approval ratings were as low as any other President in history at this point in his term with an election coming within a year. The temporary bounce from bin Laden's killing had faded with current events in the economy.

Playing the reelection card, Kurtz advised the President that the best thing he could do to shore up his poll numbers was to do something dramatic and forceful about Iran. Kurtz pointed out that the liberal base of his party would not abandon him because they would have no other candidate to back and he was still their best option for a second term to implement their domestic agenda. Doing something decisive would bring independents and liberal Republicans back into his camp. Kurtz's trump line was "That's what I would do if I were the President."

Knowing that Kurtz's backers were simply waiting for the President to stumble further so that they could make a run with her the following year, the President looked intently out the window of the Oval Office and finally said, "I think you are correct. Correct about the fact that we need to do something decisive for the Israelis," not acknowledging her political analysis.

"Mr. President, you are correct," Kurtz replied without pointing out that his base of Jewish voters had become disillusioned with his softened backing of Israel previously during his administration.

The "deal" was cut without Geno or anyone else outside of the Oval Office doors knowing that it had been done. Kurtz was a shrewd operator. Now she had to find some shrewd tactics for the other players in this game.

Having received the President's backing, Kurtz worked overtime trying to keep the Israelis as calm as possible, assessing the situation in Saudi Arabia, and working the back channels of diplomacy with Iran. She was trying to work a three-way deal that would be acceptable to Israel, Saudi Arabia, and Iran. Each nation had a set of wants and, of course, the outcome had to be with acceptable "honor" for all parties. Kurtz was confident that if the Iranians would agree to the plan, Israel would agree also. Saudi Arabia would be rewarded in the "bonus round". Kurtz was trying to negotiate a swap as part of the deal that would lead to the freedom of King Abdullah and the ruling royals who had been captured and were being held hostage in Saudi Arabia.

COMING AND GOING, TWISTING AND SPINNING

Kurtz flew immediately to Kuwait from Tel Aviv after briefing the Israelis, she then began negotiations with Iran and Saudi Arabia from there. She had selected Kuwait for many reasons; it was a secure location for her to work from, was somewhat central to all parties involved, and was neutral in location. She did not want to headquarter in Tel Aviv, which might send the wrong signal to the Iranians or Saudis. She had considered Baghdad to enhance Iraq and Baghdad's status as a new key player in the region, but she did not want to tempt Iranian militant action inside of Iraq. Cairo had been her first thought, but she did not want to risk political damage for Egypt while it was grappling with newfound freedoms.

Kuwait had been out of the international head-lines for nearly twenty years and seemed the best and safest location from which to shuttle her diplomacy. After all, it was the hidden stronghold of American military might in the Middle East.

One thing Kurtz knew with all certainty was that the past week brought twists and turns, comings and goings by her and others. The arm-twisting and political spinning that occurred had made it a grueling week and the next week didn't look as if it would be much different.

CHAPTER 33

THE UNTHINKABLE!

THE CIA HAD BECOME VERY ACTIVE IN TEHRAN SINCE THE
Green Revolution of 2009. Evidence of a high level
of bloodshed and brutality had been smuggled to
the world via YouTube, cell phones, and Skype. The
political hangover from those events affected the
West's decision to provide the no-fly zone coverage
of Libya during its uprising. The President could not
resist the call of the world community to stop the
Libyan carnage but had instructed Secretary Kurtz to
keep American involvement to a minimum and the
USA out of the NATO leadership role.

The military actions in Libya, Iraq, and Afghanistan were taxing the American military to near its
limitations. The CIA had been assigned to develop a
solution for Iran, and especially Kharmini, because
of these limitations. What the CIA learned from
Tunisia, Libya, and especially Egypt was that a small
core group of people could mobilize millions to
overthrow a government. The extremely significant
fact was that these overthrows succeeded with little

or no bloodshed, with the exception of Libya and Syria.

This was an amazing new reality and tool for the forces of change. Communication from the government had always flowed vertically from top to bottom in a society; those that controlled the communication facilities controlled the message. However, now, communication flowed through horizontal channels that the ruling parties did not control. In a sense, that is what happened in Tehran in the summer of 2009. Two years later, Egyptian protestors amped up the amount of horizontal communication and were successful. Fortunately, the Egyptian army was willing to stand on the sidelines while the demonstrators organized and carried out their protests. The present Iranian government of Kharmini would not sit on the sidelines. They would brutalize dissenters again if challenged. For that reason alone, Kharmini needed to be dealt with.

While Kurtz was conducting her shuttle diplomacy and Geno was preparing for the Iranian insertion mission, the American triangle of State Department, military, and covert agencies would come together with a plan to solve the Israeli-Iranian crisis and also to secure the release of the Saudi Arabian Royal Family. The CIA was to immediately begin a horizontal communication plan to stir unrest among dissidents in Tehran, "Cairo style". President Kharmini and the state police were to be the targets of the campaign. In the campaign, they were to display a high degree of respect to the ruling mullahs. The plan was not to replace the Islamic state government with a secular government, but simply remove the President and allow the ruling mullahs a fresh start with a new President.

The campaign focused on the isolation and suffering that had been placed upon the Iranian people because of ever-tightening sanctions brought upon by President Kharmini and his program to build nuclear weapons for Iran. Gasoline had been in short supply for years, but now food products and medicines were also becoming scarce. The campaign message targeted young people that comprise over 50 percent of the population.

The kidnapping of Abdullah and the bombing of the El Al flight accelerated and condensed the time schedule that everyone had planned to implement at some point in time. It was now necessary to accomplish in three days what would have normally taken several months or even years. The CIA extraction mission would revolve around the Friday *jum'ah* prayer time at the mosques of Tehran, especially the main mosque in downtown Tehran. The CIA planned an intense communication build up via Facebook, Twitter, YouTube, and cell phones. The initial phase of the plan would emphasize organization and propaganda on Wednesday and Thursday, before Friday *jum'ah*.

The CIA plan would produce huge crowds of protestors that would flood the streets of downtown Tehran on Friday, similar to what happened in 2009, and, following form, the protestors would be brutalized by the state police once again. It was not known if CIA agents fired weapons against the police in 2009 to induce further mayhem, but someone did, which resulted in widespread wounding and killing of protestors. The violence in 2009 escalated on Saturday and Sunday, and by Monday, the mullahs feared that there would be a total rebellion by the "heathen" youth of Iran that would lead to a total overthrow of the Islamic state.

Fearing a repeat of the 2009 Green Revolution, the Supreme Ayatollah and ruling mullahs had been feuding with President Kharmini behind the scenes about his growing political and military power. The dispute broke into the public arena when some mullahs said that President Kharmini should resign or be impeached. The mullahs had enough of Kharmini and signaled the CIA that they were willing to visit about a deal to remove Kharmini.

Kurtz immediately sent messages through emissaries to Iran that America was also willing to deal. The American delegation met the Iranian delegation at a secret location in Beirut as agreed. Iran felt secure in Beirut because Hezbollah, its sponsored agency, controlled it and meeting in Beirut would test the Americans' commitment to see how eager they were for a deal by forcing them to come to hostile Arab soil. The Americans were eager to deal and had no problem showing "submission" by going to Beirut. If she was anything, Kurtz was a practical realist. This was her once-in-a-lifetime chance as Secretary of State to solve what was truly one of the world's most dangerous, ongoing crises of modern times. It was a risky plan, but Kurtz was all in.

The mullahs demanded three outcomes for Iran. Number one, Iran must emerge from this arrangement with a high degree of respect and honor among the Arab world. Iran must be acknowledged as the nation that bargained the strongest deal with the West for the Arabs. Number two, Iran must be allowed to continue with the build up of its nuclear weapons program and with the construction of the new Syrian naval base that had previously been announced by Syria and Iran. Number three, and most humiliating for the Americans and their surrogate, Israel, all economic sanctions on Iran must be lifted immediately. Iran's demands were nonnegotiable and must be taken as a package, or there would be no deal whatsoever. Iran stated it was more than willing to wage a war with Israel if that is what the West wanted.

Kurtz didn't have any problem with Iran's demands at the secret meeting in Beirut. She fully understood the value of honor and manhood through out the Arab world. She was willing to be a female that appeared weak throughout the Arab world as long as it brought peace to the region. On the other hand, she knew that her American political poll numbers would skyrocket.

Kurtz also had no problems with Iran's demands to continue its nuclear weapons program; after all, the Worm Virus had delayed the program three to five years and by the time Iran got caught up, the West would have another virus to use. No problem. The naval base in Syria? Once again, this was a fixable problem at a later date. The base could easily be bombed and that possibility would present a very tempting opportunity to keep Iran in line. The bigger issue for Kurtz was the economic sanctions; they were finally beginning to work. Kurtz had no issue with a perception of humiliation of America by the rest of the Arab world. However, in reality, she knew the stable regimes of the Middle East would privately be grateful to Americans for removing Kharmini. He was a threat to all rulers in the region.

Kurtz would agree to remove economic sanctions because it was the real deal maker for Iran. The removal of sanctions provided honor and prestige for Iran throughout the Arab world. Sanction removal would allow Iran to increase economic growth, which was so desperately needed in a country with so many unemployed young people, the seeds of all rebellions.

The United Nations could impose new sanctions at a future date if necessary. Also, the United States could deliver technology and key industrial machinery with intentional defects, as President Reagan had done to the Russians in the 1980's while they were constructing the massive natural gas pipeline to Western Europe. There were a lot of ways to skin the cat when it came to economic diplomacy.

Everyone knew these strategies were serious, deadly serious like the present situation, but ultimately part of an overall strategy that steered world governance through sheer and ultimate power. America currently had this governing power and Kurtz's job was to maintain that position. A nuclear exchange between Israel and Iran, with all the deadly political and economic blowoff, would be a black swan event that could knock America out of the "power seat".

China and its growing economic alliance of emerging economies, such as those in South America, Africa, and India, was waiting in the wings to become the new ruling leader of the world. Kurtz knew this fact. Black swans or not, Kurtz signed off on the removal of sanctions. It was the practical thing to do.

The Iranians approved the deal in Beirut, but what about the Israelis? Kurtz and company departed for Tel Aviv immediately for more briefing about the deal, and to assure Israel that Iran would agree to Kharmini's removal. This was a bigger prize for Israel than they originally envisioned and they immediately agreed to the deal.

CHAPTER 34

A BITTER PILL

SECRETARY KURTZ BEGAN HER NEGOTIATIONS IN TEL AVIV
with the Israelis. Addressing the Prime Minister of
Israel she said, "Mr. Prime Minister, once again
America acknowledges the restraint of Israel during
the current state of affairs with Iran. America and the
world are grateful to you and the nation of Israel for
showing such restraint. The President of the United
States understands the extreme political pressures
you personally face and the cries for your resignation
because of your decision to show restraint at this time.
The American people and all freedom-loving people
throughout the world acknowledge and share your
country's loss of life on El Al Flight 4. The bond and
special relationship that Israel and America share with
each other are exemplified to the rest of the world at
this time, as they were on 9/11. These bonds will be
strengthened as we march forward together. Mr. Prime
Minister, I come with an opportunity, only needing
your agreement, to change the history of Israel and the
world forever in our march for peace and good for all."
The Prime Minister of Israel looked at Kurtz with an

incredulous look on his face.

Meanwhile, Cardinal of the CIA was waiting at the drop site in Iran with his team. Cardinal had a team of eight from the secretive Special Operations Group (SOG) of the CIA. The SOG groups within the CIA traced their history back to General "Wild Bill" Donovan during World War II. SOG operations had ebbed and flowed through the years, depending upon various Presidents' comfort levels for such clandestine activities. SOG was ramped up again in recent years by CIA Director George Tenet, with the full backing of the White House and then President George W. Bush. SOG officers were now dispersed throughout Pakistan, North Africa, East Asia, Central Asia, and of course other hot spots such as North Korea, Iran, and other countries throughout the Middle East.

All SOGs had had a minimum of five years of military experience before being recruited to SOG. Names and background records were frequently changed to match an assignment, in a process known within the agency as "sheep dipping". Most of these recruits received further training at the "Farm", the CIA training center at Camp Peary near Williamsburg, Virginia. Some were sent on to Delta Force training headquarters at Fort Bragg to learn highly specialized counter-terrorism training.

SOG teams were well stocked with weaponry and

money, often millions of dollars stuffed into suitcases used to buy agents and information. The SOGs were not bound by paperwork and had fewer regulations to abide by than regular military forces. They prided themselves in being able to get in and out of a country without detection. They called it "hiding in plain sight". It was common for the SOGs to work with Navy SEALs and other Special Forces in tandem to achieve an objective. Together with the military expertise of Special Forces and the looser regulations of the SOGs, they formed a lethal and effective team.

"Falcon," Cardinal radioed from the Iranian desert floor to the pilot of the 130W and Geno.

"Copy, Cardinal," Geno replied.

"The drop zone will be lit for you," indicating that the laser-guided equipment would guide the cargo and personnel drop from the 130W to the landing zone.

Geno looked out into the pure darkness of the desert sky as he contemplated their drop. "Copy that."

"We're approaching the drop zone," the pilot communicated through the headset to Geno.

"Copy that," Geno replied.

Geno gave the ready signal to the team. All arose, adjusted their parachutes, and assembled for the drop. The crew of the 130W would drop the supply pallets from the plane's back drop door. The team would then parachute out the back drop door after the pallets of equipment had been dropped. The red jump light turned to green. The team executed a HALO jump, high altitude low open, from 34,000 feet to avoid detection by any enemy electronics or weaponry. Air temperatures at 34,000 feet were near fifty degrees Fahrenheit below zero and required special protective gear along with an oxygen tank to supplement the low oxygen levels at high altitude. The 130W crew shoved the pallets out the back drop door and SEAL Team 6 followed accordingly, avoiding the dead zone of the aircraft's wake.

Geno and the team cleared the dead zone, executed a free fall dive for two minutes, and then pulled their rip cords. They all came in with amazing accuracy to within a few hundred feet of the drop zone, but SEALs are trained to do that. Geno and the others quickly unharnessed the jump gear and gathered in their chutes. Cardinal had directed the SOG team to secure the pallets as he strode over to the group of SEALs.

"Cardinal?" Geno inquired.

"Falcon?" Dr. Jones replied. The two shook hands in the dark desert night. "Pleased to have you here," Jones said.

"Pleased to be here, sir," Geno replied.

"Gather up your men and no more 'sirs' here, understand? My name is Jonsey, but over here it's Vasu.

We're posing as a band from India seeking black market fortunes. Vasu is translated as 'wealthy' in Hindi. Your name is Sahan, which means 'falcon.' All of your team will have an Indian name. Got it?"

"I do, Vasu," Geno replied to Jonsey.

"Gather your men together and let's do an intel report," Vasu stated, "but I have to talk to you alone first." He explained the command structure to Geno that placed Vasu in charge. Geno gave him a questioning look but nodded his head.

"Men, my name is Vasu, and this is my team," Vasu said as he went around the SEAL team. It was very dark and the SOGs were all dressed in Indian clothing and head garb. "We're here to conduct a very delicate exercise. We are not going to become best buddies and swap stories back and forth about all of our exploits and deeds. I want none of that, do you understand?" Heads nodded as SEAL 6 glared at him.

"I don't want to appear harsh," Vasu said as he flipped over to a pure British accent. He and his team had been trained in the art of voice accents. He had the ability to sound British, Irish, French, Italian, Serbian, or Middle Eastern, depending upon the circumstances.

Vasu continued, "You might think you're a black team, but we're as black as it gets. You don't know who we are and you don't need to know. We don't want you to know. There might be some stuff that none of us wants on a record. Understand?" They did. "I'm running this operation and Sahan (Geno) is my number two. Got that?"

This guy's a real arrogant ass, Steve thought. *I'd like to drop him right here!*

"We have an inside man within the Presidential Palace. We've been mining him for over a year. We know the comings and goings of President Kharmini and his inner circle quite well. The Revolutionary Guard is his most loyal force and comprises his personal security unit. They are well trained, equipped, and hardened. Your job as SEALs is to deal with them when the time comes. We will handle the snatch and grab. The target is to be taken alive and unharmed. Does everyone understand? I want to be perfectly clear." Vasu said, rather condescendingly.

Make that a real ass! I'd like to meet that son of a bitch in an alley some time! Steve thought.

Matt could see that Steve's face was beet red in the darkness. "Easy, big fella," Matt mumbled to him.

Vasu continued, "We have a deadly game of don't ask, don't tell we are playing here. Arrangements have been made and agreed upon by the highest levels of our governments. The Iranians do not know the exact logistics of the plan, but they know the plan exists and have agreed to it. We are not to ask for their participation, nor are we to tell them where or exactly when.

Any questions on that?"

"Yeah," Fats said. "You mean to tell me, Vasqoo—"

"Vasu," Jonsey corrected him. "It's very important that we use proper language on our names. It's better not to speak at all if you can't engage with proper voice inflections or pronunciations. Blending in is extremely important. You are not to act like Americans or Europeans. Act like Indians if at all possible. At the very minimum, you are Southern Europeans."

"OK, Vasu," Fats said. "You mean to tell me that this thing isn't 'greased' for us?"

"It is and it isn't," Vasu replied. "We have the green light to conduct an operation, but if we're caught, we won't be protected by the Iranian government. We'll probably be taken prisoner, tortured, interrogated, and then put to the sword or hanged in a public setting as enemies to Iran. The mullahs want to come out of this with completely clean hands, which they should. They've taken a huge risk to do what they're doing. Put yourself in their shoes; do you think the President of the United States would want his hands dirty by this type of operation? I don't think so. This is the way it's done if it's to be done at all. I can have a Delta Force team in here in twenty-four hours if you're not up to it," Vasu said. The mood was very tense and alpha male Vasu was butting heads with the alphas of SEAL 6.

Sensing the tension, "OK, everybody take a time-out here," Geno said. "We're all cool with this. We just came off an intense mission and lost two of our guys. Everybody's a little stressed. Take a deep breath. Look 6, I'm OK with all of this. These guys are experts in what they do and we're experts in what we do. We're a team. They can't do it without us and we can't do it without them. We all want to get in and get out alive.

"Everybody on 6, team up with a SOG, shake hands, and let's get on with this. Cut the crap. We're all professionals here, not a bunch of schoolgirls squabbling over our places in line out on the playground. Vasu runs it. We're here to support. Any questions on that, 6, and you will sit your ass right here in the desert and we'll pick you up on the way back! Now stop the bullshit right here and now! Understood?" Geno asked.

"Yes, sir," from 6 all around.

We'll be fine, Fats thought. *Geno's back!*

In the end the men knew it was all about a successful mission, but taking a backseat to this Vasu character was a bitter pill for Team 6 to swallow.

CHAPTER 35

SUPERWOMAN!

THE TWO TEAMS GATHERED THEIR GEAR AND GOT UNDER WAY. They were about 175 miles east of Tehran. Jonsey's team traveled in beat-up Toyota SUVs. Geno's team followed at a distance in some trucks disguised as Iranian troop carriers and equipment trucks that had been brought to the drop zone by the SOGs. They split the SEALs into the two trucks. Geno rode in truck one and put Fats in charge of truck two. Truck one carried weaponry and electronics, as well as a couple of local uniforms to fit the circumstances. Truck two carried the transport squad along with the small motor-cycles so prevalent in downtown Tehran. The SOGs drove the trucks.

Team 6 was dressed in the Indian attire the SOGs brought to the drop site for them. They ate MREs and granola bars, drank water to stay hydrated, and drift-ed off into power naps. Per standard SEAL procedure, though, one man stayed awake for watch in the back of each truck in case there was a problem. The drive was going to be about four hours, so they switched off for sack time. It was 0400, dark and cold out in the desert.

The call to morning prayer in Tehran would be in about two hours. They would be on the outskirts of the city by 0700. Taking a circuitous route, Vasu took them to a safe house after they dumped the trucks at a warehouse and proceeded from there in some beat-up sedans. The city was teeming with life and the smell of revolution was in the air because of the efforts of the CIA agents on the ground. It was early in the day and things probably wouldn't heat up with the protestors until midday.

Jonsey didn't tell Team 6 the extraction date, but they knew it would be within a matter of a few days. They knew they wouldn't have been inserted if that was not the case. As Vasu had said, the SOGs could blend in anywhere. It was different for a group of guys like 6 that couldn't throw their accents very well. Team 6 hoped it wouldn't be too long because they were amped and ready to go, and they didn't care for Vasu's command style. He wasn't a team player like Geno.

"Mr. Prime Minister," Kurtz said to the Prime Minister of Israel while in Tel Aviv. "The extraction team is in the city. You will have your honor and retribution fulfilled within seventy-two hours."

"I hope so, Madam Secretary," the Prime Minister said. "As you know, we are sitting on a tinder box and I don't know how long we can keep the match at bay."

"I understand, Mr. Prime Minister, but I assure you,

in seventy-two hours a thorn will be removed from your side forever," Kurtz said.

"We shall see. I hope with all my heart that you are correct. Otherwise, I fear Armageddon for the world."

"Mr. Prime Minister, I must take my leave, with your permission. May I reach you on your secure line?"

"Of course," the Prime Minister said. Kurtz then shuttled off to Riyadh from Tel Aviv.

In Riyadh, Kurtz began, "Prince Alsan, as you know, we take the situation in your country with the gravest of concerns for King Abdullah and the Royal Family. Our friendship and ties extend back for decades. We are working on a plan that could work highly in your favor. It will be difficult, but it is possible. As you know, I escaped from the same jihadist band less than a week ago. We learned from that experience that these terrorists are long on fanaticism but not so long on military training or strategies. If they were, I would likely still be held hostage or dead. You and your family have been like a mother to your people, providing them with twenty-first-century living and all of its comforts. Your family has worked tirelessly to improve the freedom and rights that other nations in this region are dying for right now.

"Prince Alsan, these terrorists seem to have an agenda built on recognition and rewards for their exploits. We know that Hezbollah and Iran back them. Would you be open to an exchange that would save the lives of your king and the Royal Family members currently being held hostage?"

"Of course, but how would this be possible?" Alsan asked.

"Esteemed and worthy Prince, what does the ship of the desert, the camel, crave most of all? A lump of sugar! Would you be willing to exchange your king for a lump of sugar?"

Irritated, Alsan said, "Madam Secretary, please do not toy with me at such a time. Please do not speak to me in riddles that try my patience. Let me pose a riddle to you, a rather plain-spoken riddle: Would you and your country be concerned about this situation at all if it were not for Saudi Arabia's vast oil reserves that you and the West so desperately covet? Answer that for me, Madam Secretary."

Kindly and diplomatically, Kurtz said, "Prince Alsan, we would, because Saudi Arabia has long been the voice of reason in the region. Saudi Arabia is tolerant and understanding to other nations. Saudi Arabia is important to all Muslims of the world because of Mecca and Medina. You have tried to maintain access for all Muslims of the world, even at great risk to your country from terrorist infiltration. You take this risk in the spirit of freedom and access for all, much like the United States of America does with its open borders. We stand shoulder to shoulder with all peace-seeking nations of the world, regardless of their might or their resources. I do hope you can see that, Honorable Prince Alsan."

Alsan nodded while fingering his prayer beads. "Tell me more, Madam Secretary."

Kurtz informed the prince of the plan, and he agreed to consider it if it would be possible to bring the plan to fruition. Kurtz assured him that it would and Kurtz then shuttled to Damascus—yes, Damascus—to negotiate with the crumbling Assad family. Kurtz needed a safe and hospitable exile country for Kharmini's relocation. It was a heavy price to pay, but if Syria, as the conduit for Iranian-backed Hezbollah, would accept the plan and the exchange of the President of Iran for the King of Saudi Arabia, it would be a huge political victory for Assad and could possibly perpetuate his regime for his family. Kharmini could become the head of Hezbollah or any other organization of President Assad's choosing. The main political ingredient for Assad, despite all of the risks with fundamentalist Arabs and Iranians, would be that he helped humiliate the West in this exchange and exalted Kharmini into an international jihadist leader like bin Laden was, not merely the President of Iran. This had a great deal of appeal to Assad, who could hardly believe the offer.

He accepted readily, mostly from survival instincts, but he did accept.

The arrangement was now fully set. The mullahs had grown tired and wary of Kharmini's rants and threats. They wanted to get in front of the reform curve of the Middle East and could not do so with Kharmini as the figurehead of their governing body. They had a better chance of remaining an Islamic state without Kharmini than they did with him. Kharmini was also accumulating too much military and political power for their comfort. He had to be deposed.

Israel would be rid of someone they truly feared and there was a reprisal to Iran that would be visible to the world for the downing of flight El Al 4, which made the Israelis as content as they could be under the circumstances. Saudi Arabia would get their king and the Royal Family returned. Syria would receive honor and prestige. Iran would benefit from the removal of Kharmini and economic sanctions. Kharmini would live another day to rant and radicalize. Hopefully, within seventy-two hours, the world would be pulled back from the precipice.

"Mr. President, Secretary of State Kurtz on the secure line," said the President's aide back in Washington before passing the phone off.

"It's four in the morning," the President said to his aide

"I know, sir. She asked to speak to you."

"I'll take it," he said as he got up from the sleeping quarters of the situation room.

"In here, sir." The aide escorted him to a private security room next to the sleeping quarters.

"Yes, Kathryn, what do you have for me?"

"I think we have a deal, Mr. President." Kurtz replied.

"Thank God. Are you sure?"

"As sure as I can be under these circumstances. The only one I'm worried about is Syria, but Assad seemed to buy it."

"Great. We have resources in position if we need them. I hope we won't."

"Me too, sir. I don't think we will, but I've learned recently that you can't have enough firepower on hand when you get into these circumstances."

The President looked at the phone and thought, *This is coming from my Secretary of State?* Maybe he would take her up on her offer to serve only one term, but if she could pull this off, it would virtually guarantee his reelection. "Good job, Kathryn. I knew that if anyone could do this, it would be you. Keep me in the loop."

"Are you sure you want that, sir? This could get a

little dicey with the CIA and SOGs involved. It might be better to keep your fingerprints off this," Kathryn replied.

"You're right, Kathryn, run it through my Chief of Staff," the President replied. *Damn it, she knows all these calls are recorded and transcribed! What the hell is she trying to do! If she wants to play hardball down the line, we'll be ready for her. Damn it!*

The President was now fully awake. "Get me some coffee and juice, now," he told the aide.

"Yes, sir!" the aide replied. Wow, thought the aide, *something must have crawled up his butt!*

Superwoman strikes again!

Meanwhile, back at the safe house Jonsey and Geno had their heads together. Jonsey shared the bare bones elements of the plan, "We're going to let this pot boil for a couple of days. We have operatives on the ground working the crowds. Our agent Radioman is flooding the airwaves with Facebook posts and YouTube feeds. Today is intended to incite the masses. Tomorrow will be a day of frenzy amped up further by Radioman, and the next day is our extraction day," Jonsey shared with Geno. "We're going to stay in a lock down here. It's not safe to the mission for your team to be out on the streets. We leave that up to the other teams. I only know my contact as Zebra. Zebra is the inside brain of Kharmini's circle and he works in conjunction with Streetman and Radioman. Zebra will make the call when the target is most susceptible. Zebra runs the show. I key off him. You key off me, obviously."

"Sounds like a plan to me, Vasu. We'll busy ourselves with PT and weapons," Geno replied.

"Yeah, knock yourself out. This is the hardest part, waiting," Vasu replied.

CHAPTER 36

PASSION!

TEHRAN IS A LARGE URBAN AND COSMOPOLITAN CITY OF SOME
eight million residents, tracing its history back as far
as the tenth century and increasing in importance
from 1500 forward to the present. Like all large urban
centers, the city has its high and low points, as well
as the diversity of population to match. There are
some very affluent sections where people might think
they're in the fashionable districts of Paris or London,
with exclusive shops and the latest fashion. It is
common to see drop-dead gorgeous young women
wearing skirts and sunglasses, along with a western
style hair scarf. The young men can easily be mistaken
for preppie university students.

Then there are many other sections of town
where slum-like conditions prevail. There has been
increasing migration from the rural areas to Tehran
and other large cities of Iran as the migrants seek the
conveniences of basic city services and urban living.
Tehran has undertaken a building boom in recent
decades to provide more parks, stadiums, theaters,

and other recreational facilities to meet the needs of its growing population. However, sewage and water issues are a thorn in less-affluent neighborhoods. The city has been divided into various districts in an attempt to monitor and improve these basic services.

Tension was building in Tehran. The arrival of early summer, along with the organizational activities of the CIA on Facebook and Twitter were having their effect on the people. Well placed cell phone camera operators videoed police beating and clubbing students. Those videos were quickly fired to YouTube and major news outlets of the West. CNN and the BBC were given preferred distribution status for the feeds by CIA agents. It was extremely important to the CIA and DOD to get as much carnage on the airwaves as soon as possible, especially in America, Britain, and the rest of Europe.

"Casualties" were interviewed and video feeds were sent worldwide. The casualties focused on the crude and fierce repression of President Kharmini and his henchmen. There were reports of rape and murder. The CIA handlers orchestrated the crowd to press forward into the city squares as much as possible. They knew that a mass of humanity would fuel the memories of 2009. Of course, all of the "casualties" reported that the violence and brutality were much worse than in 2009. They even reported and videotaped mock murders of children and their parents. This was an all-out theatrical production by the CIA. The world was its audience and Tehran was the stage.

President Kharmini fed right into the CIA frenzy on Thursday by going on state media and proclaiming, somewhat accurately yet unknowingly, that the protests were organized by Zionists from Jerusalem and America. He insisted that the Iranian people loved Allah and Muhammad and that they would never allow themselves to be corrupted by the West, nor would he allow so many innocent Iranians to be so polluted. He proclaimed "Death to Israel" and "Death to America", "Death to all traitors of Islam", and "Death to the infidels". Once again, he threatened to "wipe Israel off the face of the earth". "Death to Israel", he chanted as he pumped his fists repeatedly for the crowds.

The mullahs were not comfortable with the "Death to Israel" chants under current conditions. Mullahs may be somewhat political, but they are spiritual first and foremost. Agree or disagree, they are guided by a religious belief system, and that belief system does not allow for the slaughter of any Islamic nation by foreign forces, especially non-Muslim forces. It would be a desecration to Allah to allow Israel or America to destroy Iran with a nuclear attack. The mullahs understood that Israel might shoot first and ask questions later if their backs got pressed to the wall any tighter. Iran did not have a stock of nuclear weapons to threaten with or fire back. It would be a blood bath of an unprecedented scale. They had to act upon Islamic beliefs to save Iran from Kharmini and possible destruction by outside forces.

Thursday evening, the ruling mullahs gave President Kharmini one last opportunity to tone down his rhetoric for the following day, but he just could not control himself. President Kharmini felt that he had the mullahs on the run and that he could seize ultimate power if mayhem were to ensue. He had the Revolutionary Guard, the State Police force, the police force of Tehran, and several urban militias backing him. What did the mullahs really have to challenge this? The 50 percent of the population that was under age thirty had nothing, absolutely nothing to resist with, nothing! They caved in 2009 under what President Kharmini called moderate military and police pressure. They could not resist true harsh repression by his hand, with or without their social media friends. Of this he was sure.

Ego and arrogance had completed their journey within Kharmini. It had been a long journey from rural poverty, by way of the seizing of the American Embassy and hostages in 1979, to his election as President, but the journey was now complete. He fantasized that he could now seize ultimate power and create a true militant Islamic society to rule over the entire world, much like Darius the Great had done in

Persia over two thousand years ago. Islam would now be spread by the sword in every sense of his imagination. Iran would redouble its efforts to achieve nuclear power status. Kharmini would now create and lead the most powerful Islamic country in all of recorded history. He was truly drunk with power—and drunkenness is forbidden in Islamic culture. Kharmini had a problem though, he told the mullahs "no".

Kharmini told the ruling council of mullahs, "No, now is not the time to back off or back down. Now is the time to press onward with all resources. The West has reached its breaking point financially and militarily. We have managed to stretch them from Afghanistan and Pakistan in the east to Libya and Tunisia in the west, from the former Soviet 'Stan-ish' republics in the north to the central coasts of East Africa in the south. Their troops are tiring. Defections and suicides are up among their troops. More American women are divorcing their army men. Their battle stress illnesses are increasing. Their congress and their people are growing weary of constant warfare. Bush Two understood that we could engage them for decades, but his people would not listen to him; they could not listen because America is an impatient country.

"This war is ours to win now. We are on the verge of victory. Did the Americans not fear that their puppet, Israel, would start another war for them to fight? Did they not keep their dog on its leash? Yes! Because they have much more to lose than us; they are running short on resources, allies, and money. Satan has America firmly in his grasp. He will not let them go because the Americans will not let go of their prized material possessions and immoral ways. I will not let you stop Iran from fulfilling its destiny, not now, not ever! Allah must prevail!" and so went Kharmini's half-sincere, half-self-serving rant to the ruling body of mullahs.

Zebra was in contact with Vasu after the meeting between the mullahs and Kharmini Thursday evening. "Streetman will produce a big show tomorrow. Package being wrapped for delivery. I will answer the door when the bell rings."

Vasu told the men to come together. "We should be in motion in twenty-four hours or less. Our contacts within the government have told us that things are reaching a boiling point and the regime wants a change. We are pleased to provide that change courtesy of your local CIA! The trucks and vans will be here at the appropriate time. We will pick up our package at a designated location. As always, we want to get in and get out without any damage. Relax. Get your rest. Be ready to roll when we get the call."

CHAPTER 37

TENSION

THE **DOD** WAS BUSY TRYING TO COMPLY WITH FEDERAL LAWS that would not implicate it with any covert activities involving the CIA and the mission at hand. Since the actual extraction and transfer of Kharmini would be done by the CIA, the DOD ordered the Navy to pick up only its team upon completion of the mission, they were not to transport any SOGs or Kharmini in any way, shape, or form. He was a CIA package exclusively. Admiral Gates was quite relieved to have those instructions.

Gates' career was nearly torpedoed a few days ago when Geno had spoken so bluntly on the White House south lawn. Gates did not want to end his career with a scarlet letter in his file for cross contamination with the CIA. "Captain Smart, coordinate with JSOC to get our guys out of there when it's time."

"Yes, sir, Admiral," Smart replied.

Azadi Square, known as Freedom Square since the Iranian Revolution of 1979, was a monument built by the Shah of Iran in 1971 to commemorate the 2,500th anniversary of Persia, now known as Iran. The tower in the center of the square was fifty meters tall and covered in white marble.

Azadi Square was a perfect backdrop for the CIA-orchestrated demonstration that took place on the third day, Friday, of the Tehran protests. The square was filled with hundreds of thousands of young professionals and everyday Iranians who felt that this could be their "Iranian Spring", just as the Egyptians and Tunisians had theirs and Libya was fighting for theirs.

This idea of an "Iranian Spring" could happen someday for these masses, but it was not to be on day three of the 2011 uprising, day three was about brutality and a strong push back by forces loyal to President Kharmini. CNN, the BBC, YouTube, and virtually every electronic hand-held device was working over-time that day, sending videos through-out the media and world blogosphere.

As Friday evening descended, Zebra called Jonsey. "Pick up your package, please." So courteous, so lovely, so British, almost like the old days of the British Empire in India.

"Will do, my stripe-ed friend. Would you recommend a bit of early-evening air or midnight air?" Jonsey Vasu asked.

"There is nothing like the crispness of the midnight

air in summertime to clear one's senses."

"Agreed, my friend," Vasu replied.

"All right, let's get ready. The vehicles will be here in a few hours. Scrub everything. Don't leave any-thing behind that could be linked to us. NO electronic files, computers, papers, maps, NOTHING! Spread the disinformation packs in the bedrooms and main room. Distribute the Syrian propaganda brochures throughout the rest of the house. We're happy to leave our Syrian calling cards!" The CIA was throwing Syria under the bus before the mission got under way. They called it "dis-informing".

"Sahan (Geno), let's firm up the mission between us." The Indian name stuff was driving Geno some-what crazy by now.

Geno and Jonsey retreated to a corner. "Sahan, we're going to go as a caravan to the pickup point. It will be well secured, but we have assets inside. We'll have to play it by ear to some degree."

"Look, Vasu, I know you've got your job and I've got mine, but we're going to screw this thing up royally if we don't share some details back and forth. I feel like two Washington agencies that are down the hall from each other but don't talk to each other because everything has to be run through Langley for clearance. This is crazy! We're really gonna botch this thing because you're not sharing anything with me, and because of that, I can't prepare my team! What are we supposed to do, just roll up and jump out of our vehicles for a shoot-out at the OK Corral? That isn't the way we do business. We're professional Naval Sea, Air, and Land Special Forces, SEALs! Not some circus act, but professional military killers when necessary. We've had enough! Now where in the hell are we going and what in the hell are we doing?" Geno blasted as the others looked over to the corner where they were sitting.

It's about time! seemed to be the look from 6. *You tell him, Geno!*

"All right, all right. Calm down, Sahan. Like I said, we're going to leave in a few hours. We're going to caravan—"

"Yeah, I know. Caravan where and do what?" Geno interrupted.

"We're going to caravan to the grounds of the Presidential palace, get on the grounds, and snatch the President. I don't know exactly how it's all going to go down, but that is the plan."

"You don't know how it's all going to go down, but that is the plan? Are you serious?"

"Deadly serious, Sahan. Trust me if you would, please. We've done this before."

"Trust you because you've done this before?

Where, in some hut in the Sudan or a farmhouse in Bosnia? This is the fricking Presidential Palace of Iran, with some nut job inside! Does the CIA ever plan in advance, or are all of those botch job stories of the gang that couldn't shoot straight really true? I'm starting to wonder. I think they are! I think you guys are a bunch of dumbasses. Next thing we know, you'll find WMDs in there!"

"Back off, Genelli, or I'll have your ass!"

"Bring it on, Vasuuuu!"

As the two stood up to face each other, Fats ran over to the corner and separated them. "Everybody calm down…We've spent too much time cooped up together here…Everybody wants to kick some ass, let's just not kick each other's, OK? There's a really high profile dude out there that we're supposed to grab and pass off to some of the mucky-mucks so they can make their deals with each other.

"Normally I wouldn't give a damn about who gets passed off to whom by who, or when and how it gets done. But you know what? This time it's some pretty big chips we're involved with. A lot of people are going to live or die if this thing goes nuclear, including maybe my wife and kids, so if you two puffed-up asses don't mind, the rest of us would like to do our job, get it done safely, get out, and go home. Maybe even get a medal like you, *Sahan*."

Fats smiled and gave Geno a brotherly love tap to the jaw. Geno and Jonsey nodded to each other with the "look" and sat down to finish their business. It went well after that.

The vehicles came and the teams loaded. Truck one with Geno and some of the team took the lead and truck two with Fats and the rest of the team followed up the entourage. It was common to see army vehicles acting as escorts for civilian vehicles in Tehran. After all, it was a matter of providing a "service for a small fee".

In fact, there were black market security services provided by underpaid military personnel. It was also well known to the locals that some Army vehicles were actually fakes with some paint and markings, driven by men dressed in army surplus clothing. Depending on how many escorts a crew could do in a given day, it was a good supplement to low-grade pay. So 6 and the SOGs blended into the urban environment just as any good CIA crew should do.

"How far?" Geno asked the driver.

"About six klicks across town, mate."

Geno radioed to his team on their commo system that they were six klicks out from target.

"Roger."

Kharmini had a strong security detail, especially

after a large bomb had been detonated a few months earlier near the home he owned before becoming President. Kharmini was driven to the Presidential Palace grounds as nightfall approached after a tense day with the mullahs and the protestors. The palace grounds contain eighteen castles, homes, and meeting sites. The palace facilities were a safe and secure location to plot and strategize for the political moves necessary over the next several days. Kharmini had selected the Special Castle, known and used since the 1979 revolution as the Museum of Natural History, for his official presidential usage.

Kharmini felt that he needed to secure his power base as soon as possible because he sensed "an ill script was written in the sand" for him. Supreme Leader Ayatollah Khamenei had recently reinstated the interior minister that Kharmini had removed. This was a highly unusual step for the Supreme Ayatollah to take in confronting the government in such a public manner. Kahamenei may remove Kharmini next.

Kharmini met with his inner circle until late into the night and then retired to bed. Guards patrolled the interior and exterior of the castle, as well as the perimeters of the grounds. Motion detectors and surveillance cameras dotted the landscape and lighting flooded the area.

Big as brass, the caravan drove north from Tajrish

Square on Ayatollah Maleki Street to the southern entrance to the compound. The square was filled with debris from the protests that had also taken place during the previous day. Government workers were cleaning up the mess to make things look normal for the next day. The security police were reinforcing barricades and checking water cannons and other crowd control measures. Vasu presented his paperwork to the guards and the caravan drove into the complex.

Vasu and Sahan were posing as additional security forces and Special Operation forces to protect the President from any assassination or hostage-taking incidents instigated by the massive protests. Team 6 and the SOGs motored to the Special Castle and presented their papers to the Iranian commander on duty.

Within the palace, President Kharmini lay in an exhausted sleep.

CHAPTER 38

INTO THE NIGHT

VASU TOLD THE COMMANDER IN PERFECT FARSI THAT HE
needed to see the layout of the palace so that they
could set up their stations. The commander gave him
a quizzical look, but Vasu explained to him that the
military commanders at higher levels were concerned
that an attempt might be made on President Kharmini's
life at any time. He also mentioned that they were
concerned that the Israelis or the American CIA might
attempt a plot.

It took everything Geno had inside of him to not
show the shock on his face; he simply nodded in agreement to the commander. Their papers were in order
and it was nearly two a.m. The Iranian commander did
not want to awaken a senior officer because he didn't
want to seem inept at reading the proper papers that
had been stamped by the Chief of the Revolutionary
Guard *himself*, so he took the two squads on a tour of
the facility and the grounds.

Vasu assumed a command role and instructed
various members of the team to take positions at

appropriate points on the exterior of the palace. He told the commander that he was concerned about having escape routes in the event there was an attempt on Kharmini and that he would count on the commander's security forces to ward off any intruders. Vasu's team was there for escape purposes only. Vasu inquired where the helicopter pad was in the event they needed to escape by air. The commander felt comfortable sharing the information, after all, Vasu's papers were in order.

With the outer perimeter established and Fats in charge of it, Vasu instructed the commander to take them through the interior of the palace, which he did. Vasu stationed men appropriately on the interior as well. He then instructed the commander to take them to Kharmini's sleeping quarters. There were two armed guards stationed at the entrance to the hallway of the sleeping quarters and two armed guards at Kharmini's bedroom door.

"This looks quite secure, Commander. I think our President is quite safe," Vasu said. "May we retire for a cup of tea?"

"Of course? Down the hallway. Follow me please," the commander replied.

Vasu, Geno, Artie, Mad Mike, Miggs, and the commander adjourned for a cup of tea. Vasu and the commander engaged in a discussion of the previous day's events and agreed that events seemed to be escalating. Setting the SOG plan in motion, Vasu asked for a status check over the communication system from his troops as a signal that it was time to put the plan in motion.

Shortly thereafter, Fats radioed a false report of movement on the perimeter to Vasu. Vasu and the commander rushed to the sleeping quarters with Geno, Artie, Mike, and Miggs in tow. Fats and the outside forces fired flares into the air that they had stowed in their backpacks. The flares alerted the Iranians on duty on the grounds and soon there was a massive amount of activity outside. The Iranian captain of the outside guard radioed for assistance and alerted HQ that a possible event involving the President was under way. It was, but they didn't know the event was from the inside, not the outside.

"Commander, we cannot take any chances," Vasu said. "Neither one of us wants to die. If the President is captured or harmed, we and our families will pay with our lives. We must act now!"

"I agree!" the Iranian commander replied.

Vasu said, "Please do what you are told by me and instruct your men to do the same. The future of Iran is in our hands! We will secure the President. Instruct your men and return immediately!" Vasu said with a commanding tone.

The commander nodded and ran down the hallway instructing the men on guard to follow the instructions of Vasu. The SOG plans were going beautifully.

"Come here," Vasu told the guards. "We are going to awaken the President and take him out of here. He is not safe here. We are being attacked. He must leave the grounds. Shoot to kill any intruders. Station yourselves here and do not leave your post." Though hardened troops, they were stunned at the events under way and nodded their heads in agreement.

Vasu and Geno entered the quarters and awakened Kharmini. Vasu spoke perfect Farsi. "Mr. President, we must leave. There is a possible event under way. We don't know if it is the Israelis, Americans, or forces from inside the government, but your safety is in jeopardy."

Kharmini knew that there were many long knives out for him from external and internal sources, so he agreed. He was dressed for travel in a few minutes and they walked out of the room into the hallway. The commander was returning to the hallway as Vasu and the others came out.

"We are going to move the President for his own personal safety," Vasu told the commander. "Lead us to the helicopters." The commander led them outside where the rest of 6 and the SOGs had gathered. They made their way to the helicopters.

Vasu stopped short and said, "This is exactly what the enemy would expect. If this is an internal plot, we will be shot down. We must leave in the vehicles, not helicopters! It will be much safer. Commander, we need the armor-plated vehicle for the President, two armored personnel carriers for the guards, and two Ranger tactical vehicles with machine guns for protection. Also, you must accompany us. We may need you to wave us through any checkpoints that may be set up. Instruct your commanding officer to hold this compound as if the President is still here. That will make the enemy think that the President has not left the grounds. Hurry, hurry!"

Astoundingly, the "Presidential Party" motored off into the night. *Maybe this Vasu guy wasn't so bad after all,* thought Team 6.

CHAPTER 39

LOST

THE CARAVAN SPED OUT OF THE GATES OF THE COMPOUND into the nearly vacant streets of Tehran. The Presidential Compound sat on the north central border of the city of Tehran with the Elburz Mountains as a backdrop. The caravan drove south toward the center of the city as a decoy maneuver, but as soon as they cleared vision from the compound, they turned due west to get out of the city. They would then turn and speed quickly to a pickup point sixty miles northwest of the city.

Vasu called Langley to notify them that they were en route. Steve drove with Artie up front, and Vasu and Geno rode in the back of the armor-plated vehicle with Kharmini and the commander.

It was imperative for the team to get to the pickup point before sunrise for a secure handoff. They turned onto the Hemmat Highway and sped west, then dropped south, connecting to the Karaj Qazvin Highway. They then dropped south off the Qazvin and headed into the desert.

Kharmini soon smelled a rat because they were headed away from the city. He protested and began to ask questions, becoming more concerned as they headed into the desert.

Suddenly, the Iranian commander pulled his weapon and shot Jonsey dead. Geno grabbed the gun out of the commander's hands and shot him in the side of his head. Blood and brains flew everywhere in the back of the vehicle. He then put Kharmini in a headlock and screamed at him to sit or he would kill him too! Geno knew that Kharmini understood English.

"Artie, get back here and lend a hand!"

Artie climbed to the backseat and helped Geno cuff Kharmini's hands and feet. They also put tape over his mouth to shut him up.

Geno said to Artie, "Jesus, we're on a frickin' CIA mission and we've got a head of state on our hands, and the CIA idiot gets blown away. Kiss your ass good-bye, Artie. We could all end up in front of some tribunal if this thing blows up!"

"What d'ya want to do, Cap?" Artie asked.

"Give me the damn CQ set…Langley, we've got a big problem here. Your man is dead."

"Kharmini?"

"No, Jones. Put me through to DEVGRU."

"Can't do that sailor. This is not a military op."

"It is now," Geno replied.

"Sorry, sailor. Meet at the pickup point. Birds on the way."

"Steve, beat it to the pick up point!" Geno barked.

Irritated, "Fine, but I don't have a clue where we are because 'Mr. Vasu' wouldn't trust us with any info."

"Look, we're supposed to meet them at a pickup zone near some place called Ebrahimabad. There's supposed to be a small landing strip there. Look at the map," Geno shouted.

"OK, boss. We'll give it a whirl."

"Langley, this is Falcon. Have you got a GPS fix on us? Your man Jones has us in a jam because he didn't share directions with anyone. I guess that would be too much red tape for you guys, but we're driving blind here."

"Sorry, no GPS coverage. We don't want our personnel tracked," Langley replied.

"Great! Put me through to DEVGRU or we're gonna wander out here until the entire frickin Iranian Army and Air Force find us and their President!" Geno shouted.

"Keep moving and let me get back to you," Langley replied.

"Moving? Moving where? We're frickin lost out here!" Geno shot back.

No response from Langley.

"We need to get this mission under control or we're all toast," Geno told Artie and Steve. Geno relayed the news to the trailing vehicles. "Steve, pull over. We need to get organized.

"Everybody, Jonsey was killed by the Iranian commander. We're 'lost' by Langley without GPS coordinates. I'm trying to get a patch through to head-quarters at Dam Neck, but Langley is resisting, claiming it's their mission. I've told them that it's a SEAL mission now. They're checking up the chain would be my guess. We're secure right here for now but not for too long. I'm going to wait a few minutes to see what the outcome is with Langley. Hopefully, they'll turn us over to Dam Neck. Set up a perimeter defense until we hear something. There's no point in wandering around blind out here."

They waited. Finally, about ten minutes later, "Team 6, this is DEVGRU. Do you copy?" Cheers went up!

"We copy," Geno replied.

"How's your fuel status in your vehicles?"

"Pretty good. We're in Iranian personnel carriers and Humvee-like vehicles with machine guns. We have an armor-plated vehicle that we brought Kharmini out in but it's full of blood and brains," Geno replied.

"Good," DEVGRU replied. "Dump the armor-plated vehicle in the desert, fairly close to the road. We want them to think that Kharmini might be dead or wounded. Rub his jacket or some piece of clothing in the blood and leave it in the vehicle. Bring Jones's body with you. They'll see a dead Iranian commander and a bloody jacket of Kharmini's. We'll be back to you shortly." Team 6 did as instructed.

"Team 6, DEVGRU, we want you to proceed to a new pickup zone. The chatter is starting to pick up out of Tehran. You need to get out of there. Get back on the Qazvin and proceed to Abyek. Then turn right at a sign marked Ziyran, about ten clicks beyond Abyek. Then head due north across the desert. Due north, do you copy?"

"We copy."

"You will be southwest of the Elburz Mountain Range, headed to the Caspian. This is a desolate region, ideal for pick up. We'll be in further contact with you."

"Copy, 6 out."

The SEALs and SOGs moved out with Geno in firm command. They made their turn beyond Abyek and headed due north as instructed. It was a desolate region, but desolate was good. The sun was rising in the east and the temperature began to rise. Geno was now in the second personnel carrier with Kharmini. He took the tape off Kharmini's mouth and allowed him to drink water. It was crucial that he be kept alive. He offered him a power bar to eat, but he refused.

"Suit yourself. We're not worried about you starving to death."

"Where are you taking me?" Kharmini asked in broken English.

"Classified. You know how that goes, don't you?"

"My people will hunt you down and kill you. You know that, Mr. American, don't you?" Kharmini said with spite.

"Salty little fella, aren't you? Tell me, just between us boys out here in the middle of the desert, you're the guy in the picture of the American hostages being led out of the Embassy back in '79, aren't you? You could be tried at Guantanamo for that. Maybe that's where we're headed?" Geno taunted.

"Propaganda! I was not present and I do not fear your show trials!" Kharmini said.

"Yeah, and the Pope isn't Catholic. Tell you what I'm gonna do. Since you're such a nice guy, head of state and all, I'm going to leave the duct tape off your mouth. How's that sound?"

"I am grateful for that, Mr. American Soldier, but I have nothing to say."

"That's fine. Just enjoy the view. We might have to blindfold you, or do you prefer a hood? You were there in '79, weren't you?" Geno was enjoying himself.

Dam Neck and Langley were not enjoying themselves, that's for sure. There was a turf war going on while a team of Americans and the key to peace in the Middle East were sweating in the desert. The Attorney General signed off, with the President's arm-twisting, that the mission was now a "rescue mission" by the Navy. The CIA was ticked, but realized that if things did go wrong from this point, the Navy could be blamed. The CIA had done their part. They had peacefully extracted the target without bloodshed. The target was intact and in good health when the handoff took place. Their hands were clean.

That wouldn't be the case if the real facts ever came to light. They had kidnapped a foreign head of state, but those were mere semantics. True to form for the CIA, the facts would not come to light and if they did, it would be many years later. The CIA was confident that none of the players involved wanted to go public with this. There could be jail time at home or executions waiting in less civilized countries for some. However, there was always the presidential pardon, if necessary—unless the administration didn't mind a

Harvard *student activities* record surfacing just in time for the upcoming elections.

"How we doin', Steve?" Geno asked.

"Great! I thought we were lost, but it looks like we've now been found!"

CHAPTER 40

INTENSE PRESSURE

THE PRESSURE WAS BUILDING ALL AROUND. DEVGRU HAD a team—two teams, in fact, including the CIA SOGs—in the middle of the northwestern Iranian desert. Secretary of State Kurtz was under intense pressure to keep her three-way deal going between Israel, Saudi Arabia, and Iran. The government of Iran was under extreme pressure, not only from the younger population protesting for greater democracy but now their President had been kidnapped.

Imagine if the head of state of France, Germany, Great Britain, China, the United States, or any other country had been kidnapped. Any country facing that circumstance would immediately mobilize their full military, intelligence, diplomatic, and all other resources to focus on one objective: the safe return of their head of state. That was exactly what Iran did. Even though the mullahs had given the "wink and a nod" to the plan, they had to go along with a full rescue effort to keep up appearances.

"Team 6, DEVGRU. Do you copy?"

"Copy."

"Things are really starting to heat up in your neighborhood. The locals are scrambling aircraft of all sorts to find their missing man. We are also monitoring major troop movements throughout the country. It appears there's a fanning procedure under way to cover as much ground as possible in a search effort. Embassies around the world are starting to light up like Christmas trees with communiqué traffic. We've got a real hot situation developing. You must keep moving as quickly as possible. This is very important. Proceed to coordinates twenty clicks west and north of the Taleghan Dam. The area is very remote and should be a safe pickup zone."

"Roger, DEVGRU."

The Iranian military was getting up to speed and realized that they had been tricked in the most embarrassing manner possible. General Ozalan, the overall commander of the military, briefed the ruling body of mullahs about what had taken place. He assured them that no resources would be spared in rescuing President Kharmini. The general offered his resignation, but the mullahs chose not to accept it at this time. They wanted to keep all appearances of normalcy within the military for the moment. However, they would use this event as a watershed event to reform and de-fang the Army and Revolutionary Guard, as well as militias throughout the major cities of Iran.

Kharmini had pushed the envelope too far and the mullahs realized that they had to regain control of the country if they wanted to maintain an Islamic state. In the days and months that would follow, they would grant many concessions to the young people of Iran but maintain their powers by professing a slightly moderate form of Islam that would be more acceptable to the majority of the Iranian population. It was a new time, a new generation, a new set of circumstances. The mullahs realized this, just as Muhammad realized circumstances that changed during his life and just as the ayatollahs and imams had realized through the centuries. The mullahs realized that Kharmini had marginalized Iran's influence in the world with his ranting and threats and that Iran was becoming a pariah even among Arab states, let alone elsewhere in the world, where they appeared "bizarre".

The mullahs further realized that if Iran was to grow in power and influence throughout the world, and if Iran was to be seen as a serious force in the Middle East, these changes *had* to be made. The mullahs felt pressure to get Iran invigorated so that Islam would grow and prosper throughout the world. Their pressure was not political or economic, but spiritual. They could use the successes of economic and political reform to further their religious efforts. The mullahs' focus had always been primarily religious, but they had allowed Kharmini to accumulate too much political power.

Secretary of State Kurtz was concerned that the President of Syria was still a weak link in the Kharmini arrangement. The main concern was his ability to work with Hezbollah to contact their splinter group within Saudi Arabia that kidnapped King Abdullah. Kurtz and the CIA both worried that the radical splinter group might not respond to the order to comply with the arrangement.

Kurtz contacted Assad and told him that she would be arriving in Damascus as soon as a flight could get her there. She took millions of U.S. dollars with her, as well as a diplomatic agreement that would outline the demands that Syria and Hezbollah had made to comply with the agreement. The millions of dollars in cash was money to be given to the leaders of Hezbollah to gain their support for the agreement. Assad would then work with Hezbollah to contact the splinter group.

Hezbollah would send agents to Saudi Arabia with the agreement in hand that secured positions of power within Hezbollah for the members of the splinter group. Kurtz did not care if the agreements between the two were honored in the future, she was only working in the moment. Syria, Hezbollah, and the splinter group could determine their own fates after the moment had passed.

As an added "incentive" to Assad, Kurtz informed him that the CIA had left Syrian papers and plans in the safe house in Tehran and that the CIA had tipped the Iranians to the safe house. Also, she informed him that Syrian paperwork had been left in the bloody armored vehicle stranded in the desert. She assured Assad that every measure of U.S., Saudi, and Israeli resources would be used to convince Iran that Syria was not involved in the capture of Kharmini, but Iran could be left to draw their own conclusions if Assad did not cooperate.

Bastards, Assad thought, but he understood the deck was stacked against him and he was desperate to hang onto power in his own country. In his heart, he was grateful for the opportunity to be perceived as a regional power broker with the Americans. Perhaps this event would save his ruling dynasty.

Kurtz also lobbied heavily to get the Saudis to allow the Hezbollah agents into Saudi Arabia. The Saudis would be allowed to monitor the agents from their arrival to their departure. They would also be allowed to monitor and verify that all terrorists holding Saudi prisoners, including King Abdullah, left Saudi Arabia. The Saudis were likely to agree, but Kurtz presented an added incentive to the Saudis to solidify their commitment: They would receive America's latest air defense system as a security measure for them throughout the region.

Kurtz instructed the CIA, with the full authority of the President, to contact the ruling council of Iran to inform them that America looked forward to a new working relationship with Iran and that America would back a relaxation of UN sanctions against Iran. America would also work to enhance Iran's reputation in the region. The ruling council was also told that Secretary of State Kurtz would visit Iran if invited, even though the two nations had severed diplomatic ties over thirty years ago. The visit would be a coup for Iran and its new government.

Events were unfolding with blinding speed as Israel watched from the sidelines. Kurtz had kept them informed of developments as they unfolded. They liked what they saw so far. They only hoped that Kharmini would not somehow resurface later, if he did, Mossad would take care of him.

Meanwhile Iranian jets were combing the country-side and patrolling major highways throughout Iran. The Iranians had put their air defense facilities on a state of high alert. Kharmini and his captors would soon be found if they were still in the country.

The pressure was intense for all players involved, time was ticking away.

CHAPTER 41

SUCCESS AT A PRICE

GENO AND 6 AND THE SOGS WERE RACING TO THEIR
destination point when an Iranian jet streaked across
the horizon. "Uh oh!" Geno said. "Looks like we might
have company if we don't get picked up pretty
damn soon."

Kharmini began chirping about the jet immediately
so Geno taped his mouth shut and put a hood over his
head. "We don't need that," he told Steve and Artie.
"Team 6, bird on the horizon. We need to slow it down
a bit so we don't kick up dust clouds. We'll take point,"
Geno relayed to the two teams.

"Roger."

DEVGRU was arranging resources for the pickup.
The 130W, F-15 Eagles, and F-16 Falcon escorts flown
by the Air Force would leave from Kuwait. A KC-135
Stratotanker would be prepped for them in Baghdad,
ready to refuel on the return flight. Because of extenu-
ating circumstances, DEVGRU doubled up on fighter
escorts. They didn't want to be outgunned! The 130W
also carried DPVs and supplies in the event a landing

would not be possible. The 130W, an extraction aircraft by design, was also equipped with electronic warfare and jamming equipment. The aircraft would fly north from Kuwait to Tikrit, former home of Sadam Hussein, and cross the Zagorsk Mountain Range of western Iran from there. The peaks were in excess of fourteen thousand feet and were not suitable for placement of air defense systems. The door was open for the extraction.

If Iran had an Achilles' heel, it was that it relied on its northern and western mountain ranges as a defense barrier for invasion rather than a true air defense system. The DEVGRU squadron would fly over the peaks to the landing zone.

The planes were cleared for takeoff. The flight was a routine procedure. They were up and through the mountains into Iran when Iranian jets were picked up on radar. The Iranians were patrolling north to south midway between Tehran and the Zagorsk mountain range.

"Bogies dead ahead," came the call from the electronics officer on board the 130W.

"Roger," replied the fighter jets.

"Ten minutes to landing zone," the pilot of the 130W radioed. The commanders back in Kuwait, the DOD in Washington, DEVGRU in Virginia, and the situation room at the White House were helpless at this point, except to order an abort of the mission, which they were not going to do.

"We've got you covered for descent," the commander of the fighter squadron radioed to the 130W.

"Mission on plan," radioed the pilot of the 130W. "Beginning our rapid descent."

"Roger, we've got you covered." It was white-knuckle time for all.

Geno had made it to the pickup coordinates. He ordered all the men out of their vehicles and a perimeter defense set up to await the extraction. Geno kept Kharmini in the center of a huddle formation with Fats, Artie, Steve, Harley and himself. Mad Mike, J'effie, Miggs, Lou, Nick Vee, Matt, and the others were in a circle defense with the SOGs. They had a lot of firepower with them but were definitely in the crosshairs.

Suddenly they were strafed by one of the Iranian jets. Large caliber bullets tore up the desert sand and two of the vehicles caught fire and exploded. Two of the SOGs and SEAL Josh Jones were killed by the strafing. The huddle covered Kharmini with their bodies.

Geno radioed DEVGRU. "Live fire and casualties! Where's the bird?"

"Five minutes out. You should see him de-scend soon."

"Eagle One. Live fire on the LZ! Do you copy?" Geno relayed.

"Yes, we copy," replied the pilot of the 130W. "Fighters in pursuit to take bogies out."

"We're on descent now. Everything looks clear." Radioed the 130W.

The American fighters knocked the two Iranian jets out of the sky just after the Iranians radioed to their base and informed them of their discovery.

As in any combat situation, the action was intense and cramped into a small timeframe. Sometimes literally only seconds or minutes pass. Yet simultane-ously, the mind seems to be processing in slow motion allowing the combatants to do what they do within such a brief moment. This duel over the desert was no different.

It was another matter for Geno and the men on the ground. It seemed like an eternity before they saw the 130W and even longer for it to drop down to the desert floor. They quickly gathered the dead and Kharmini and ran for the back ramp of the 130W. Mike, Miggs, and Artie provided rear cover as everyone raced to the 130W. The SOGs carried their dead comrades while Lou and Matt carried Josh Jones up the back ramp into the guts of the plane. Mike, Miggs, and Artie ran up the ramp into the plane once everyone else was inside.

"We're in!" Geno shouted, and the ramp door closed.

"Strap in for takeoff. We're moving!" the pilot radioed to the crew. They took off well before everyone was strapped in and left a huge desert sandstorm in their wake. Everyone grabbed their seats while the plane climbed out of the desert at a thirty-degree angle with full throttle on the four huge turbo props and banked to the west. Cheers went up from Kuwait to D.C.

"We're not out of here yet," the radar officer on the 130W radioed. "I've got Iranian fighters coming from the east."

"Full throttle. Give it everything you've got!" barked Kuwait.

"I am!" the pilot replied. "We're approaching top end speed at 390 knots. We're gonna need help with the fighters on our tail!"

"We've got you," radioed the commander of the fighter escort, and four of them peeled back to the east for an intercept. The Iranian jets were no match for the F-16s and they soon returned to formation. "We're gonna need some juice soon," the commander of the fighter squadron radioed.

"Baghdad, get your birds in the air, now!" came the

command from Kuwait. "Tankers and escorts. To the border now! We'll refuel on the Iraqi side and return everybody back to Kuwait as planned. No touchdowns in Iraq for security reasons."

The team had achieved success, but at a price—again.

CHAPTER 42

PEACE

GENO AND HIS TEAM LANDED IN KUWAIT. THEY TAXIED TO a hangar at the far end of the complex. They were met on the tarmac by a security force, agents of the CIA and the commander of Special Operations for the base. Kharmini was secured and led to a black SUV with darkly tinted windows. He was whisked inside the hangar and placed in a windowless room with representatives of the CIA. The hood and tape were removed from his head and mouth. He immediately demanded to be released and for his government to be notified. The request fell on deaf ears.

Geno, 6, and the SOGs filed out of the 130W and formed an honor line from the back of the plane to the three vans waiting to take their three fallen comrades away. The medics and others went into the plane to cover the bodies with American flags prior to their removal. Geno and the men stood at full attention and saluted the three men as they were carried to the vans.

It was 3:00 p.m. on August 12th, Dolly's birthday, and

Geno thought of how his mother always insisted that he attend mass with her when he was young boy. Tears flowed from his eyes. He brought his hand down from his salute as the last body passed and fell into the arms of his men. They embraced the SOGs and all wept together. To think, less than a few hours ago these men were as hard as nails facing death on the desert floor. To have seen that image, and to see them now was the stark contrast of war and peace.

Geno walked off to the hangar, maybe to another mission, maybe not, clutching his Saint Christopher medal and humming Happy Birthday.

------------- EPILOGUE -------------

Kurtz made her arrangements and everything flowed according to plan. There would be collateral damage to contend with after this mission of peace. Some of it would last for many years, but the world had been pulled back from a nuclear holocaust. Dead Americans and dead Iranians had paid the ultimate price for this peace, if one could call it that. Everyone knew it would simply be a matter of time before the next crisis would occur and lives would again be placed at risk to solve it. Events in Libya and Syria almost guaranteed it.

Would Israel and the Arabs ever be able to co-exist together? Could the mullahs in Iran reform their country? Would Iran give up its pursuit of nuclear weapons? Would the peaceful elements of new democracies sprouting in Egypt and Tunisia be allowed to spread throughout the Middle East, or would they be overrun by radicals? Would Saudi Arabia be able to continue walking the fine line between the Arab world and the Western world?

Was oil worth dying for, or would there be solutions in

the future that would make Middle Eastern oil less crucial to the free flow of commerce in the world?

Would traditional Islam work to convert the world in a peaceful, religious manner, or would radical Islamic violence continue?

How could the West be a positive leader in the eyes of the Middle East?

These were all questions that needed answers, but that was for another time. This was a moment of "peace".

Made in the USA
Charleston, SC
25 August 2012